continued . . .

PUTT TO DEATH

"[An] author who's succeeded in demonstrating her knowledge of golf, while still attracting readers who have never done more than putt balls over a moat and through a spinning windmill . . . *Putt to Death*'s mystery thread unravels at a healthy clip . . . A fun read, one that's several strokes ahead of the competition."
—*January*

"A very entertaining mystery . . . an exciting, enjoyable ride."
—*Mystery Morgue*

"A very entertaining and clever mystery."
—*Deadly Pleasures*

"Isleib has created an endearing, and surprisingly somewhat complicated, character in Cassie."
—*New Mystery Reader*

A BURIED LIE

"A fun new mystery heroine in Cassie Burdette, LPGA player and amateur detective."
—*Hole by Hole*

"A winner, a tightly-woven and briskly-told amateur sleuth tale that will please fans of the game as well as readers who love their soft-boiled books a little well-done."
—*Cozies, Capers & Crimes*

"Golf enthusiasts and fans of amateur sleuth novels will definitely enjoy *A Buried Lie* . . . Roberta Isleib knows how to write an interesting who-done-it that is a hole in one for the audience."
—*Midwest Book Review*

SIX STROKES UNDER

Nominated for the Agatha and Anthony Awards

"Isleib expertly captures the myriad personalities of professional golf and the unique world of the country club and spins it like a Hollywood thriller." —*New Haven Register*

"Murder, suspense . . . and golf. What more do you need? Roberta Isleib hits the sweet spot with this impressive debut." —Steve Hamilton,
Edgar® Award–winning author of *North of Nowhere*

"So intelligent and engaging, even readers who don't know a driver from a nine-iron will love it."

—Abigail Padgett,
author of *The Last Blue Plate Special*

"Isleib handles her subject well, like a pro. Even the non-sports fan will enjoy this book. Recommended."

—Reviewingtheevidence.com

"Even if you are not a golf enthusiast this is a must . . . you really will enjoy the read."

—*Murder on Miami Beach Newsletter*

"Cassie is a fresh face in the mystery world . . . A fast-paced book mystery- [and] golf-lovers will enjoy."

—*Knoxville News Sentinel*

"A stunning debut, chockablock with all the passions and perils of the Pro World and the clever Cassandra Burdette in competition." —*Mystery Scene*

"Near-perfect . . . A first-rate mystery." —*I Love a Mystery*

FINAL FORE

Roberta Isleib

BERKLEY PRIME CRIME, NEW YORK

THE BERKLEY PUBLISHING GROUP
Published by the Penguin Group
Penguin Group (USA) Inc.
375 Hudson Street, New York, New York 10014, USA

Penguin Group (Canada), 90 Eglinton Avenue East, Suite 700, Toronto, Ontario M4P 2Y3, Canada
(a division of Pearson Penguin Canada Inc.)
Penguin Books Ltd., 80 Strand, London WC2R 0RL, England
Penguin Group Ireland, 25 St. Stephen's Green, Dublin 2, Ireland (a division of Penguin Books Ltd.)
Penguin Group (Australia), 250 Camberwell Road, Camberwell, Victoria 3124, Australia
(a division of Pearson Australia Group Pty. Ltd.)
Penguin Books India Pvt. Ltd., 11 Community Centre, Panchsheel Park, New Delhi—110 017, India
Penguin Group (NZ), Cnr. Airborne and Rosedale Roads, Albany, Auckland 1310, New Zealand
(a division of Pearson New Zealand Ltd.)
Penguin Books (South Africa) (Pty.) Ltd., 24 Sturdee Avenue, Rosebank, Johannesburg 2196, South
Africa

Penguin Books Ltd., Registered Offices: 80 Strand, London WC2R 0RL, England

FINAL FORE

A Berkley Prime Crime Book / published by arrangement with the author

PRINTING HISTORY
Berkley Prime Crime mass-market edition / March 2006

ISBN: 0-425-20896-6

BERKLEY® PRIME CRIME
Berkley Prime Crime Books are published by The Berkley Publishing Group,
a division of Penguin Group (USA) Inc.,
375 Hudson Street, New York, New York 10014.
BERKLEY PRIME CRIME and the BERKLEY PRIME CRIME design are trademarks belonging to
Penguin Group (USA) Inc.

PRINTED IN THE UNITED STATES OF AMERICA

10 9 8 7 6 5 4 3 2 1

For Andrew and Molly

And for Yvonne,
Cassie's other mother

Acknowledgments

My heartfelt thanks go to all who helped me with this book:

Gina Finocchiaro, who shared her huge enthusiasm for Mount Holyoke College and showed me the scary places in the library. Twice.

Amy Lillibridge, good sport and friend.

My entertaining golfing companions—Heather Brown, Mary Pat Maloney, and Mary Ann Salatto—completely willing to take a road trip to the Orchards on an author's whim. Curt and Gina for company at the Open.

The friendly folks at Mount Holyoke College: Audry Longo, Mount Holyoke golf team captain; Laurie Priest, Director of Athletics; Rochelle Calhoun, Executive Director of the Alumnae Association.

Golf psychologists Richard Keefe, Dick Coop, and Joseph Parent; my favorite golf guru, Don Gliha, for a decent golf swing; golf journalists Kiel Christianson and Joe Morelli for showing me the ropes; Matt Pepin for giving me a chance; Bob McHugh, golf professional at the Orchards; Diane Tusek and Marlene De Santo for their meditations; Cindy Johnson and the staff at Fran Johnson's; Joan Grenier and the Odyssey Bookshop staff; Andrew Blau, my favorite rules guru, and his wife, Kelly; good sports Julie Nothstine and Lucien Beccia who donated their names for charity; the ever-punny Reverend Dwight Juliani for the title.

The fabulous players on the LPGA and Futures tours including Heather Daly-Donofrio, Diane Irvin, Kate Golden, Donna Andrews, Brittany Lincicome (along with her mom Angie and friend Rhonda), Jeannette, and Allison Hanna—all so graciously willing to share their experiences on tour and at the Open.

The fantastic organizations who've supported me along the way: Executive Women's Golf Association, Women in the Golf Industry, GWAA, Mystery Writers of America, and Sisters in Crime; RJ Julia Booksellers—home is where the bookstore is; the Shoreline Writers' Group—Chris Falcone, Angelo Pompano, Karen Olson, and Cindy Warm; my mystery writing companions and confidants, including Susan Hubbard, Jessica Speart, Hallie Ephron, Deborah Donnelly, and Libby Hellmann.

My cheerful and optimistic agent Paige Wheeler; the great folks at Berkley Prime Crime, including editors Cindy Hwang and Susan McCarty; skilled and ruthless independent editor Nora Cavin.

Most of all, thanks to my family for their love and support—Isleibs, Bradys, Ceruleans, Cantors, Chantons all—and always, to John. He never ever complains when I interrupt his shower to discuss the plot.

Roberta Isleib, May 2005

"Most players have dreamed about winning the Open since childhood. They can't stop thinking about what it would be like to win. And that is exactly the worst mindset for good golf."

—Dr. Richard Keefe,
On the Sweet Spot

"There's nothing really you can do for your man. You realize that at the end of the day you can give him good yardages, tell him how you see the knobs of the greens, is it uphill, is it downhill, all that; you can throw your grass clippings in the air until the sky falls down, tell him the direction of the breeze and how hard it's blowing. You can warn him that he's got a flier lie or that the green is as hard as a motorway or that the pin position is for suckers only. You can make all the calculations, do all your considering. You can put the club in his hand, tell him to hit the soft six or the hard seven. But you cannot take the bloody swing for him."

—Michael Bamberger,
To the Linksland

"Winning for women becomes a mixed pleasure because women are trained not to hurt anyone's feelings. If you are concerned that the people you triumph over will not like you, you have no choice but to be a loser. In order to compete to win, you have to learn to tolerate other people's discomfort and dislike."

—Adrienne Mendell,
How Men Think

"There is nothing to do.
There is nowhere to go.
There is no one else to be."

—Ajahn Buddhadasa

Chapter 1

A wash of light-headedness hit me as I walked off the eighteenth green. The flush of heat and sweat that followed left me clammy and tense.

But we'd all suffered this week with the early season heat wave. Besides, I'd been edgy lately anyway. This damn day meant too much. Every one of us—veterans, rookies, and amateurs—wanted to qualify for the US Open. Desperately wanted to qualify. It's only the most prestigious tournament in women's golf. Solid middle-of-the-pack professional golfers who earn money every week on the tour have nightmares about missing the cut in a qualifying round and losing their place to an unknown who has one great day. No one wants to hover at the bubble—where I was right now—waiting for the other players to finish their rounds and find out whether you'll be facing a sudden-death playoff for one of the last three spots.

The group playing in front of us hadn't helped. I knew I wasn't supposed to be thinking about anyone else's performance. Play one shot at a time and all that good mental hoo-ha. But all morning we'd watched the gallery swell ahead of us. And had to back off our balls when we heard their roars—the kind of noise a crowd makes when a hot player is racking up birdies and eagles and heading for a record round.

Dizzy made sense under the circumstances.

Today I'd been paired with a skinny seventeen-year-old who'd competed in enough junior golf to know her 85 stood no chance. We dragged into the blue-and-white striped scoring tent that had been set up just off the eighteenth green.

I handed the girl her scorecard and patted her bony back. "Tough day out there." Her eyes filled with tears.

I slumped into a folding metal chair to check my own numbers, sign my name, and wait. The pencil trembled in my fingers. I took a deep breath, grimaced a pseudosmile at the official waiting for my card, and tried again. My hand only shook harder and I could feel the sweat beading on my forehead. I supported my right wrist with my left hand, scribbled my signature, and stumbled out into the bright sun. A horde of reporters blocked the way to the clubhouse.

"Congratulations, Amber!" one deep voice called out. "Can you take us through the highlights of your round?"

I recognized the player in the crowd's center—a slight girl with coffee-colored skin and a long braid: Amber Clancy. She's golf guru Lucien Beccia's most recent rising star. Shooting star is more like it—he'll have to hold on for his life if she keeps the pace she's on. Amber, a college freshman out of Arizona with intentions to turn pro in the future some day, alienated half the women's golf world this year by comparing herself to Tiger Woods. (Female stars aren't good enough?) Her father, an African-American man with an Indian wife and a chip on his shoulder the size of Plymouth Rock, was even worse. Thing is, Amber probably will make history. But let's see a few years of golf before voting her into the Hall of Fame.

Two reporters broke off from the outer fringes of the mob and headed my way.

"Miss Burdette, are you planning to accept the offer to play in the PGA's Buick Championship?" A fellow in an Atlanta Braves cap and a striped polo reached toward me with a small, portable tape recorder. Then he laughed. "And a follow-up to that question, please: Did you find any dead bodies out on the course today?"

"Cassie! What's your game plan for a play-off for the final position if it's needed?" This man stood short and squat, his pen poised above his notebook.

"Sorry, guys. I'm not feeling so great."

I turned and bolted toward the clubhouse. My heart banged against my chest and I gasped for air. Then I was choking and grabbing at the pain that gripped my heart and squeezed. A heart attack, I was sure of it.

Unusual for a healthy woman in her twenties, tried my logical mind. I ran past the security guard, flashing my LPGA badge, and burst into the locker room. Two women on the bench in front of a row of lockers were talking about dinner menus. The mention of seafood made me instantly queasy, and I ran for the toilet, slammed the door closed, and threw the bolt.

Pushing down a wave of nausea, I lowered the seat cover, sat, and leaned sideways to rest my head on the cool metal of the stall. I tried to breathe, forcing air into my lungs. I pictured a pink balloon rising softly as the good air flowed in. But the sharp pain in my chest started up again and began to spread down one arm. I dropped my head to my knees, dizzy and sick and scared. This was it. I knew it.

"Cassie?" Fingernails tapped on the metal door. "Cassie, are you okay?"

"Not really," I croaked, slumping to the floor. "I think I might be having a heart attack."

"Oh my God! Stay right there—I'm calling 911!"

Julie Nothstine, a sophomore-year golfer who'd made four cuts already this year, held my hand in the back of the ambulance all the way to the hospital. She kept up a steady calming stream of chatter, stories about her little brother, a shopping trip she'd taken for new shoes, a recipe for her grandmother's cake that she'd made to impress a former boyfriend. It hadn't risen and he'd asked for maple syrup, thinking she was serving some sort of pancake.

I didn't mind. As long as I could hear Julie's voice, I wasn't dead yet. Then she sat in the waiting area for two hours along with her caddie, Jason, and my best friend and caddie, Laura, while hospital personnel tested me from head to toe.

Physically, I was fine. The psychiatric resident they

called in to consult suggested that mentally, I might need some work.

"Panic attack," he announced. "Your symptoms are classic: heart palpitations, sweating, choking, trembling. And the feeling that you were dying or"—he set his clipboard on the counter and made quotation marks in the air with his fingers—"going crazy."

Quite the bedside manner on this bozo.

"No way," I said. "My symptoms were classic heart attack."

"People say it feels like that. I'm sure it's very uncomfortable." He squeezed my shoulder and adjusted the stethoscope that hung around his neck. "But you're a fine physical specimen. Now let's talk about follow-up. There are new medications that are quite useful for some patients with this condition. I'm going to recommend a clinician who can monitor the meds and work with you on some cognitive behavioral adjustments. We'll have you back on that golf course in no time." He gave me another reassuring pinch and turned to reach across the desk and pull out a directory from a shelf along the wall. "What town did you say you lived in?"

"I already have a shrink." I dug through my wallet, found a dog-eared business card, and presented it to the resident. "I'll call him when I get back home and set something up."

The resident scribbled Dr. Baxter's particulars on my chart and handed me a release form. "Sign here and we'll send him the test results."

He put the chart down on the desk and crossed his arms over his chest, looking worried. His scalp glowed pink through carefully arranged strands of blond hair.

"Perfect." I slid off the examining table and signed the paper before he could change his mind.

Julie, Laura, and Jason stood when I emerged into the waiting area.

The two women rushed over.

"Are you okay?" asked Julie.

Laura pushed past Julie to hug me. "What did they find out?"

"Anxiety." I rolled my eyes. "How embarrassing is that? I feel terrible that you guys waited so long."

"Nothing would have ruined this one's day," said Jason, punching Julie's arm lightly.

Julie grinned. "We both made the cut. We're going to play in the US Open, girlfriend. Mount Holyoke College here we come!" she crowed. Then she picked me up and whirled me around the reception desk.

My heart felt a thousand pounds lighter than when they'd wheeled me in.

Chapter 2

According to my shrink friend Joe Lancaster, relaxation is supposed to be incompatible with anxiety. That's his theory anyway. No point in arguing with him—he'll quote a host of experts at you to prove his point. So I'd been halfheartedly practicing yoga for the past month, hoping the stretching and concentration it demanded would translate into good golf shots when I needed them under pressure. And beat back any possibility of the panic attack that had swamped me after the US Open qualifying round. As far as I was concerned, by now I practically had a Ph.D. in relaxation.

Then Julie talked me into coming to her favorite yoga institute the weekend before the US Women's Open began. Kripalu is in Lenox, Massachusetts, about fifty miles from the golf course in South Hadley, but a million miles away in ambience. I folded once she told me she'd placed in her first top ten after completing a weekend yoga retreat. No phones, no e-mail, no fans, no other players, just time and space to get centered, wind down, and then gear back up.

The bearded man at the front of the room murmured into the microphone that hovered in front of his mouth. "Remember, my name is Bloom. I'll stay here a couple of minutes after the session in case anyone needs to connect."

"His parents were hippies. He has siblings named Summer and Rain," I whispered to Julie. "Or do you think that's his Sanskrit name?"

"Notice your prana, listen to your body's inner wisdom," said Bloom. "What is it telling you about a position you might need to take before we begin our meditation?"

"How about a fast walk out the door?" I muttered, thumping cross-legged to ground.

"Shhh . . ." said Julie.

I stared glumly out the window while Julie balanced the crown of her head in the center of her sticky mat and lifted her legs up into a perfect and graceful V. In a million years a headstand would not have crossed my mind as the position my prana body craved. Even if I knew what a prana body was.

After she and Laura and Jason helped me back to my hotel last month, Julie had taken an interest in my well-being. And stuck to me like a burr in a dog's tail. She kept quoting a Chinese proverb that says if you save a life, the person is your responsibility for a lifetime. I would have left me in the john.

I called Dr. Baxter after my visit to the ER and described the overwhelming feeling of foreboding—I honestly thought I was going to die. He confirmed the panic attack diagnosis—bad news on top of my ongoing battle with low-level neurosis—and prescribed returning to Myrtle Beach for more therapy. Sound advice, but I wasn't willing to drop off the LPGA tour and return home to the safety of his office cocoon.

Bloom murmured into the microphone again. "Now we'll move into meditation. During this time, you'll empty your mind of thoughts and solidify all the good things that your body has done over the past hour. Please sit up on your mats, close your eyes, and breathe." He inhaled noisily and let out a big gust of a sigh. "Mmmmm . . ."

My mind was not about to clear. It swirled right back to Baxter.

"Several of my other patients have found medications to be useful," he'd said when I stopped home for a quick visit.

I took a pass on those, too. In my opinion, I'd made a lot of progress over the past year understanding how I used alcohol to manage my ups and downs: I wasn't about to consign my mental status to better living through some other chemical. We agreed to work on the phone when I was out of town, a compromise neither one of us really liked.

Identifying some of the reasons behind the attacks was elementary. The stress of competing in my first ever US Women's Open, for example. Much better players than I had succumbed to that kind of pressure over the years. Also stressful was an unwanted invitation I'd received to play in the Buick Championship, a men's tournament in Cromwell, Connecticut, just a month following the Open.

Bloom breathed heavily again into his microphone, drawing my mind back to the room. "Quiet your inner chatter," he whispered.

Chatter. That's the word the government uses whenever there's an uptick in terrorist activity. It fit like a glove here, too: The thoughts crowding my brain were like terrorists plotting to sabotage any dreams of success I might have.

Ollie Crum, a legendary caddie for one of the PGA's top golfers, had died of liver cancer last February. The Buick Championship office came up with the idea of inviting another PGA caddie to compete in their tournament to honor Ollie. A special assessment was to be levied on the tickets, with proceeds going to the American Cancer Society.

Then the tournament brain trust hatched the idea of inviting a *female* former PGA caddie to play in the event. That pretty much narrowed it down to me. They seemed to imagine my transformation from caddie to LPGA player to PGA player as a great Cinderella story that would become a huge media coup that would boost attendance and make sponsors delirious. And somehow honor Ollie. I'd look like a heel if I refused. Only a couple of other lady golfers had preceded me down this cart path: hitting from the championship tees with the male golfers, watched by galleries worthy of Tiger Woods. And only one had made the cut and gone on to play like one of the men: teenage phenom Amber Clancy—the same girl whose dust I choked while she set the course record at the USGA qualifying round last month.

Along with the publicity surrounding my PGA invite had come an onslaught of attention. Over the past month I'd received a steady barrage of mail—everything from prepubescent girls wanting autographs to middle-aged women whose personal goal was to break 100 for a round of golf. These women seemed to want a hero. They wanted me to do and be what they couldn't manage themselves.

The unpleasant letters had been more surprising. There were a couple of proposals—marriage, that is—and warnings, too, should I decide to follow through on the PGA event.

The so-called opportunity reduced me to a quivering mass.

Bloom's amplified voice nearly scared me out of my wits. "Namaste. May the highest point of my spirit meet the highest point of yours." He placed his hands together in prayer position and bowed his way around the room.

"Let's go take a hot tub," Julie whispered.

At Kripalu, you speak sotto voce after meditation so you don't invade someone else's zone.

I followed her down the stairs into the basement and along a hallway lined with white pipes and painted with a rolling blue sea.

"I'm going to start with a sauna," Julie announced when we reached the locker room.

My whole body stiffened. "I think I'll just head up to lunch. See you back at the room."

I wouldn't be caught dead in a sauna. I'd been nearly strangled in a steam room at the Pinehurst spa last fall. As with Pavlov's rats who were shocked any time they pressed a lever, the steam room would never provide a relaxation response for me. This layout was a lot less posh than the Pinehurst spa, but my subconscious recognized the space just the same.

For a moment, I considered the clothing-optional whirlpool. I peeked in. A couple of women were already soaking, moaning, sighing, and splashing as though orgasm wasn't far away. There was a lot of that at this institute—moaning and loud breathing, that is. Expressing your feelings was encouraged. So was noticing. We were to notice every physical change and not judge. Stay in the present. Avoid judging.

I trudged back up the stairs, passing posters of the Dalai Lama, Rosa Parks, Mother Teresa, and Albert Einstein on the landings. When I stepped away from my usual tendency to harsh judgments, I had a glimmer that this place might really help me survive the upcoming week.

My ex-boyfriend Mike Callahan had just laughed when I phoned to tell him I was going. Crapalu, he called it. But that's another story and precisely why we finally broke things off. He can't help the negative edge that runs through his personality and his relationships—he hardly even sees it. But it had a bad effect on me. Oddly enough, Mike and I have talked more about our lives and our golf and our families since we've broken up then we ever did when I was caddying for him or when we were "going out." My friend—and maybe more—Joe Lancaster, a golf psychologist, can't understand that at all.

I stopped into the mailroom while waiting for the cafeteria to open. A series of tall, thin open boxes lined the left wall. A neatly printed sign explained that mail would be filed according to the first initial of our first names or our Sanskrit names. Not having the latter, I looked in the *C* box. Cerise had a ride to Albany confirmed by Robert for Wednesday at noon. And there was a note for me.

Cassie, hit 'em straight!

No signature on the message. I shrugged, pushing back a little spike of discomfort. Someone at the yoga institute must be a closet golf fan who—praise the Dalai Lama—did not want to be intrusive. I jammed it into my back pocket.

I entered the lunchroom, grabbed a tray, and pushed it through the line, choosing salad and a lumpy-looking lentil burger. After burying the burger under layers of Tabasco sauce, mustard, and organic lettuce, I waited for my turn to get a cup of herbal tea.

The middle-aged woman ahead of me looked like she'd been crying, her eyes swollen and red. "That was amazing," she said to her friend. "Something is starting to break open." She thumped her chest. I noticed they both had Teddy bears squeezed under their arms.

"Wait until you have your turn to experience the womb," said her friend. "We're reaching out to our inner children," she explained to me, and rubbed her cheek on her bear.

"Would you like to join us for lunch?" asked the first woman, smiling sweetly at me. "I'm Eloise from Connecticut."

"Thanks anyway," I said quickly. "I—I'm fasting today."

She glanced at my full tray.

"I mean meditating."

I carried the tray to the "silence-only" dining area. I'd go to the yoga classes, but I couldn't see myself sharing childhood memories with Connecticut housewives squeezing stuffed animals to comfort their inner Teddy bears. God knows it might help, but it just wasn't me.

I gobbled lunch and left Julie a note in the room. *Don't squeal on me—I've gone for coffee!*

Chapter 3

I drove into town and parked behind the Lenox Coffee Shop. Honey-toned floors and furniture, mustard-colored walls, and Georgia O'Keefe prints in gilt frames gave the shop a warm and laid-back feel. The young men behind the counter, one tall with acne-pitted skin and a black knit ski cap, and the other sporting bleached white hair with black roots, argued over technique and speed. I ordered a double latte and took a seat at a small back table. A cluster of women grouped at the table next to mine were debating whether gay couples should have children.

"The kids will resent it later," insisted one of the women, clutching a baby in a sling protectively to her chest. "You're taking on a huge responsibility."

"Kids will resent you no matter what kind of parent you are," said another.

The remaining ladies broke in with loud counterarguments as the boy in the ski cap shouted that my latte was ready. This town was not as laid back as it first looked. Maybe it was the caffeine. I fetched the latte and sat back down, sipping it. A sigh of pleasure escaped me.

Fortified by the comforting double jolt of espresso, I powered up my laptop to take advantage of the coffee shop's wireless Internet. First, I typed in the address for the Ladies Professional Golf Association Web site.

I have a new ritual, days I start to feel sorry for myself— or when the yardstick of success on the tour seems impossibly long. I click on the LPGA Web site and scroll through the "Qualifying School," starting with the sectional qualifying event—the one I attended in Venice, Florida, several years ago. At the bottom of the list are the girls who withdrew after shooting a first round of 89 or 91—numbers that might not even get you into the championship flight at a private country club. On our first day in Venice, the tournament director informed us that any score 88 or higher meant automatic withdrawal. It wasn't a score I'd wanted to even consider possible, but feeling insecure already and with everything on the line, the risk hovered in the back of my mind.

Next I roll back up the list, skimming the names of the girls who were cut, starting with those so far off the mark, they'd have to think long and hard before shelling out several thousand bucks to try Q-school again. Then I scan the players who missed the cut by one or two shots and had a year to consider which lipped-out putt or chunked chip or approach shot off line made the difference. Then last, I linger on the name of the girl who was in a five-way tie for the final four positions. And lost her chance in a sudden death play-off. By then, I'm remembering that I'm on the tour, that I intend to make enough money this year that I don't have to go back to Q-school, and that I'm lucky as hell. And besides, I'm playing in the US Women's Open in less than a week.

Feeling a tad better, I logged onto Web mail and downloaded the messages to my laptop. I had plenty of time to sort through them while the other Kripalu guests were exploring their energy chakras through "sounding." From what I could tell from a safe distance, this afternoon's special seminar had to do with how to plumb the depths of the mind by chanting. Frankly, I didn't want to go that far down into mine.

I opened a message from my brother, Charlie. With apologies, he'd forwarded on two articles about my invitation to play in the Buick PGA tournament, on behalf of my mother.

Matt Pepin, the sports editor at *The New Haven Register,* had written an essay arguing that my intimate knowledge of the course in Cromwell, Connecticut, gained while caddying for Mike Callahan, would prove to be a great asset. I should definitely accept the invitation to play.

The Hartford Courant pointed out that even though Suzy Whaley's husband managed the golf course in 2003, and while she played as well as her considerable abilities allowed, she hadn't come anywhere near the cut. Why would I think I could do any better? Face it, Amber Clancy's amazing performance this spring had been a freak of nature. As with Suzy Whaley, Michelle Wie, and Annika

Sorenstam, I should understand that my shorter length off the tee and the psychological pressures of playing with professional men would result in humiliation. And humiliation of me would mean humiliation of my entire sex by proxy.

My head started to throb. Everyone else's passion about this decision seemed to far outweigh mine.

Almost worse, my brother had included a link to an article about the "golfing detective." That was me. I hit Delete, not wanting to rehash the deadly scrapes I'd gotten involved in over the past couple of years. My part in these incidents had been unintentional and terrifying. I certainly wasn't recruiting new business.

"Cassie! How's it going? Aren't you supposed to be in yoga class?"

I looked up, guilty, and smiled at Julie's caddie, Jason Palmer. "I'm easing into it. The vegetarian swill is healthy as hell, but I'm salivating for a prime rib. Meanwhile, I needed a hit of caffeine and e-mail."

"Me, too." He lifted his laptop in salute. "Can I join you?"

I gestured to the empty chair across from me.

"I just got back from Cranwell," said Jason. "Their practice green matches the stimp readings we'll find at the Orchards almost exactly—slick. And they're excited to see a couple of LPGA stars—hope you don't mind signing autographs." He flashed his all-American grin, revealing two cheek dimples and a little gap between his front teeth.

Julie and I had a date later this afternoon to hit balls in the field behind the main building at Kripalu and then drive five miles to the Cranwell resort to borrow their putting green. Julie was lucky to hire Jason this close to the Open—they'd agreed he should come with us to Kripalu to work out the kinks in their new relationship—before one of those kinks cost her the championship. Jason had been on the golf team at the University of Florida with Mike, two years ahead of me. He knew the ropes and he had a nice way about him. If he could keep his beer count under control (like I was one to talk), he'd probably do just fine.

I clicked through a series of spam e-mails—who had any idea what college girls and bored housewives were up to these days?—and moved another dozen messages to the trash.

"How's your baby?" I asked.

Jason pulled out his wallet and showed me a photo of his little girl—sweet chubby cheeks, a toothless smile, and a pink ribbon that looked as though it had been glued to her bald head.

"She's a doll," I said. "She's got her daddy's smile. How's your wife holding up?"

Frown lines creased his forehead. "We split up a couple of weeks ago. Still working out the custody details. You know how these things go." He tried a smile, but his face was clouded with anger and sadness.

"Really sorry to hear that," I said, placing my hand briefly over his. I'd read somewhere that children are the biggest stress on a marriage outside of money. In my case, even managing a relationship where I have no overlapping responsibilities with the guy seems hard. "I know what you mean. Mike and I called it quits—finally. And I don't have much hope for me and my friend Joe, either." This thought had been floating through my mind lately, but I surprised myself, saying it out loud.

A new e-mail chimed in with "Following the rules" as the subject line. I skimmed a quote from *The Rules of*

Golf, USGA Rule 6-4: "Caddie. The player may be assisted by a *caddie,* but he is limited to only one *caddie* at any one time." Two lines followed in bold type: **"Cassie, don't play where you don't belong. You could get hurt."**

My stomach clenched and a backwash of latte burned my throat. I glanced up. Jason was watching me. He looked concerned—and kind.

"What's the matter?" he asked. "Bad news?"

He'd already witnessed my panic attack and subsequent ER visit. Besides, we'd shared more than one embarrassing moment, usually drunk, at the University of Florida. I shifted the laptop so he could read the e-mail.

"Is this someone you know?" he asked, looking more worried.

I glanced at the e-mail address: ruleswhiz@topmail.com. "No. Probably just another crackpot. They've all been weighing in about whether I should play at the Buick next month."

"Decided what you're going to do about that?" he asked.

"I'm trying to ignore it," I said. "Everyone else seems a lot more interested in the outcome than I am."

He tapped the top of my computer. "Are you getting a lot of this crap?"

I nodded.

"Jesus! You try to do something nice to honor someone. . . . You should increase the level of your spam filter. Or better still, complain to the folks at your e-mail server."

"What could they do about it? That's why God invented the Delete button." I laughed, unconvincingly, and pulled the computer back across the table. I glanced at my watch. "Time to get cracking, huh? I'll meet you back at the ranch shortly."

I drove slowly to Kripalu. As I crested the upsweep of the curved drive, the imposing redbrick structure came into view. Who thought of designing the place to look like a minimum-security prison? Or a high-end mental hospital? I grinned. Notwithstanding this morning's admonition against judging, I'd already seen plenty of possible inmates among the yoga students. I wasn't far from qualifying for a good long stay myself.

I parked Julie's car and veered into the coat and mailroom area to avoid the women I'd snubbed at lunch. I checked the *C* box again and found a second message.

"Call Laura Snow."

My stomach did a belly flop, this time bringing vestiges of lentil burger to my throat. Laura is my caddie, my longtime friend, and the most unflappable human I'd ever met. She wouldn't leave a message at the institute without a very good—or bad—reason.

I returned to the parking lot, turned on my cell phone, and checked for voice mail. There was a breezy greeting from Joe saying he hoped I was feeling relaxed and that he missed me. My teeth clenched reflexively. Then a borderline whiney message from my mother reminding me to look for an e-mail from my brother, Charlie, and for the snail mail she'd forwarded to USGA headquarters at South Hadley. And last, an urgent request from Laura.

"Listen, Cassie. Call ASAP. We have a problem. My father had a stroke this morning and he's in the hospital. It's touch-and-go here." Her voice caught and I heard her take a ragged breath. "I'm not at all sure when or if I can get to Holyoke. I'm really sorry, friend. I know how much this means to you. I wanted to give you as much notice as I could so you can round someone else up. Maybe a fresh face on your bag will be just the ticket. Call me when you can."

I felt instantly sick. Laura is as attached to her father as a daughter can be without being labeled unhealthy. She'd stuck close by him when they lost her mother in a freak accident and he is her biggest fan. I'd met Mr. Snow many times—a skinny little guy with smooth, nut-brown skin and a wicked sense of humor. There was none of the usual parental tension between him and Laura, only transparent affection. If he was ill, she'd be terrified. She'd need my support.

My mind shifted into selfish gear: Laura was a huge part of my game plan at the Open. She was my rock, my sanity, and my sense of humor. She knew how far I hit every club in my bag, even down to fine discriminations between full swings and punch shots. She knew when to hand me a granola bar and when I needed M&M's. She could tread the fine line between sympathizing over a bad shot and ordering me to leave it behind and just find a way out of the trouble I'd created. I speed-dialed her cell phone and reached her voice mail.

"So sorry to hear about your dad," I said after the beep. "Don't worry about me. I'll try again later."

Damn. I was worried. Who could I turn to now? Dr. Baxter and I had agreed that it was important for me to feel more independent from Joe. I dialed Joe's number.

"Laura can't caddie," I said as soon as he answered. "Her father's in the hospital. Stroke."

"Is he going to be all right?"

"Too early to tell," I said.

"Well, don't panic," Joe said, then snorted. "That's helpful, isn't it? Sorry."

I laughed. "I am panicked. But just the garden variety."

"What about Evelyn Gates? You used her last year, right?"

"I used her all right. Don't you remember I was carrying the bag myself by the end of the round? She kept asking if she could take stuff out of the pockets and come back around later to pick it up."

"Scratch Evelyn, then. They always have a few local caddies available on site. With all the amateurs and Futures Tour players on the roster, not everyone comes with her own man. Some of those guys probably know the course pretty well. You don't need a baby-sitter at this point, Cassie. Just someone who's familiar with the layout and can carry your bag."

Fifteen minutes later, after we'd generated a short list of interview questions for potential caddie candidates, I felt reassured and a little silly. I could have done that on my own.

Turning to Joe was going be a hard habit to break.

Chapter 4

ⵔ **Julie** and Jason met me at the back door of the institute by a stone Buddha positioned to oversee the back patio. This Buddha seemed to have particular responsibility for the smokers, gathered in the afternoon sun to enjoy their guilty pleasure. Jason picked up our two golf bags and a large sack of range balls and started down a grassy hill.

"I suppose he's expecting a big tip," I joked to Julie.

"Nah, there's no place else he'd rather be," she answered, laughing.

"In your dreams," said Jason. "How's it going in there?" He tipped his head back at the brick building.

"Fabulous," said Julie. "I feel so relaxed. How about you, Cassie?"

"I just got some bad news—Laura might not be able to

carry my bag. Her dad had a stroke." I heard my voice quiver with the fear I hadn't wanted to show. Or feel.

Julie stopped stock-still and stared at me, blue eyes wide. "Is he okay?"

"He's in the hospital." I shrugged, my eyes brimming with tears. "I haven't actually talked to her yet."

Julie put her arm around my shoulder.

"Who's going to carry your bag?" Jason asked.

"Something will work out. I just have no idea what it'll be." I could feel tendrils of panic begin to crop up and wind through my body. Breathe in, breathe out. Shaking off Julie's arm, I walked quickly ahead.

"Do you know anyone who's available?" Julie asked Jason.

"Nobody I'd trust with Cassie," he said. "She's a hot ticket, what with the invitation to the PGA tournament and all." He grinned a lopsided smile. "She needs someone who can handle the pressure of a big gallery. Let me think about it."

"It's okay," I repeated. The pressure of a big gallery. Jesus. All I needed was to start thinking that way. *Nothing special, nothing extra,* was supposed to be my motto. "It's no big deal. I'll figure it out." I pointed to a maze of low shrubs that lined a twisting and well-worn path. "What's this?"

"It's a labyrinth," said Julie. "Go ahead and get set up, Jay, we'll be there in a sec."

"What's it for?"

Julie wrinkled her nose. "It's hard to explain. The idea comes from an ancient tradition of Christian pilgrimage. You see it in Greek mythology, too—myths about the minotaur at the center of the labyrinth."

I was trying really hard to keep an open mind and squash my usual sarcastic commentary.

"I know it sounds a little goofy," Julie said, glancing at me. "See, as you walk the labyrinth, you're supposed to meditate or pray. Your internal journey is reflected in the external movement. As you move into the center, you are preparing to arrive. So you might start out with a thought or a question, and as you arrive in the center, you have the answer."

"Woo, woo, woo," I said, feeling bad the second the words left my mouth.

Julie ignored me and pointed to a collection of faded objects as we reached the middle of the maze.

"Throughout history people have left things at the end of a pilgrimage. It's symbolic of laying down your burden."

I squatted to examine the leavings: a charm bracelet, a plastic rose, and several notes that had been washed almost blank by the elements. What had the owners wanted to unload? Dumping a psychological weight, leaving it for someone else to handle, sounded quite appealing. Though I couldn't imagine who would be willing to take me or my burden on.

I stood, knees cracking, throat constricted with unshed tears. "Better get to work," I said curtly. "No one's going to help us chip onto those Donald Ross greens. It's all about accurate irons and staying below the hole."

Julie's face flooded with sympathy. Apparently, my tough-woman act wasn't hard to see through. But I wasn't going to survive the most challenging week in women's golf by weeping each damn time a negative thought crossed my mind.

Jason had stacked a pile of balls for each of us and laid

towels out in the field every fifty yards as targets. We hit balls for a couple hours. My right hand began to cramp up.

"I've about had it," I said.

"I'm going to work a little longer," said Julie. "We'll meet you in the lobby in half an hour?"

I nodded, gathering my clubs together for Jason, and started up the hill toward the institute. I slowed as I reached the labyrinth. Making my way back to the center, I looked over the soft blues and greens of the Berkshire Mountains. Baxter and I had worked out a simple survival program for the next week. Step one, as in this morning's yoga class, I had to notice when my anxiety started to rise. Step two, Baxter called reframing. Laura's having to pull out because of her father's illness, for example, wasn't a disaster. It was a challenge. Step three, stay in the present. I was not to waste time worrying about the Buick Championship decision. I should enjoy the experience of playing in my first Open, a privilege other golfers would give their eyeteeth for.

Baxter's program was a Band-Aid approach, and he wasn't happy about dispensing that much concrete advice. He's the type that thinks almost everything circles back to the family who raised you. In my case, that meant sorting through an unhappy mother, a runaway dad, two difficult stepparents, two teenage half brothers, and my real brother, Charlie, who hasn't had a full conversation with our father in years. Every one of them was making an appearance at the tournament this week. Which got me thinking more about Julie. How could someone that young be so together? Did she have a "normal" family? Maybe I could learn something by watching her.

Tucking my hands into my pockets, I jingled an

assortment of change, tees, and a divot repair tool. One golf ball nestled in the bottom of my right pocket. I pulled it out and fingered the dimpled surface. It was a Slazenger Select, with CB marked in permanent blue below the cat on each side. I rolled the ball between my palms, then knelt down to place it at the base of the shrub that centered the labyrinth.

I was on a pilgrimage of sorts. I'd be very grateful if someone, anyone, helped me find the way.

Chapter 5

Monday morning the sun crept over the horizon to paint the Massachusetts Turnpike with rosy light. Jason had the wheel of Julie's Cabrio convertible, which she had purchased with her recent top ten winner's check. Beet red with a black top, tan leather seats, and a touch of mahogany trim. You could still smell the new. No way would I let some guy drive my brand-new car. But maybe he wasn't just some guy—maybe there was a nuance in their relationship, besides caddie/player, that I hadn't caught.

We exited off the highway onto Route 202, passing a sign that read "Holyoke: the Birthplace of Volleyball." The buildings looked tired and some of them, abandoned. I wondered who picnicked at a table set up with umbrella and chairs on a dirt square along the road.

Julie shouted back over her shoulder. "This used to be a factory town, textiles I think. Now there's a pretty good-sized immigrant population."

Julie graduated from Mount Holyoke several years ago and was thrilled to be returning to the golf course on campus to play the Open.

"A few of the students bring their own horses to college," she explained.

My mind whiplashed from the trappings of poverty to privilege.

"I was way too busy with golf to get involved with that. Did I tell you the story of the golf course? The Orchards was commissioned by Elizabeth Skinner's father—he wanted her to have access to great golf so he hired Donald Ross to design the first nine holes."

Jason slowed for a stoplight. If she hadn't been completely sincere, I would have had to suppress the urge to open the car door and fling myself out, just to get away from the travelogue. But she wasn't bragging. She adored the place and wanted to share every detail. With me. And some of my grumpiness could probably be explained by the contrast between her intimate Ivy League college experience and mine—four hard-drinking, anonymous years at a big state school.

"The campus starts here," said Julie, the excitement in her voice rising. "This is Abbey Hall. I lived here senior year. I think it's where we'll be staying."

The campus was stunning. Handsome red stone buildings with gargoyles and turrets all crawling with ivy. Just what you'd imagine a New England private girls' school to be. Light-years from the hot, flat, brown, crowded landscape of the University of Florida. I wished I'd had the vision to look outside the obvious choices for playing college golf. Or maybe a parent who could see beyond scholarship funds. I slapped my wrist. Self-pity was not in Dr. Baxter's program.

Jason grinned. "It's not much like Gainesville, is it? Not that a couple of lushes like ourselves would have noticed the fine points anyway."

I didn't particularly like being lumped together with him in the "lush club," but it wasn't worth the energy to take him up on it. Yes, I had a track record in that department, but he'd spot the change in me soon enough.

"We would have noticed the golf course. How the hell did the US Open end up at a rich girls' school anyway?" I asked, unable to keep the little barb from slipping out.

"Not everyone's rich," Julie said sweetly.

Jason pulled into the small parking lot next to the Willetts Conference Center. "Back in a sec," said Julie, scrambling out and heading into the building before I could offer to accompany her.

"Have you seen the course?" I asked Jason.

"Came up last week for a day. It's a beaut. A good old-fashioned setup. Keep it in the fairway and sink some putts and you'll be in the hunt."

"Thanks for the tip," I snorted. A golfing virgin could come up with that advice. "What about the greens?"

New England had suffered a serious old-fashioned winter and rumors ran rampant on our tour about whether this golf course could handle the US Open. The players were nervous enough about fast greens, heavy rough, and big galleries without having to survive lousy course conditions. I'd heard as recently as last week that the newest superintendent had been canned and the whole operation was moving to another venue.

"Maybe a little patch of winter kill here and there, but overall, it looked good to go."

Julie returned waving two key cards and settled back into her seat. "Cross over the creek and take a left onto campus."

"I'm a little worried about staying in the dorm," I said. "How private can it be?"

"I checked everything out." Julie took a barrette from her backpack, wound a hank of blond hair around her hand, and clipped it to the top of her head. "There'll be a couple of older alumnae on our floor who are volunteering at the tournament. They'll be thrilled to meet us and then they'll know enough to leave us alone. The media shuttle runs just a block from our doorstep."

"Swell. So we'll start each morning peppered by journalists hungry for dirt."

Julie laughed. "You're absolutely right. Jason can swing by and take us over to the players' lot near the golf course. Or get your own courtesy car if you think you'll need it. You're going to love it here. Tons more privacy than a hotel. And prettier, too."

We carried our luggage to a large double room on the third floor. More spacious than a hotel, but a lot more Spartan. I stretched out on my single bed and felt the bones of the mattress press a chicken wire pattern into my back. Julie had been correct on one count—the third floor was empty and quiet as a tomb.

I plugged in my Internet cord and powered up the laptop while Julie unpacked the contents of her suitcase into a battered wooden bureau, chattering with excitement as she worked. I logged online and downloaded my e-mail. Spam— I had had my nonexistent mortgage application approved, and horny dates of both sexes were eager to meet me—good wishes from two old friends, and a message from Joe.

"Good morning, Cassie! Hope you had a safe trip and are settled into MHC. Let me know what happens with the caddie master. Or if there's anything I can do to help. Joe."

For both of our sakes, I needed to tell him I had things under control. Even if that was a lie. Before I could hit Reply, a new message chimed in from Ruleswhiz. Subject: "Rub of the Green."

I felt weak and a little shaky. Damn the bastard who sent me this garbage.

I looked over at Julie, who was folding underwear into her top drawer. "Are you receiving e-mails from someone calling himself Ruleswhiz?"

"I didn't look this morning. But nothing up till now. Unless I deleted it accidentally."

Julie came across the room to sit on the bed next to me, took my computer, and scanned the note. She read aloud:

"Rule 19-1. By Outside Agency. If a ball in motion is accidentally deflected or stopped by any *outside agency,* it is a *rub of the green,* there is no penalty and the ball must be played as it lies."

"That's it?" I asked, letting go a heavy sigh.

"Yeah." She glanced at me. "How many have you gotten?"

"Two. This one, and one yesterday about sharing caddies. I thought maybe the USGA was sending them out to everyone." I didn't mention the threat attached to the caddie e-mail—didn't want to worry her, or worse yet, come across like an emerging mental patient.

She shook her head and stretched out on the bed. "Nope. Maybe you have a secret admirer." She sat up and reached for my computer again. "Let me see that a minute." She typed in the LPGA Web site address and clicked on my name. "Now I get it."

"Get what?"

"You changed your photo. It's a sexier picture. You're bound to get more attention with this."

"I don't want more attention," I snapped. "Unless it's for great golf shots. Since when were you looking at my Web site photo anyway?"

I took the computer back from Julie and studied my picture. The LPGA was working hard to market professional women golfers as friendly, accessible, and let's face it, attractive athletes who deserved the full support of sponsors and fans. The LPGA commissioner called it the "five points of celebrity" program. And it was working, too—there'd been a record number of hits on the LPGA Web site lately.

So I'd been willing to have a new photo taken, and didn't despise the result. It was still me, though the photographer's assistant had done something weird with my hair that I'd never try at home. And lipstick—she felt strongly that I should not go out without it. But in my opinion, lipstick and golf bags just don't mix. After four or five hours in the beating sun, the tube melts into a colored mush that ends up staining whatever article of clothing I might be wearing, especially if it's new. Besides that, foreign substances chap my lips.

All things considered, it was a nice photo, but nothing that would bring *Playboy* running. Julie was overreacting. Someone I knew must be sending those e-mails. Come to think of it, they had the stink of my sponsor, Lloyd Pompano. He'd stepped up this year to bankroll my season. And he was terrified that I'd blow his investment by overlooking some minor but important detail.

I scrolled through the rest of the messages, deleting spam. "Did you leave me a note the other morning in the coatroom at Kripalu?" I asked suddenly.

Julie looked confused.

"In one of the mailboxes? 'Hit 'em straight' or something like that?"

Julie shook her head. "Why would I leave a message there? We were sharing a room."

I shrugged and looked at my watch. *Forget it, Cassie. You're getting paranoid.*

"Are we going to try to squeeze in a couple of practice holes? I told Lloyd I'd meet him at the Amherst Brewing Company at seven." I pressed my fists against my cheeks. "Please, please say you and Jason will come with me. I can't stand to be alone with that guy."

"Lloyd's your sponsor?"

I nodded.

"Sure we'll come. Gotta eat somewhere. Maybe he'll pick up the check."

I laughed. "And add it to my balance."

We collected hats, sunglasses, and backpacks and returned downstairs to meet Jason. "I told Cassie we'd have dinner with her and Lloyd," she told him as he pulled back out onto the main drag.

"Who's Lloyd?"

I sighed. "Lloyd Pompano. He's a lawyer and a golf nut. Since he can't play worth a damn himself, he offered to put some money up for me this year. I figured any strings he could tie on would be an improvement over taking money from Dad."

"Not so?" Julie asked.

"He's not horrible. Just full of suggestions. Things I

should eat, exercise regimes, ideas about new clubs, and tips on mental toughness."

Julie groaned.

In truth, the psychological tips were the worst. I could justify my club choices to him fairly easily and just flat-out lie about the exercise and diet. But listening to his mental tips meant trouble. The suggestions wormed their way into my fragile mind like computer viruses, replicating and then popping out at inopportune times. One thing for sure—real players wouldn't have to put up with someone like Lloyd.

My cell phone rang.

"Cassie, it's Mike. Michelle and I are in the area. Any chance you're free for dinner?"

"Hang on a sec." And then to Julie, "Do you mind if Mike Callahan and his girlfriend join us?"

Julie shrugged. "It's your party."

I lifted my hand off the receiver and gave Mike the address of the restaurant in Amherst. "See you at seven. We're going to take a look at the course now and try to rustle me up a caddie. Laura's father is in the hospital."

"What's the matter with her dad?"

"He had a stroke. She thinks he's going to be okay, but she doesn't want to leave him. So I'm SOL in the caddie department."

"I could carry for you. I'm free this week."

I started to laugh and laughed until hysterical tears ran down my face, letting the phone drop into my lap. When I'd finally regained control, I picked it back up. "I'm really sorry. That was so rude. It just struck me funny. No offense intended."

"Not that funny," said Mike, his voice stiff. "We'll see you at seven."

Chapter 6

We parked Julie's convertible in Lot A and loaded into a new Honda minivan, driven by a tournament volunteer. During the short hop to the golf course, he elaborated on the weather forecast and the condition of the greens—both reported to be excellent. He dropped us off next to a small practice putting green encircled by a blacktop drive. Two girls I'd met on tour and several I didn't recognize were rolling balls across the small space. A movable waist-high fence gave the impression of exotic animals in a cage. I felt a twinge of claustrophobia, even standing outside.

"Let's register and get our lockers," said Julie.

"And see what's for lunch," I added.

"I'll take your bag up to the caddie shack and tell them

you might be looking for a looper, at least today," Jason told me.

"Thanks." His offer reminded me again that I had no caddie—not that this problem was ever far from my awareness. I pushed down the gathering panic. I would check in with Laura and deal with the fallout of her situation right after lunch.

Julie and I showed our LPGA badges, entered the clubhouse, and found the locker room. I unloaded four-dozen new Slazenger balls, some clean underwear, granola bars, three shirts, six pairs of socks, and my second most comfortable golf shoes from my backpack into the locker between Ashli Bunch and Audra Burks. Then I went upstairs to the dining room and slapped together a sandwich—turkey breast, Swiss cheese, a helping of salad, and hot peppers on whole wheat. I passed up potato chips in favor of watermelon squares. Even Lloyd couldn't have quibbled. I backtracked and scooped out a large handful of chips. It would be hot out on the course—I'd need the salt.

We ate our sandwiches on the deck high above the first tee. Enormous white tents housing concession stands fanned out between the first and ninth holes. The smell of grilled meat was overpowering. A grandstand had been constructed at the back of the ninth green. I imagined that later in the week some fans would stake a spot out early and stay for the day—watching player after player drop her putt. Or not, depending on the kind of round she was having.

That kind of dedication is a puzzle to me. I'd had posters of rock stars on my teenage walls, at least until Mom flipped out about the tacks making holes in the wallpaper.

And I had favorite golfers—Donna Andrews, Fred Couples, Nancy Lopez—players whose swings and behavior on the course I most admired. But Tiger Woods had spawned a new kind of golf fan—folks who had little previous interest in the sport. They wanted to see Tiger the star, Tiger the ball-crusher, Tiger the black man crashing into the pale arena, Tiger the best damn golfer in the world.

The LPGA had caught on to this and was doing what they could to cultivate their own stars.

Joe doesn't think the rock-star phenomenon explains it all. He says people like golf's structure and fairness, too. With the world a chaotic mess, real life doesn't come with the comforting structure that the USGA rules provide.

"I'm going to stop in the bathroom. I'll meet you downstairs," I told Julie.

Amber Clancy was splayed in a wicker chair in the dressing area of the locker room. She appeared both younger and older than when I'd seen her last. The short-shorts and eyebrow piercings were a teenager's; hard to even picture her on a college campus. Her eyes, on the other hand, shadowed by dark hollows, looked more like a worried adult's. Three other young golfers closed the circle around her.

"Did you get to play with Tiger?" asked an Asian girl with delicate features.

"No. But he did ask me to play a practice round with him." Amber giggled and ran the tip of her braid across her cheek. "He's so hot."

"Awesome," said a redhead in Amber's audience. She wore a short, short skirt made out of stretchy fabric decorated with scissors and knives. These girl golfing phenoms with their rigid practice and travel schedules had to figure out some way to rebel.

I mumbled a quick "How's it going?" and edged around the girls into the bathroom. Why do teenagers always take up more space, both physically and psychologically, than they rightfully deserve? When I emerged from my stall, Amber was alone in the room, rustling through a messy stash of belongings in her locker.

She looked up. "Aren't you that detective golfer?"

I shrugged. "Sort of. It was a dumb article, though."

"Cool," she said.

"Have a good round." I headed toward the door.

Her voice stopped me. "So what, you like found a dead girl and figured out who killed her? Do you, like, have a license or something?"

"Oh no." I laughed. "Just wrong place, wrong time."

"Oh." She looked in the mirror and adjusted the beads woven into her cornrows—then glanced back at me, touching the ring in her left eyebrow. "So you don't, like, do this for a living?"

"I'm trying to earn my living playing golf."

Not something she would have to worry much about. Where was this conversation going? Based on recent dealings with my nephews, I knew that teenagers hardly ever tell adults directly what's on their minds. You have to take the few clues provided and make educated guesses.

Two golfers burst into the locker room, laughing loudly. They stopped when they saw Amber and me.

"How's it going?" asked one, flipping her ponytail over her shoulder. She turned away and continued her conversation with her friend before either of us could answer.

A USGA official pushed open the door and poked her head in. "Amber? Your father's looking all over for you.

Half an hour to tee time. He wants you to meet him on the green ASAP."

Amber shrugged, her eyes flashing with icy teenage scorn. "Whatever." The game face was back, the one I'd watched handle a hundred TV interviews.

I trailed her and her escort to the putting green. She sailed into the caged putting enclosure like royalty, waving off autograph requests and ignoring her father's obvious annoyance. Two burly men in jade shirts shadowed her just outside the fence as she putted around the green.

At the caddie shack, Julie introduced our third practice partner for the day—one of the golfers who'd been tapped to write the rookie diary on the LPGA Web site this season. She was juggling two children, a husband, and a Winnebago during her first year on tour. Either she'd go mad, or she'd develop a perspective about professional golf that few of us managed.

I punched in Laura's cell phone number as we waited for our bags. "It's Cassie," I said. "How are you doing? How's your dad?"

"He's hanging in there." I recognized the forced cheerfulness that probably came from sitting beside his hospital bed. "Let me step outside. We're not supposed to have phones on here." The phone crackled and buzzed.

Her voice dropped a little lower and the background beeping and hissing was no longer audible. "We're still in the ICU. His speech is slurred and they're not sure how extensive the damage will be." I thought I heard her crying. "He's a tough old bird. He's pulling through."

"That's great," I said. "I bet he's really glad you're there. Wish I could be there with you."

"I'm so sorry, Cassie," she said. "I know how much you're counting on me, but I can't leave. Not yet."

My eyes brimmed with tears. Dammit. "Don't even think about it. Tons of caddies are hanging around here looking for a bag and one of them is sure to work out. Just send him my love and keep me posted."

I hung up feeling blue in more than one way. A little part of me had hung on to the hope that her dad would make a miraculous recovery, releasing her to my side. Wasn't going to happen. And even through this crisis, I envied her connection to her father, clear and true, free of the history of abandonment, competition, and disappointment that choked my family's relationships.

The caddie master approached. "Cassie Burdette?"

I raised a finger.

"I have a couple guys that I think will do a good job for you." He ushered me to a small cluster of men wearing assorted polo shirts. "Martin plays on the local high school golf team. He's young and strong," said the caddie master, pushing a teenager toward me. The kid's hand shook as he reached for mine. How would he handle an audience of 25,000 if he was that anxious about saying hello? One very nervous caddie and one very nervous player spells O-U-T O-N Y-O-U-R A-S-S in the US Open.

"And this is Tony," said the caddie master, drawing me over to the next candidate. He clapped the back of a middle-aged gentleman wearing wrinkled khaki pants and a Ryder Cup 2004 hat. Tony had apparently misplaced his razor.

He gripped my hand and began to reel off his caddie gig résumé. "I nearly won the Dinah Shore with Kate," he finished, shaking his head sadly. "I told her that putt broke left to right, but she couldn't see it."

Blockbuster ego aside, there was little mystery about why this man got the frequent boot. The smell of stale alcohol billowed out as he talked. If he wasn't pickled now, he'd be back in the jar soon.

I smiled weakly at Tony and walked back over to the kid. "Martin, do you mind carrying my bag for just nine holes today? I'm hoping my regular loop will be able to make it tomorrow."

Tony looked furious, but I had to do what was right for me.

"Awesome!" Martin grabbed my equipment and we started back up the hill to the first tee, where he pulled on a yellow USGA bib. Odd to see my name stretched across the back of a stranger.

I selected a granola bar and a bottle of water from the stand on the tee while we waited for the group in front of us to clear the fairway. "Have you played this course before?"

"Oh, yes, ma'am," said Martin. "My team practiced here a couple times this spring."

Ma'am. I cringed. Did I look like a senior citizen?

"I can tell you all the places you don't want to be."

Great. I knew he meant well, but he was already rasping on the few nerves I had remaining. In Golf Psych 101, you learn to put things in positive terms, never negative. If you tell a player "Don't hit it right, there's water over there," nine times out of ten she hits it right, into the drink. Joe says our brains aren't wired to hear "don't."

"I've only seen two ladies hit driver off this tee today," Martin continued. "One was Annika Sorenstam. The other was Amber Clancy. Unless you're the number one player in

the world, or gunning to take her spot"—he smiled slyly—
"trying to go over this creek is risky business." He pointed
down the hill to the stream that crossed the fairway, maybe
250 yards out. "It plays with every golfer's mind."

"Thanks." I slid my three-wood out of the bag. "I'll use
the three."

No point in telling him that on a new course, in a new
tournament, on a Monday, I'd be using the three-wood
anyway. My driver and I were just starting to be friends,
and I didn't like to put too much pressure on the relationship. Laura would have known that without a word exchanged. I rushed through my preshot routine and yanked
the drive into the rough.

"See what I'm saying, though?" The corners of Martin's lips curved up into another knowing smile. "You pull
a shot like that with a driver and the little extra mustard
puts that puppy in the creek."

How had this kid gone from being afraid to shake hands
to the world's greatest authority on absolutely freakin'
everything?

By the time we finished nine holes, I was famished and
frazzled. Jason spent the afternoon making notations in
his green yardage book, pointing out preferred landing
spots, and laying targets on the green for Julie to practice
putting at potential future pin placements. He'd walked
the course backward on his previous visit and obviously
had a mental command of Donald Ross's devious undula-
tions and hazards. Julie would have every advantage he
could offer.

Martin was outgoing, to say the least, and apparently
knew the rules of golf. But he was oblivious to the ground-
work that Jason was laying. Let's face it—I wouldn't trust

him to carry my bag on a course featuring Astroturf and windmills.

He had to go.

"Thanks an awful lot for your guided tour," I said, stuffing a wad of cash into his hand and trying to make it sound as though there'd been no possibility that I might keep him for the week. Surely the caddie master could drum up more reasonable candidates. Wasn't this the most prestigious tournament in women's golf? "I'll pass your suggestions on to my regular gal when she gets here tomorrow."

My phone buzzed on the short hop back to Lot A. Hearing the voice of my only and older brother, Charlie, felt like coming home. I described the fairways (narrow) and the greens (undulating) and the performance of my temporary caddie (impossible).

"I'm arriving on Wednesday with Mom," Charlie said. "I could start then."

I sighed. The only thing going for my brother as caddie would be his sense of humor. He'd taken a stand against golf back in high school when he was pushing away from Dad, and he'd never returned to the game. He claimed his law practice and bicycle racing kept him too busy, but even I could see his knee-jerk reactions to golf came out of unresolved feelings about our father. Not surprising. Just before Charlie went to college, good old Dad had left home and started a new family. Even the thickest parent should realize that his kid deserves a chance to launch his own life path before he flics the coop himself.

I'd come close to forgiving my father lately, thanks to steady pressure from Baxter to explore the shadows of my sadness and rage. And thanks to Dad himself, who'd nudged his way back into my life. He gave up his dream of professional golf last year and offered to pour his heart (large) and funds (limited) into mine. Lloyd was my attempt to keep some independence. Sheesh. My Declaration of Independence appeared to apply to all the men in my life.

"What do you say?" Charlie asked.

"Thanks anyway," I told him. "Someone has to manage Mom."

I shivered just saying those words. Mom and my stepfather Dave had never attended one of my tournaments. Honestly, I preferred it that way. But I couldn't very well tell my own mother not to come to the US Open. It was a small miracle that (a) she understood the importance of the tournament and (b) was willing to travel away from home. So I made Charlie swear in Burdette blood that he would not leave her side.

"Just bring Mom on Wednesday—that's a big enough job."

Chapter 7

With a couple hours to kill before our dinner reservation, Julie had Jason drop us off at the Mount Holyoke library.

"I want to say hey to the research librarian. She was such a doll when I was writing my thesis. You can look around or check your e-mail and then we'll walk back through campus. Sound okay?"

"Okay."

How did I end up with friends who were so damn perky, when most of the time I felt like the anti-perk personified? Jeanine, who'd insisted I play the maid of honor in her Pinehurst wedding to Rick Justice last fall, had the same chipper way about her. Only Laura shared my sense of the absurd. And Laura wasn't here.

I swore on my father's Cleveland sand wedge that I would not think one more grumpy thought.

Inside the library the walls of a stone courtyard stretched three floors to the skylight. Even more important was a small coffee shop. I ordered a latte, one ear open to Julie's excited chatter.

"Be patient with us, will you?" asked the chunky young woman behind the counter. "Daren is going through our training program today." A lanky boy with a crew cut and a grubby apron waved.

"Each incoming class is assigned a class animal and a class color," Julie explained while we waited for Daren to grasp the mysteries of espresso. "There's mine—the yellow griffin." She pointed to the flags that hung in the courtyard.

I added two packets of brown sugar to my coffee and followed her up the steps to the reference area.

"See the stained glass on the back wall there? Those are the seals of the seven sisters and Mary Lyon's missionaries. She's our founder," Julie explained. "The entire campus is centered around her grave."

Which seemed a little gruesome to me. The reference room was imposing—also several stories tall, with dark beams sporting buttresses and gargoyles. Two dark oak staircases spiraled through the center of the space.

"I'll be right here, take your time," I said, settling behind a large computer screen with my illegally imported coffee. The sign outside had been very clear about forbidding food and drink in the library, especially near the computers. But I considered this a medical emergency.

I logged on to my e-mail. Another message from Joe.

"Hey there, Cassie! How's the course? How's Laura?

Did you find a caddie? Hope everything's going well! Give me a buzz when you get a minute. Your friend, Joe."

In six simple lines, how did he manage to leave me feeling terribly guilty, practically smothered, and horribly lonely, all at the same time? It was obviously killing him not to be here. And even though I was the one who'd suggested he back off, it was odd for me, too.

My mind drifted back to our interactions in Maui last winter. I'd finally realized that touchy, grouchy, erratic, brilliant, prickly Mike Callahan was not the man for me. Another woman might be able to tease him out of his mood swings. But I took every shift to heart. Like two people struggling in quicksand, with each argument we sank lower.

Joe, on the other hand, was a steady optimist, not to mention smart, caring, and handsome in a professorial sort of way. With our respective romantic rivals set aside, and after he told Laura he had the hots for me, we'd made the crazy decision to share a room in Maui—a "faux honeymoon." I thought getting together in Hawaii, of all places, would be a slam dunk.

It wasn't.

My friend Jeanine had put a lifetime's worth of planning into her Pinehurst society wedding last year. Then after a series of fiascos, the festivities were canned—almost taking the marriage with them. Eloping to Hawaii with Joe and me as witnesses was the compromise.

This time, Jeanine and Rick's wedding was perfect: waves lapping softly in the background, the perfumed scent of flowers wafting in on a subtle breeze, the sun dropping through wisps of clouds to the horizon. Jeanine looked like a goddess in a white silk shift, carrying a huge spray of tropical blooms. She cried when Rick slid the gold band on her finger. I did, too.

During dinner on the patio, we toasted everything: a long and happy marriage (duh, that was me, but someone had to say it), a successful season on the tour (Jeanine, for her new husband), God for bringing him such a gorgeous and kind wife (Rick, of course, still scrambling to butter Jeanine up after her fancy wedding got ruined), good mental health for all of us (Joe, who couldn't help his occasional outbursts of dork-hood, and besides, the champagne was going to his head).

Then Joe asked me to dance. I might have the grace of a swallow-tailed kite with a golf club in my hand, but I've got three left feet on the dance floor.

"I'm afraid I'll hurt you," I told Joe after we'd stumbled around the room once. We retreated to a couple of lounge chairs on the sand with more champagne. It was a perfect night. And Joe and I had a lot to look forward to—three years we'd dodged our mutual attraction and now was the time to fish or cut bait.

So how come I felt sick to my stomach? I wanted to blame it on the bubbly, but it was a different kind of sick. A lead weight in my gut that, if I was honest with myself, felt like dread.

Joe pulled me to my feet and led me down toward the water. "Mmmm. I've waited a long time for this." He reached out to take my hands and leaned in for our first kiss.

The result was a real clunker—something from a bad comedy rerun where the noses and lips just don't fit. If we'd been wearing braces, they would have locked. Joe was breathing harder.

I pulled away and tapped my heart. "I'm really sorry. I

don't think I can do this right now." I was close to tears and his confused expression only made it worse.

"I don't know what's wrong. But I'm afraid we'll ruin things for good."

Joe dropped my hands and took a step away. "Let's sit down and talk about it."

"I can't talk about it just now." I started to hyperventilate. He always, always wanted to talk.

Now his voice sounded professional. "No problem. We've been friends a long time. Waiting another night won't hurt."

Then I remembered we were sharing a room. A room with a king-sized bed. The sick feeling got worse. I was having trouble getting enough air.

"Do you think they might have a second room available?"

He had to be disgusted, or at least disappointed, but he didn't let that show. "I'll go check."

The front desk had bad news—like it or not, we were in this night together. The resort was sold out to goal-busting salesmen from an electronics data storage company. "They did switch us to a room with two double beds. Or I could always sleep in the car."

"Don't be silly."

We went back to the wannabe love nest, swept our stuff into our bags, and rolled the suitcases down the hall to the new digs. This room was next to the elevator and lacked a water view.

"I'm sorry," I said again. "I can't believe I'm doing this to you."

"Not to worry," said Joe. "Do you mind if I take a shower first?"

While he was in the bathroom, I washed my face and

changed into sweats. Slipping under the silky birds of paradise coverlet of my bed, I flipped on the TV. I wanted to fill my mind with loud voices and silly sitcom plots, not think about what bit of twisted family history led to this moment. Or hash anything more out with Joe. How come I could sleep with a cad like Mike, no problem, but it was hands off with a perfectly nice gentleman like Joe?

Joe finally resurfaced with wet hair, wearing a pair of blue cotton pajamas. He got under his covers, inserted a pair of earplugs, and slid on a black eye mask.

"I didn't know we were coming to bed in costume," I said. Always the smartass.

He pulled out the plug from his left ear and barely smiled. "I've got thin eyelids."

"Oh?"

The way he described it, if there's any light in the room at all, it's like normal people lying in a tanning bed with only a strip of white gauze over their eyes.

Normal people. Why couldn't I be one of them?

"I'll turn the TV off," I said.

"I'm fine like this." He patted his ears and the mask, and adjusted it over his eyes.

That's when the image of a giant lizard lounging on the bed next to me came to mind—hooded lids, flickering tongue. It wasn't fair, I knew that, but I was learning too much about the private details of Joe's life. And not handling it one bit well.

Dr. Baxter, of course, diagnosed a more serious case of fear of intimacy than we'd even imagined before. The white flag has been waving over my relationship with Joe ever since that night. Even if it hurt his feelings, I couldn't afford to consider changing anything now.

I clicked through the remainder of my messages. Dammit. Ruleswhiz again.

"Rule 28. Ball Unplayable. The player may deem his ball unplayable at any place on the *course* except when the ball is in a *water hazard*. The player is the sole judge as to whether his ball is unplayable." And further down the page in bold: **"Who's your daddy, Cassie? Who's your caddie?"**

Who the hell was sending this shit? I picked up the latte, but my hand shook so badly I had to set it back down. Someone was trying to rattle me—and doing a damn good job. *Get a grip, Cassie.* I thought back to Dr. Baxter's plan: notice the anxiety, reframe the circumstances, stay in the present. The noticing part was easy—my stomach hurt, my heart pounded, and I was near tears—again.

Reframe the circumstances: I tried to think logically about the three messages I'd had from Ruleswhiz. He obviously knew my e-mail address. He didn't want me playing in the PGA-sponsored tournament. And he knew I had no caddie here at the Open. None of those factors alone were overly alarming.

Half the country thought I'd be an idiot to try to play in a professional men's event—that hardly narrowed things down. And the caddie problem was no secret after the practice round today. This tournament was a small world, and every even slightly interesting diversion was fodder for gossip.

But who wanted to shake me up? And why? And what did the stupid *Rules of Golf* have to do with anything? I remembered Jason's advice about tracing the e-mail and wished I had a clue how to go about it. I drummed my fingers on the desk.

There were other golfers who got attention for their celebrity—Annika Sorenstam, for one, and calendar girl Natalie Gulbis, for another. Natalie was a beautiful and talented young golfer who had followed tennis player Anna Kournikova's footsteps as a glamorous athlete/star, only with less accent on bare flesh and more on the talent side of things. She'd released a full-color calendar in time for the 2004 Open that had been banned from the USGA merchandise tent at the eleventh hour.

I typed her name into the Google search bar and surfed through her Web site. She had included a diary, sexy but decent photos, a detailed appearance schedule, and some very annoying background music. No message board, no e-mail address—all her correspondence was funneled through her agent. Though fans were invited to download an application for the only *official* Natalie Gulbis international fan club.

Then I moved on to a couple of articles about Annika Sorenstam's divorce. This was the real drawback to fame—people started to think the private details of your business were public property.

Buried in among the articles about Annika, I came across one about Amber Clancy's soon-to-be-released calendar. Amber had a calendar? I clicked on the link. "Amber Bares All for Golf" was accompanied by a photo that the author claimed was the calendar's front cover. You could call it soft porn or art, depending on your perspective. She was naked from the waist up except for a Pebble Beach golf towel draped around her neck. She appeared to be humping her golf bag.

"Women golfers need a sexier image," Amber had been reported to say. "I'm proud of my game and proud of my body and not afraid to show them both."

Good God. What was she thinking? What was she after? And wouldn't this tank her amateur status? The message board following the article was jammed with excited replies.

"Maybe the entry requirements for the LPGA tour aren't just based on golf skills!" said Ladygolflover.

"Hooray for girl golfers! Next year, let's suggest a calendar with Amber completely in the buff. She could pose in Lucien Beccia's twelve positions of the golf swing," wrote Golftalk. "I for one would like to see her release."

"Better have your copy laminated," commented Eagerbeaver.

Good lord. How were the LPGA mucky-mucks reacting to this?

"How hot is Amber?" asked Bogeyman. "Hot enough to burn this blogger's fingers."

"Are those boobs the real thing or is there silicone in them there hills?"

I winced. No eighteen-year-old should have to be the subject of creepy Internet crawlers with nothing better to do than fantasize about her sex life. On the other hand, hadn't she asked for it by putting herself out in the public literally half-naked? Did her parents know about this?

I had nothing to worry about. Not like Amber had, with pages of rude comments written about her fantasy sex life—and her body. I was working myself into a groundless frenzy over a couple of stupid e-mails.

"Ready to go?"

I yelped and jerked my arm away from the keyboard, banging my elbow on the chair.

"Gosh you're jumpy, girl," said Julie. "Let's go get dressed for supper."

Chapter 8

As we crested the third flight of stairs, I noticed that the door to our dorm room was cracked ajar.

"Did you forget to lock it?" Julie asked.

I shook my head. "Housekeeping services maybe?"

Julie snorted and pushed the door open. "In your dreams. Let's just make sure none of our stuff is missing."

As far as I could see, nothing had been disturbed. The two hundred-dollar bills I keep tucked away in my suitcase were still there. And my laptop and my iPod. Except for my golf clubs, which were stored safely at the caddie shack, I don't own anything else valuable.

Julie shrugged and grabbed her towel and cosmetics bag. "Just make sure it latches when you leave next time." Like I was the one who couldn't be trusted.

We took quick showers in yellow-tiled cubicles, where the white plastic curtain wrapped itself around my legs. Judging from the many small signs taped to the tile—*If you sprinkle when you tinkle, be a sweetie and wipe the seatie*— the housekeeping staff focused their anal—bordering on obsessive—attention here. I still regretted forgetting my flip-flops. Public showers make me think of fungus, whether or not the cleaning crew is top-notch. While we toweled off, Julie reviewed the golf holes on the back nine for me.

"The last three holes are so challenging—just wait, you'll love them! We'll be playing sixteen as a long par four with a creek just in front of the green. You absolutely have to stay below the hole or you've got a very slippery putt going down. Seventeen's a pretty little par three. And eighteen, wow! Not only is it uphill but it usually plays into the wind. Remember to stay a little left with your tee shot and you'll have no trouble with the stream on the far right side."

"Umm, thanks."

Julie laughed. "Information overload, right?"

"No, no. I'm grateful for any local knowledge." I tried to smile.

We padded back down the hallway to our room.

"You're awfully quiet. Is everything okay?" she asked.

"I'm a little worried about the caddie business," I said.

More to the point, in spite of my attempts to reassure myself, after reading crude comments about Amber Clancy for an hour, my imagination had pulsed into overdrive. The weird e-mails were starting to really bother me. It wasn't fair to unload this on Julie. She worried about me too much as it was. I could give her a different concern, something less toxic.

"And I just realized, I feel a little funny about seeing

Mike with another girl. Even though it's absolutely the right thing for us not to be together."

"I still feel bad about springing that Mike thing on you in Pinehurst." She looked embarrassed—cheeks pinked up and eyes watery. She'd stunned the heck out of me last fall by asking for dating advice about Mike, when as far as I knew, Mike and I hadn't even officially broken things off.

I flicked my wrist. "Forget about it. You didn't know the situation. It's ancient history now." I couldn't help being curious. "You guys didn't hit it off?"

She laughed. "A brief lapse of judgment on my part. Have you met the new girlfriend?"

"Oh yes." I sighed through gritted teeth and tugged a shirt over my damp hair. "Michelle and I go all the way back. She was dating Mike when I carried his rookie year bag. She drove him bonkers, blowing hot and cold. She actually slept with his best friend, the golfer he'd be paired with the following day, during a tournament."

"And he's taken her back?" said Julie. "Unbelievable."

"He says she's changed. All I can figure is that he craves that weird kind of intensity. She's a challenge in a way I could never match. I'm too damn dull."

"You wouldn't want to compete with that," said Julie. She glanced at my blue jeans and T-shirt. "You're wearing *that* to dinner?"

"I'm not dressing up for Lloyd. Or Mike. Or Michelle. I'm going comfortable." And safe, I thought. Not one extra molecule of glamour or sexiness.

We heard Julie's car horn beeping and went downstairs to meet Jason.

"You girls look good enough to eat," he said, eyes pinned on Julie. "And I'm starving."

"Cut the crap," said Julie, with a smirk.

"Who is this Lloyd character?" Jason asked, meeting my eyes in the rearview mirror.

"He's my sponsor. He's staking me some expenses this year to take the pressure off." I grinned. "So I have to be nice to him. My friends do, too." I tapped his shoulder. "It's part of the deal."

"How do you know him?" Julie asked.

"He was a fan. He watched me play last year in the ShopRite Classic, and he liked my swing. So he got in touch with me through the LPGA office."

"He liked your *swing*?" Jason asked.

"Yes." I wrinkled my nose. Honestly, I'd been so grateful to have someone outside my circle of friends enthuse about my potential that I hadn't looked too closely at the possible down side. "All I can say is, it seemed like a good idea at the time. He loves golf. And he's got the big bucks. He considers me to be part of his portfolio." Enough. I was getting annoyed. Time for a diversion.

"Tell me more about what it was like here as a student," I suggested to Julie.

And she was off.

After a fifteen-minute drive through the countryside, we passed the Amherst green. Jason maneuvered the convertible into a spot across from the Amherst Brewing Company. Like South Hadley, this was clearly a college town, also harboring a smattering of the possibly homeless and the definitely hippie. Lloyd was waiting outside the restaurant, looking at his watch.

"Hey, Lloyd!" I leaned in stiffly for a hug. "This is my roomie, Julie, and her caddie, Jason. Julie's a Holyoke grad and Jason went to Florida a couple years ahead of me."

"Dartmouth man here," said Lloyd, shaking their hands briskly.

He was overdressed for the Brewing Factory—for Amherst, period—in tasseled loafers, pale blue seersucker pants, no socks, and a pink shirt. He had a crested navy blazer slung over his shoulder, decorated with the Dartmouth seal, I was guessing now. His thick brown hair had been buzzed short and then gelled into tiny spikes.

"How did it go out there today?"

"Great!" said Julie and Jason in unison.

Lloyd peered over his sunglasses at me.

"Terrific," I lied. "None of the rumors about potholes in the fairway and dead greens appear to be true. It's a beautiful course, my swing feels good, not a care in the world."

Two blocks up the sidewalk I spotted Mike and Michelle heading our way. Michelle's a redhead, but with a skim-milk complexion, not the kind with freckles. And stacked, as I'd overheard one of Mike's friends comment one day when he didn't know I was listening. They were holding hands, actually *swinging* their hands like kids on a playground. How the hell did she manage that?

I made the introductions, receiving a real hug from Mike and an air kiss from Michelle. Laura insists the girl is seriously threatened by my history with Mike. Which is fine. I kind of like the idea of getting under her skin—she's sure gotten under mine. Either way, I don't want him back. But it all felt awkward as hell.

"Long time no see, man," said Jason to Mike, with a neck-snapping back clap. "How you hittin' em?"

"Can't complain," Mike said. "Except when my old friend Snappy comes back." They chuckled in unison, Mike with more enthusiasm than Jason. In college those two had spent many hours at the range stamping out their common flaw, the dreaded snap hook. Mike had conquered it, mostly; Jason had not.

"You must be Michelle," said Julie. "Jason and Cassie have told me so much about you."

Michelle arched her pinkish brows. "Really?" She flashed a smile at Jason. "I wouldn't have thought you'd remember me."

"Unforgettable . . ." Jason crooned, then waved the waitress over to request an emergency order of double nachos for the table. "Come back right away—these people need beer!"

We studied the menu's lineup of home-brewed draft beer.

"What's your favorite?" Jason asked the waitress when she returned.

"The Boltwood Bock has the toasted malt flavor. But I like our Heather Ale. It won a silver medal at the beer brewing festival."

"Budweiser," I said when my turn came, ignoring Lloyd's no-alcohol-during-a-tournament glare.

"So who's your caddie, Cassie?" Mike asked when the waitress had taken our drink order back to the bar.

I tried to cut him off with an eye roll in Lloyd's direction—too late.

"What's that supposed to mean?" asked Llyod. "Where's Laura?"

My chest tightened and I felt a twinge of pain radiating down my arm. "Her father's sick. She probably won't make it up this way, not anytime soon."

"I offered to carry for her," said Mike.

Jason laughed louder than I had when Mike made this

offer on the phone, only without the same edge of hysteria. "I've seen players throw clubs and scream at rules officials, but the caddie doing it—now that would be something for the history books."

"Tiger's caddie will go after anyone who interrupts his player's concentration," said Julie.

"That was one incident," I started. "And the photographer was shooting right through Tiger's swing. With Mike on the bag—"

"Enough!" Mike said, scowling. "This is what you get for being a nice guy."

I patted his hand across the table. "You're sweet. I tried out one of the local caddies today and it went fine."

"He was a dweeb," said Jason. "For Christ's sake, this is the US Open, Cassie. You can't have a freakin' skateboarder on your bag."

"He might be trainable," I said, crunching a tortilla chip loaded with melted cheese, onions, and one glistening ring of jalapeno pepper. My eyes watered with the heat and I took a gulp of beer.

Lloyd slipped a small notebook out from the pocket of his blazer. "What was this fellow's name? Mike, what's your caddie doing this week? Would he be available?"

I groaned inwardly, wishing I had explained to Mike ahead of time that I didn't hash problems out in front of Lloyd. He tended to panic and push to take over, a lesson I had learned the hard way.

"I'd suggest you let Cassie figure this out herself," said Mike. "She's done all right so far."

"Thank you." I nodded at Mike and flashed a real smile.

"*All right.* Those are the operative words," said Lloyd. "Is she satisfied with all right, or is she reaching—"

"Can we talk about something else, please? I'm under doctor's orders to relax."

"Do you know the story about why the tournament is being held here?"

Without waiting for an answer, Julie started in on the fable of how Mount Holyoke College had come to host the biggest women's tournament in all of golf. It involved another tournament venue pulling out a year before they were due to host the Open, either because of terrorist concerns or an unwillingness to turn their locker rooms over to the USGA, depending on which version you believed. Third time I'd heard it, but what did I care—as long as it wasn't a discussion about my caddie, my diet, or my golf swing.

"Speaking of thinking outside the box," said Lloyd as we paid the check, "I had an idea. We should set up a Web site for you. And even consider a calendar, like the one Natalie Gulbis sold."

"Oh, please."

"If you want advice on your clothes and makeup," said Michelle, raking me from head to foot with a critical eye, "I could help you there."

She had eyelids layered with three different shades of purple and lashes so long and so loaded with black gunk that I wondered how she kept her eyes open. After dinner, she needed five minutes to repair the damage a cobb salad had done to the paint job on her lips.

"Great idea, I'll get back to you on that," I said. When golfers returned to playing with wooden clubs and balls stuffed with feathers, that's when I'd solicit any kind of advice from Michelle.

"Did you see the article about Amber's calendar? Ooh-la-la," said Mike. "What are you girl golfers coming to?"

"What's with her calendar?" Jason asked.

"She's naked," said Mike.

"She's *naked*?" asked Lloyd.

"Well, half-naked, anyway."

"Is she out of her mind?" Julie asked. "What are her parents thinking?"

"Dollar signs," said Jason.

"She may not have told them about it," said Julie. "Would that be legal if she isn't twenty-one?"

I noticed Lloyd's face grow animated. "Don't even go there," I said. "I'm only interested in promotion through golf. Period." I held both hands up. "Besides, if you idiots could get past the mammary glands, you'd see that she's an incredibly buff young lady. She should show that bod off. No suet ass there."

"So how many times have you worked out this week?" Lloyd asked, his notebook on the table again.

"Four," I lied again. "I did the three you suggested and an extra run."

He nodded and scribbled in his notebook. I hated the way lying to him had become automatic. At least it was only for a year.

Back in the dorm by eleven P.M., I pulled on an oversized T-shirt, brushed my teeth, and slid under the top sheet of my single bed.

"Aren't you going to obsess over your e-mail?" Julie asked.

"Nah. Laura would call if she had news. Anything else

can wait." I was tempted to tell her about my other creepy messages. But why cause her more worry? This wasn't her problem.

"Do you mind if I ask what kind of deal you have with Lloyd?" she asked.

I pressed a pillow over my eyes and sighed. "He's staking my expenses in exchange for ten percent of winnings." I threw the pillow off to the side.

A strange expression crossed her face. "You don't have to turn in all your receipts and stuff, do you?"

"He wanted it that way at first. Thank God I had the sense to tell him it was a lump sum or nothing. Can you imagine? Every time I had dinner with him, I'd be worrying about what I ordered. It's bad enough this way."

"Did you sign an agreement about your practice or workouts, that kind of stuff?" Perched on the bed across from me, she rubbed cream into her face and then began to slather it onto her legs. "It kind of bothered me, the way he talked to you."

"Aargh," I groaned into the pillow. "I wish I'd never met the guy."

With a little frown, she hiked her nightshirt up and began to massage her thighs with pink lotion.

I sighed. "I've got to earn some money this year so I can show him the door."

"I'm sure he means well," said Julie, her voice soft and reassuring. "He's the sort that's just uncomfortable if he isn't in control of all the details."

I knew all about that. I used to be one of those people myself. Until the panic attack happened, forcing me to realize how little control a person really had.

My cell phone rang.

"It's Joe. How are things going up there?"

"Going great guns." I forced as much optimism into my voice as I could manage. "The course is terrific. We had a nice dinner tonight with my roommate and her caddie. And Lloyd was there, of course. He had a minor run-in with Mike, but other than that, no casualties."

"You had dinner with Mike?"

"Not just Mike. Michelle came, too. You remember her from a couple of years ago? I'm not sure even you could straighten out her personality problems, but he seems to like her."

"I didn't know Mike was such a fan of the LPGA."

"Don't tell me you're jealous?" I laughed. "Look, there's not a chance in hell we're getting back together. I learned my lesson on that one. Besides, Michelle was watching him like a hawk."

Joe said nothing, which was unusual—to put it mildly.

"Look," I said again. "It might seem odd, but Mike and I are better friends now than we ever were when we were dating. It's nice having him in town, actually. Especially with Laura out of commission. I really miss her."

"I miss you, too," said Joe.

Too late, I realized I had trampled his feelings. Again.

"Can't wait for you to get here," I added before hanging up. Lame.

"Mike was awfully sweet to you tonight," Julie said.

I glared and turned off the light. Just enough moonlight leaked past the white plastic shade in the window to make out the outline of her features across the room.

"Sorry," she said. "Just calling 'em like I see 'em. And

what's the matter with that Amber Clancy? Why in the hell would you want to expose yourself to all the weirdos in the world? I gotta see this picture."

As I shifted around trying to find the least wiry spot on the mattress, Julie slipped into soft snores.

Who's your caddie, Cassie?

Who's your caddie?

Somewhere in the earliest hours of the morning, a thunderstorm rumbled through. I listened to the firm drumming of the rain against the windows and the traffic flowing past the dormitory, and finally slept.

Chapter 9

"**Wake** up, Sleepyhead! We tee off in two hours." Julie bounced on the end of my bed. "You were out cold."

I stretched my full length and massaged a crick in my lower back. "Did you hear the storm last night?"

She shook her head. "It's a beautiful morning. I bet the rain softened the greens a little, too." She spun around the room, twirling her putter, singing, her blond hair streaming behind her. Seventy-thirty A.M. and my roommate believed she was starring in a Broadway musical. *Putt on a Hot Tin Roof*, or maybe *Phantom of the Orchards*. I, on the other hand, was stiff, tired, and crabby.

"Can I use your computer while you're in the bathroom?" Julie asked. I nodded and headed down the hall for another short, but claustrophobic shower.

"I left it on for you," she said when I returned.

I unwrapped the towel wound turban-style around my head.

My hands had broken into a thin sheen of sweat.

I hadn't planned to check my e-mail. Rulings from anonymous sources, sad notes from Joe, bad news from Laura, editorials about my future, even congratulations from unknown fans—I wanted none of it. A wave of panic hovered on the edge of my consciousness and anything—any little thing—might usher it in. But now it seemed worse not to look; I'd only imagine that something did lurk there, waiting to ambush me later. And e-mail addict that she knew me to be, Julie would find my abstinence odd. She'd ask questions, lots of them.

I logged on and found spam and a good-luck message from a golfer I'd met in Q-school. Relief flooded through me. Another message chimed its arrival.

"Hi, Cassie! Hope you have the caddie situation all straightened out. Don't forget, I'm here if you need me. I'm not just a big brain—I could carry fifty pounds eighteen holes, too! Love from your friend Joe."

Thank God it was only him.

He was obviously scrambling to recover from our pitiful and uncomfortable phone call last evening. Having him caddie for me wasn't the worst idea . . . I'd take him over Mike. I deleted the entire inbox and closed the computer down. I pulled on G-Star originals—capris in a casual, rumpled fabric with punkish zippers stretching from knee to mid-thigh. I'd achieve the rumpled effect anyway by the end of the day. Might as well start out looking like I'd planned it all along.

Jason drove us back to the players' parking lot, and we transferred over to the clubhouse shuttle. The grounds were busier today, bustling with players, volunteers, spectators, and the first wave of sports media. Maybe if I avoided eye contact, they wouldn't stop me to ask questions and unleash the jackhammer of fear and doubt that lay just underneath my surface calm.

How's the golf course? How's your game? How low do you think someone's going to have to go this weekend? What number do you have in mind? Have you made a decision about the Buick Championship? Solved any new murders today? Yuk, yuk.

As Joe pointed out, the media are always trying to drag their subjects into the future—the worst possible state of mind for your golf game. I thought back to a closing meditation that had caught my attention at Kripalu. It was a yoga guru's way of saying "Hit one shot at a time," though definitely more poetic: *The present moment is the precious gift that often goes unnoticed and unappreciated. The present moment is the only moment where we are . . .*

We escaped into the clubhouse dining room for a quick breakfast of scrambled eggs and French toast, then headed out to the small practice green near the first tee. Only a seriously focused player would get any real practice done here today. The fans felt closer than usual. The area was small to begin with, and the bars of the guardrail had been moved in to hug the perimeter of the green.

Suppose you didn't like your "present moment"?

I pulled up a Zen mantra that Laura had tried with Mike several years ago: "Don't complain, about anything, even to yourself."

It hadn't worked very well back then, either.

I took a long deep breath and leaned back with half-closed eyes to enjoy the puffy white clouds and a slight breeze. I inhaled again and remembered yet another technique from my weekend yoga adventure.

As we lay on our backs on our sticky mats, we had been instructed to imagine each problematic thought being carried away in a bubble. Someone sending you weird e-mail? Watch the worry float away. Strain between you and your golf psychologist buddy? Up, up, and away. No caddie for the US Open? That bubble wasn't lifting off. I knew I had to go talk with the caddie master about which dregs of the caddie barrel were available today, but I just couldn't face it yet.

Across the green, a dainty Asian player was experimenting with putters, an equipment rep hovering hopefully nearby. You don't change equipment at a major tournament unless there's a serious problem, like a case of hand-jerking, score-busting, putting yips. And that problem would be in her head, not her putter. Once a player has a basic stroke under her belt, putting is all about confidence. If a golfer sinks a series of putts with a garden hoe, that's what you'll find in her bag. I snickered, thinking about the press conference that would follow such a round.

"Miss Burdette, could you walk us through what's in your bag?" Reporters always want to know exactly what clubs a tournament leader has used.

"Sure. Callaway woods, driver, three, five, seven, Ping irons, and my grandmother's garden hoe."

But the USGA would squash that. It would not quite conform to their strict rules about artificial devices and unusual equipment.

Just behind the display of demonstration putters on the other side of the green, I spotted a tall, dark-headed figure with familiar wide shoulders and baggy plaid shorts. Charlie. I slipped through an opening in the fence and pushed through the crowd to throw myself in his arms.

"What are you doing here? I'm *so* glad to see you." The next thought tumbled in quickly. I looked behind him. "Oh, my God, you didn't bring Mom and Dave to the tournament this early?"

He chuckled. "I'm picking them up tomorrow night in Hartford. Today I'm carrying your bag. Unless you have someone else lined up?"

I hugged him again. One huge problem solved. "Just promise you won't try to read any putts."

After I'd introduced my brother to Julie and Jason, we waited briefly on the first tee. A USGA official approached, a gray-haired woman dressed in tan pants and a blue-striped polo shirt. "Would you mind if Lindsay Hanson joins you? She's an amateur from Oklahoma, turning pro this fall."

We'd scheduled this practice round weeks ahead of time. Most players did. Maybe Lindsay Hanson was an alternate who'd just squeaked into the tournament. In that case, she could probably use some basic kindness. I met Julie's eyes and shrugged. "Fine. Glad to have her."

Lindsay was a midwestern blonde, cheerful and upbeat to the edge of irritating, as was her caddie father, who beamed with pride every time she swung. She could have shanked her ball into the concession tent on the first tee and he would have been proud. I tried not to notice that she hit most of her drives thirty-plus yards farther than me.

"Drive for show, putt for dough," I muttered to myself. I couldn't afford to waste competitive energy on any one girl. I had to focus on the golf course, not the golfers in my group. One hundred and fifty-six players were desperate to win the tournament this weekend, not just the two sharing my tee box.

Charlie tried hard to stay out of my way during the round. And I tried not to mind that he didn't know my game well enough to do anything more than simply carry the bag. But the contrast between us and the two women playing beside me and their caddies was impossible to overlook. Charlie, too, carried a yardage book; but all he could do was stare at the diagrams and mutter things like "You need a goddamn advanced degree in statistics to understand this thing."

We waited fifteen minutes after putting out on the fourth green. With the tees for the fifth and sixth holes less than a hundred yards away, delay was inevitable. And the traffic jams would only get worse as the tournament pressures mounted and each putt counted. Besides, we'd caught up to Amber Clancy—and the fans in her gallery jostled and pushed four and five people deep.

"Who's that?" Charlie pointed to the girl.

"Amber Clancy. She's the amateur who gets all the press," said Lindsay's father. "See the guy in the straw hat? That's Lucien Beccia." His voice was filled with a mixture of awe and disbelief.

My brother shrugged.

"He's only the most exclusive golf coach in America," I explained to Charlie. "My brother doesn't really get the whole golf scene," I told the others. "Having Lucien Beccia follow your practice round is like having O.J. Simpson's defense lawyer accompany you to traffic court. He's a heavy hitter."

"But no one's as important as he thinks he is," said Julie. "They actually had *his* swing featured in *Golf Country Magazine* this month. Honestly, if he was that fantastic, wouldn't he be out here playing himself?"

Jason laughed. "Trust me, I've met him. The guy's a horse's ass."

"Our daughter takes lessons from a little old man at the driving range down the road from our home," said Lindsay's father. "And we've read a couple books about golf psychology. Lindsay has a preshot routine and all that." He puffed his chest out. "I'd like to see that Amber's golf game before the million-dollar coaches all had a crack at her."

Two large men wearing green shirts, khaki pants, ear wires, and black fanny packs flanked the fairway as Amber started down the hill off the sixth tee.

"Wow, did you see how far she hit her drive?" asked Charlie.

"I'm trying not to notice," I said.

"What's with the uniformed dudes?"

"Must be security," said Julie. "She was drawing a lot of attention, even before this nude calendar stunt. They say she's handling it like a pro."

Charlie's eyebrows lifted. "Nude calendar?"

"I'll tell you about it later," I said. "It's hard enough keeping you on task as it is."

He laughed. "You think so little of my skills and assets."

We caught Amber's group again as they walked up toward the grandstand behind the twelfth hole. Above the bleachers flanking the green, flags flapped furiously, alternating those of the United States, the United States Golf Association, and the Orchards' logos. Amber had banged her drive to the middle of the fairway, more than halfway up the hill. One of the other players had missed her tee shot right and was stomping through a large area of naturalized grasses with her caddie.

"That's So Won Lee," I told Charlie. "She went to Q-school the same year I did." So Won and I had gotten off on a disastrous foot at the LPGA qualifying school tournament several years ago when an illegal club had been stashed in her bag. She'd been thrown out of the tournament, and although she'd never said anything directly, I was certain she blamed the incident on me. "Things have gone a little better for her since then—I think she's number twenty-five on the money list."

"You'll get there soon enough," said Charlie, reaching over his shoulder to scratch the middle of his back with my putter.

"What do you suppose they have in those fanny packs?" Lindsay crossed one long leg over the other and leaned into her driver.

"Guns," said Charlie. "No question." He laughed. "But what the hell do I know? I'm a lawyer, not a security expert."

Guns. Good God. I was thinking special phones, or maybe even snacks. Of course they were guns. This was serious business.

"Not everyone out here is so thrilled about all the attention she's getting," said Julie. "A lot of players have done a lot of special things. Why is she on the cover of *Women's Golf?* She's not even a professional yet. She's still a college girl."

I stared at Julie, trying to sniff out whether she was one of the golfers who resented this girl. Hard to picture. It just didn't fit her style. Besides, I'd never heard Julie complain about other amateur teens—Michelle Wie or Morgan Pressel, for example. There was something about *this* girl.

Would Amber even care? I doubted that a prima donna teenager would waste much mental energy worrying about her competition's feelings. Or even notice them. Truth is, she probably didn't believe we *were* competition.

We limped through to the end of the practice round. A good attitude was critical to surviving and thriving this week. Still, it was hard to feel positive about my chances. I'd lost a half dozen balls today—four in patches of knee-deep rough, one so far out of bounds it was off the property, and one swimming with the fishes in the creek on 18. I hadn't kept my tee shot left, as Julie suggested last night and reminded me again today.

And Charlie? He tried. But he stood in other golfers' lines across the green while they putted. And he identified yellow-eyed warblers and sharp-shinned hawks instead of handing off my putter. And he talked about how much it would mean to win this tournament to anyone who'd listen. He was so proud of me and such a disaster as a caddie.

"What do you want to do, sport?" he asked once we'd hiked the last hill from the eighteenth green to the clubhouse.

"Retire?" I asked. "Just kidding. I've gotta to get over to the range and hit some drivers. The course is too damn long to have to use a three-wood off the tee all the way around. And approach shots, too. I blew every chance I had to get it close to the hole."

"I mean about your caddie." Charlie grabbed my shoulders and squeezed. "I'm a big bruiser and perfectly capable of carrying the bag, but you aren't going to light anything up with me looping. Let's face it, you need a real caddie."

"Joe offered to carry," I said, pressing back the threatening tears. If I didn't appear hysterical about the caddie problem, maybe I wouldn't feel that way, either. The last thing I needed was to set off another anxiety attack.

Charlie rolled his eyes. "What about David? You said he was a peach at Pinehurst."

"Wouldn't work." I shook my head. David, my teenage half brother, had carried the bag for me in the three-tour tournament at Pinehurst No. 2 last fall after I'd loaned Laura to Mike. "That was a silly season tournament with a couple of bucks on the line—not even the same universe as here. It's not reasonable to expect a kid to handle the pressure of the Open."

I sucked in a deep breath, feeling the blood pound in my temples. "Let me go pick up my mail and I'll meet you over at the range. We'll figure something out." My voice sounded cheerful, though Charlie probably saw right through it. He started off with my bag over his shoulder, the head covers still in the bag's pockets, and my scratch-'em-if-you-breathe-on-'em titanium shafts clanking against each other.

"Miss Burdette! Excuse me, but could I ask a quick question?" A reporter wearing boat shoes and khaki shorts thrust his miniature tape recorder toward my face. "I'm with *Western Massachusetts Golf Magazine*. Are you planning to play in the Buick Championship?"

"Not sure yet. But I'll certainly let you guys know as soon I decide. I'm trying to keep my focus here."

"How'd it go out there today?"

"Fantastic. Beautiful old-fashioned golf course. Vintage Donald Ross." I grinned and made an about-face before he could follow up with intrusive questions about my game or my life. Geez, what a job: poking golfers for soft spots in hopes of breaking news. My cell phone rang.

"Hey, Cassie. Hi. It's Joe. So . . . how's it going?"

"Fantastic. It's a beautiful old-fashioned Donald Ross design." This was bad, if I was reduced to talking to Joe as though he was one of the media. I needed to let someone in. "Charlie caddied for me today, but it didn't go too well. Besides, I need him to referee between my parents and stepparents."

"I called Laura earlier," said Joe. "She feels terrible about leaving you in the lurch, but she needs to stay with her dad."

"I know that. Hang on a minute." I slipped the phone in my pocket and stepped up to the mail desk. "I think my mother sent some things to this address. Burdette?" The volunteer returned with a large yellow envelope decorated with Mom's neat script. I tore open the corner. She'd sent letters, clippings, and a white business envelope with my name and address typed on it. I opened the envelope. At the request of my bag sponsor, Birdie Girl, I'd promised to make an appearance at Fran Johnson's Golf and Tennis Shop in Springfield later tonight. Detailed directions to the event were enclosed.

"I'm back," I said to Joe as I walked toward the caddie shack. "I've decided to hire that kid who worked for me yesterday. I've seen the course twice now so I don't really need a lot of tips. I just need him to carry the bag and stay out of the other players' way. I know he can manage that."

"I've been thinking you should ask your father."

"Everyone has an opinion, but I'm the one that has to live with the results," I snapped. I rolled my neck in a slow circle. No need to take my nerves out on him. "I'll see you tomorrow night, okay?"

I pressed End and snaked through the crowd by the first tee. I stopped next to the practice area to chat with the caddie master on my way to the range. Bad news. The kid who'd carried my bag yesterday had landed a gig for the week. The older man, Tony, had landed back in rehab after a twenty-four-hour bender. I'd probably done the guy in by refusing to give him a chance.

"There may be a couple of others that turn up. Check back first thing in the morning."

I stumbled along the road in the direction of the driving range, trying not to melt down. I absolutely could not tolerate someone new the day before the tournament began. Two girls thrust visors out for me to autograph. Chances were they had no clue who I was, but I scribbled my name and marched on. I shuffled through the rest of the mail from my mother to avoid eye contact with the other fans lining the walkway. As promised, she'd sent articles about the Buick Championship, an editorial about athletes using performance-enhancing drugs, and several letters that had been delivered to my home address over the past week. I shoved the papers into my backpack and pulled out my phone. Enough moping, it was time to take charge.

I dialed my father's cell phone number and took a deep breath before he answered.

"Dad? It's Cassie. Could you possibly caddie for me in the practice round tomorrow?"

"I'm there. What time do you need me?" Dad's voice was brisk and excited. And I felt hugely relieved. We might still have our problems, but no one knew golf like Dad. Any boneheaded mistakes tomorrow would be all mine. He started pelting me with questions about the course as I walked toward the range.

Charlie was waiting at the end of the practice area with my clubs, a pyramid of brand-new balls, and a sign with my name on it in large block letters. Two sets of bleachers had been set up behind the hitting stations—if you wanted to fix your slice in private, you'd better go elsewhere.

I covered the phone's mouthpiece and whispered to Charlie: "I called Dad and asked him to caddie tomorrow. He's pretty excited." I grinned. "I have to go hit some wedges," I told my father. "All day today my hands felt like blocks of wood."

Charlie handed me my pitching wedge and I rolled a ball off the stack. Just as I started my waggle, a muffled scream echoed across the range.

"What the hell is that?"

A crowd began to cluster around one of the practice stations, and then we heard the wail of an ambulance. Moments later it tore up the side road and bumped across the entrance to the range. Blue and red lights flashed off the faces of the milling fans. I jogged over to where I could just see Amber Clancy through the crush of the crowd. She was laid out on the turf, her father and her coach crouched beside her.

"What's going on?" I asked a worried-looking volunteer.

"It's Amber," the woman whispered, wiping her red face on the sleeve of her striped shirt. "She looks like she's having some kind of convulsions." Prickles of sweat broke out on my own face and hands.

I edged a little closer. EMTs tried to restrain Amber as she began to flail on the ground.

"Get the hell back!" her father screamed at the crowd.

Amber's spine arched backward into a giant *C*. Police pushed back the onlookers, and paramedics gently loaded her onto a stretcher. A woman with blond curls and a US Open visor stuck a tape recorder out as they rolled Amber to the waiting ambulance. Her father batted away the woman's hand.

Poor Amber. With the media following every move she made, she'd no doubt be the lead story tonight, flopping around like a mackerel on deck on the six o'clock news. Not the kind of publicity a girl would be looking for. Even Amber, who appeared to be in search of the spotlight, at any cost.

Chapter 10

A group of us milled near the station where Amber had collapsed, trying to process what we'd just seen.

"Do you think it could be heat stroke?" said Julie, dabbing her own forehead with a peach-colored golf towel.

"It's not that hot," said Jason, "and she's only—what—eighteen? She's got to be in top shape."

I remembered a boy in seventh grade who had grand mal seizures at least once a month, usually in the cafeteria or during an assembly. Poor kid, there was always an audience. Male teachers were called in to pin him flat while the nurse plunged a tongue depressor into his mouth. This creeped us out the most—could someone really swallow his own tongue and choke to death?

"Maybe she's got epilepsy," I said.

Except that I imagined her father would be fairly calm if he'd seen this before. Instead, he had a fierce grip on her arm and he was screaming at the fans to get back. And then he'd given a serious shove to that nosy reporter. No, his golf diva daughter banging her head against the flattened grass of the driving range was not old hat. Beside him, coach Lucien Beccia had also looked pale and stunned— maybe even more upset than Amber's dad.

Lloyd joined us, dressed in sharply creased khaki slacks and a black silk shirt. "Can I give you a ride to Fran Johnson's?" he asked, glancing at his watch. "Aren't you due over there about now?"

"I'm going to take her," said Charlie. "We're having dinner after."

We hadn't made any such plans, but they sounded good—riding with my brother would be a thousand times better than listening to Lloyd's nagging for a couple of hours.

"I'll handle this one solo," I told Lloyd. "I swear I won't make any important decisions without consulting you first. Take the night off and I'll see you tomorrow, okay?"

I grabbed Charlie's arm and we peeled away before Lloyd could protest. We took a shuttle to the parking lot where Charlie had left his car.

"Thanks for bailing me out," I said. "You think fast on your feet."

"All those years of courtroom training," he said. "And this works for me, too. Otherwise I'd have to go back to my hotel room to face my e-mail. You have no idea how tedious a lawyer's inbox can be. It was going to be a very dull evening."

"Any time." I smiled. We both knew I was a nervous wreck and he was looking out for me.

After a day in the sun, the black leather upholstery in Charlie's Audi broiled through the thin cotton of my shorts and golf shirt and I started to sweat all over again. Those fans at Fran Johnson's who wanted to get close to a real athlete might get more than they'd bargained for.

"I hope Amber's going to be okay," I said.

"What was all this about a calendar?" Charlie asked.

"I came across it on the Internet yesterday on a golf chat Web site—there was a half-naked picture of Amber that's supposed to be the calendar cover shot. You wouldn't believe the disgusting comments from the apes on the Web site. Why don't men golfers have calendars?"

"Who the hell wants to look at that?"

We'd driven about five miles down I-91 toward Springfield when I remembered the mail jammed into my backpack. I flipped through the clippings Mom had gathered and read a few of the headlines aloud to my brother:

"LPGA Tour to be subjected to a rigorous antidoping regime" from *Golf Country Weekly,* "Another Milestone for Women (Yawn)" from *The New York Times,* "Golf Needs Cassie Burdette" from *The New Haven Register* (double underlines in red, courtesy of Mom), and "Women's Game is Looking Good: Sorenstam, Wie, and Clancy have helped the LPGA attract new fans" from *The Boston Globe.* But Mom had added her own editorial comment—*Is Cassie Burdette chopped liver?* And last, from the South Carolina *Sun News,* "Detective Golfer Bids for her First US Open."

Mom had gone through with her yellow highlighter and marked the lead sentence of each paragraph. She loved her daughter getting attention—almost not caring what it was for. I thought of Amber's calendar—had her dad been for or against it, if he even knew about it? How far would he push his daughter for fame, or more likely, money?

"Mom's Chinese water torture, isn't she?" Charlie said with a grimace. "So the press is grouping Amber Clancy with the best golfers in the world?"

"Yup."

"Are these gals using performance-enhancing drugs?"

"I wouldn't think so. Steroids aren't going to help your golf game—not that I'm aware of anyway. And who wants to look like a football player?" I flapped the papers in my lap. "Isn't it weird that Mom is so into this?"

My mother has never played a single hole of golf. Her hatred for the game gained momentum during the years she and my father were married—she was clearly his second love. Golf absorbed his interest in a way the family never had. Later on in their marriage, as he was gathering the nerve to leave, golf provided a bond between me and Dad that she envied, resented, and plain did not understand.

"Are you thinking of playing in the men's tournament?"

The question felt so different than when asked by badgering reporters over the last few weeks. Charlie was just interested, and concerned—big brother watching, in the nicest way.

"I'm having trouble seeing the positive side of playing in that tournament. I don't have Annika's game, so I can't say I need to test myself against the best male golfers in the world. For me, there's more than enough challenge right here on the women's tour."

Charlie said, "There's always the money."

"Yeah. Money's good. But what if I bomb completely?

You think that's going to help me find equipment sponsors?"

Equipment sponsors were a sore spot in my golfer's psyche. Birdie Girl, the same bag manufacturer whose rep begged me to meet and greet tonight, had let my contract lapse after my rookie year. To be fair, my performance had plummeted rock bottom over the first twelve months. But what about giving a girl the chance to build her career over the long-term? I accepted back the company's bag and cashed their checks when they offered to sponsor me the second time around, but their fickleness still burned.

"Don't let the decision get bigger than it needs to be." Charlie glanced over and smiled. "It's just golf. Your sanity and happiness are the most important things here."

I nodded—easy to say, not so easy to live out—and opened a pink envelope with my name and address lettered in purple ink. It had been sent to the local newspaper and forwarded to Mom. I read it aloud:

> *"Dear Miss Burdette,*
>
> *I heard about your golfing career in* The South Carolina Sun News *last week and just had to write. I am 56 and have been married for 35 years. I dropped out of college because I was pregnant and my husband did not want his children to have a working mother. Since then, I have never been employed outside the home. He gives me an allowance, but most of that goes to food and household expenses. I don't know why I'm telling you this except you should grab your chance while you have it. Yours very truly,*
>
> *Alicia Berens"*

I dropped the letter on my lap and groaned.

"That's pathetic," said Charlie. "The poor woman sounds emotionally abused."

"You see what I mean about the pressure? If I don't play in the stupid men's tournament, it's no longer just my business. I'm carrying the handkerchiefs of women I've never even met."

I read the second letter.

"Dear Cassie,

I was trying to decide if I should play on the boys' golf team at my school next year. Then my mom showed me how you are playing in the PGA and how girls can do anything they want to do if they only try hard. Good luck in the tournament!

Luv, Luellen."

"Exhibit number two in the people's case against Cassie's sanity," said Charlie.

I laughed and slit open the last envelope in Mom's stack of mail. It contained a sheet of plain paper.

"Rule 8-2. Indicating the Line of Play. A. Other Than on the Putting Green. Except on the *putting green*, a player may have the *line of play* indicated to him by anyone, but no one may be positioned by the player on or close to the line or an extension of the line beyond the *hole* while *stroke* is being made."

And just down the page, again in bold: **"Remember what happens to girls who don't play by the rules. Girls just want to have fun."**

I could feel the blood drain from my face.

Charlie looked over again. "What is it? What did she send you now?"

I pointed ahead. "Here's our exit, take a right at the stop sign and it's less than a half mile on the right."

Charlie pulled off the highway and swung into a parking lot belonging to an Italian restaurant. He put the car in park, but left the engine running. "Give it here."

I handed him the paper.

He read it and dropped it on the center console. "What the hell is this? And why do you look like you've seen the ghost of golfers past?"

I slumped against the door. My throat tightened. A familiar pounding started in my chest. I'd be damned if I'd go back to spend another night in the emergency room. *Get a grip.* I straightened up, closed my eyes, and breathed a long breath in. Then out. Then in. The paper with its typewritten words drifted away in an imaginary bubble. Once my heartbeat felt almost normal, I opened my eyes and focused on Charlie.

"I've gotten a couple of these—the others came by e-mail. First I thought the USGA was sending them out to all the players, but Julie hasn't received anything like it." I picked up the letter and stared out through the windshield toward the restaurant. It was just past five P.M. and the first early birds, a stooped and white-haired couple, were being seated at a table with a view of the highway.

"What else?" asked Charlie in his serious courtroom voice.

"Someone left a note for me at Kripalu—'Hit 'em straight,' or something like that. Just a fan I guess." I wiped a damp spot off my cheek and turned to face him again. "But this came to my home address. They sent this to Mom's."

"Are you certain the rules notices didn't come from the USGA? That's the most logical explanation. And e-mail is notoriously unreliable. It's quite possible Julie just never received hers."

"Two of the others had stuff added at the end—a little threatening, like this one. 'You'll get hurt if you don't play by the rules,' and so on."

He glanced at my hands, which shook like quaking aspen. I slid them into my pockets.

"Jesus, Cassie. Why didn't you tell me about this before?"

"Because I'm trying to play in the US freakin' Open, in case you hadn't noticed!"

He shifted the car into reverse and began to back out. "We're going to the authorities. We'll lay it out for the security people and see what they think. At least we'll know whether we should be worrying or not. One way or the other, we'll know."

"Charlie." I gripped his forearm and forced my voice to come out even and calm. "I'm due at the golf shop"—I looked at my watch—"fifteen minutes ago. I'll sign a few autographs. You can watch me the entire time. Then we'll get some dinner and talk this over. I'm probably making too much out of it."

He gave a small nod and switched on the right directional signal. "We are not fooling around with this, Cassie."

"Fine."

The parking lot for Fran Johnson's Golf and Tennis Shop was jammed. A uniformed police officer directed us to an empty spot.

"See, the cops are already on the case," I said, trying again to lighten the mood.

Charlie didn't smile.

"Welcome to Fran Johnson's!" An older man with tanned, leathery skin and a wide smile swung open the glass door. "The party's all the way through the store in the back tent."

We walked past shelves of golf clothing and golf clubs and a rack of books describing how to putt like a champion, drive like Tiger, and take the five easy steps to mental toughness. If only it was all that simple.

The tent was hot, dark, and crowded with cheerful fans. I found the store's owner, Cindy Johnson, and introduced Charlie and myself.

"Thanks so much for coming. We have you ladies set up over here." She waved at four other golfers already stationed behind a row of tables, with individual welcome signs hanging above each one. FRAN JOHNSON'S WELCOMES CASSIE BURDETTE! read the sign over the empty chair.

"We have golf balls and posters for you to autograph. Grab a snack or a drink on your way over. Charlie, please get something to eat and make yourself comfortable while Cassie signs."

Charlie didn't look like he would be comfortable any time soon. He backed up a few yards to lean against the wall and watch. I felt bad about worrying him. But it felt good to have him firmly planted on my side. I filled a paper plate with cheese, crackers, and guacamole, grabbed a Coke, and settled in between Laura Davies and Audry Longo, a sunburned rookie with a strained smile. The line of fans was enthusiastic and polite, for the most part equal-opportunity autograph collectors. But their awed eyes were on Laura Davies, the golfer who'd won major tournaments, carried her European team to more than one Solheim Cup victory, and ranked number two on the European women's golf tour.

"How's it going?" I asked Audry during a lull.

"Pretty good." She sighed. "Not really. Everyone says how stressful it is to play in a major and turns out they're right. Feels like I'm swinging a sledgehammer." Her face brightened. "The good news is, I finally got the chance to talk with Lucien Beccia. I've been trying to connect with him for months. He's gonna take a look at my swing tomorrow before I tee off."

"Great," I said. "Hope it helps. Meanwhile, like the yogis say, try to enjoy the moment."

Chances were, the consultation wouldn't help. Not right before a tournament. Unless Beccia was better than I gave him credit for and managed to convince her that she'd be fine using exactly the tools she'd brought to South Hadley. You just can't groove a swing change that fast and have it operate smoothly under pressure. "Dance with the one that brung you," I'd once heard a golf shrink say.

We signed about thirty more autographs and had our pictures taken with a parade of little girls. As I chatted with two women from the Executive Women's Golf Association about the pros and cons of using an eight-iron to putt from just off the green, Charlie tapped my shoulder.

"Let's get going."

"What's the hurry?" I was beginning to enjoy my semi-celebrity status in the friendly crowd. He frowned and jerked his head in the direction of the door. I shook hands with the ladies, thanked the staff, and followed him out.

"Why the big rush?" I snapped, once we'd reached his Audi. "I'm here to schmooze with the fans."

He unlocked the car doors. "I called the tournament headquarters and got someone from security to agree to meet us at the clubhouse in an hour. They weren't all that gracious about it, and I don't want them to get annoyed with you."

"Let's cancel. Like you said, probably Julie just didn't get her messages. That's all."

Charlie gave me a long, stern look. "When my sister turns white and her hands shake after she opens a piece of mail, I figure I ought to pay attention. Now, maybe you were having another panic attack—"

"I wasn't—"

"But whether the stress is inside or outside, you can't play good golf if you're scared."

He was right. Better to check it out and put the problem to rest. But I felt embarrassed about making a stink in front of the Powers That Be. And they probably had their hands full with people upset about more important things, like Amber's illness. Amber's father, for example, was most certainly a wreck.

"There goes dinner," I groused.

Chapter 11

A tired-looking volunteer pulled up to shuttle us the quarter mile from Lot A to the clubhouse. "Trying to get your last licks in on that putting green?" He swung the shuttle van's door closed.

"You never know what an extra half-hour might mean on the weekend." I sprawled on the bench seat across from my brother and closed my eyes.

With no crowds to contend with, the van drove up the hill, circled the practice green, and deposited us twenty paces from the clubhouse. The yellow shingles glowed in the last soft shafts of daylight. A uniformed man with big ears and a bulging holster examined our badges on the front stoop.

Sarah Washington met us inside—a stocky woman with

short brown hair painted with gray streaks. My kind of hair coloring: definitely natural, not purchased in an expensive salon. She was dressed in plain black slacks and polo, with sensible shoes and a fanny pack the same size and shape of the guys who had followed Amber Clancy. Which brought the memory of Amber's unintended acrobatics on the practice range surging back to mind. I felt a pinch of fear. Sarah Washington's phone trilled.

"Washington," she answered in a gruff voice. She listened a minute. "We'll wait." She ushered Charlie and me into a back office that opened off the pro shop. "Alice Maxwell from the USGA is coming over to join us."

Jesus. My palms felt instantly damp.

Everyone I knew was a little scared of the United States Golf Association. Hard not to be. Each pairing of golfers in the tournament would have an official assigned to follow along and interpret sticky situations with the rules as they arose. And more officials would be on call for second opinions, and even thirds. Although these folks were mostly friendly, they wrote the rules, and they were dead serious about enforcing them. Tough but fair, they had the authority to throw a player out on a technicality or add victory-killing strokes to her score. I preferred to stay below their radar.

"This is really not necessary," I started.

"She just likes to be kept informed. Not a big deal." Sarah smiled, a deep dimple forming in her left cheek, and motioned for me to sit. "How do you like the course?"

"It's terrific," I said. "We'll have a lot of fun out there. After the rumors this spring, it's a relief to see the shape it's in."

A sharp knock sounded and a stern woman in a knee-length khaki skirt, blue blazer, and a floppy safari hat opened the door and stepped into the room. She had thin lips and a smoker's fine grid of lines fanning out across her cheeks.

"Alice, thanks for stopping by. Meet Cassie and Charlie Burdette."

"Do you want me to tell them what's going on?" Charlie touched my knee.

I couldn't fault him for falling back into our childhood roles, but I was afraid he'd jack the drama up to an even higher level. Besides, if he did the talking, I'd look like the biggest basket case in the field. And there was plenty of competition for that honor this week.

"I'm fine." I offered him a weak smile and turned back to the women. "I've gotten some odd e-mails over the last few days."

Sarah tapped a short golf pencil on the desk. "Fan mail?"

"Not exactly. Someone calling himself Ruleswhiz is sending me sections of *The Rules of Golf*. I say 'him'—I guess I'm assuming it's a man." I glanced at Alice Maxwell. "I was kind of hoping the messages were coming from your USGA office, but my roommate says she hasn't received anything like it."

She pinched her lips tighter and gave her head a small shake.

"What exactly did the e-mails say?" asked Sarah. "Did you bring them in?"

"Sorry." I shook my head. "Dumb. I trashed them as soon as I read them. The first one was something about how you can only have one caddie—"

"Rule 6-4," said Alice. "The player may be assisted by a *caddie,* but he is limited to only one *caddie* at any one time."

"That's it. And there was an addendum about how you can get hurt if you play where you don't belong." I forced my shoulders to relax.

"You're probably aware that Cassie has been invited to play in the PGA Buick Championship next month," Charlie inserted.

"The next e-mail was about an outside agency," I said. Quick study, this time I paused for Alice's recitation.

"Rule 19-1. If a ball in motion is accidentally deflected or stopped by any *outside agency,* it is a *rub of the green,* there is no penalty and the ball must be played as it lies—"

"I always wondered what a rub of the green was. Who thinks all this stuff up anyway?" Charlie asked.

From the fierce expression on Alice's face, it appeared that she had been part of the task force.

"There are exceptions to that rule," said Alice. "Were they included in your e-mail?"

"No. Just the introduction." I sighed, removed my US Open baseball cap, and tucked my hair back behind my ears. The clinging curtain of the dormitory shower couldn't come fast enough. "Two questions were added at the end about who's my caddie and who's my daddy." This all sounded ridiculous.

"Cassie's caddie's father had a stroke and can't be here this weekend," Charlie added. "We're trying to sort that all out."

"And the third message arrived today, but in the mail. Snail mail. It was sent to my mother's address in Myrtle Beach. The first section of Rule 8-2."

"Rule 8-2. Indicating the line of play. A. Other Than on the Putting Green. Except on the *putting green,* a player may have the *line of play* indicated to him by anyone, but no one may be positioned by the player on or close to the line or an extension of the line beyond the *hole* while *stroke* is being made. Any mark placed by the player or with his knowledge to indicate the line must be removed before the *stroke* is made." Alice leaned back in her chair, looking satisfied.

"So two by e-mail, and one in the snail mail," said Sarah. "Anything else in the third note other than the text of the rule?"

I pulled it out of my backpack and handed it over. "You can take a look."

Sarah skimmed the note and then trained intense brown eyes on me, leaning forward, one elbow propped on her thigh. "What are your thoughts about this?"

"I really don't . . ." I shifted in my seat, trying to gain back the space between us.

"Frankly, we don't know how seriously to take the threats, if that's what they are," said Charlie, "which is why we came to you. My sister has had some difficult—"

I waved him silent. "It's more a matter of just wanting to let you know. I just thought you should be aware that this was going on. In case, well, I don't know what case there might be." My eyes filled with tears. Damn. Ammunition for the Basket Case award, speaking of cases.

Sarah nodded. "I understand. It's your first Open. A lot of pressure. More fans than you're used to. And some of them not as stable as we'd like." She smiled at Charlie, the dimple in action again.

"We have a very good security system in place. You've probably noticed that no one gets into the clubhouse without a player or family member badge on his or her person. We're

100 percent strict on that. We've got over two thousand volunteer marshals to help keep the crowd separated from the players. We have police officers stationed at various points around the course. All media credentials have been carefully screened. We won't allow any oddballs or nut jobs in the tent." She laughed. "That came out wrong. Let me say when you've worked these events as long as I have, you get a feeling when you're up against something out of the ordinary."

Alice Maxwell crossed her arms over her chest, careful not to wrinkle her blazer. "Can you get us copies of these e-mails?"

I shook my head. "I deleted the others as soon as I got them."

Sarah rustled through the desk drawers, came up with a plastic bag, and dropped the note into the bag. "You get anything else unusual—letters, e-mails, whatever—you'll bring it right over to me?"

I nodded.

"Way I see it, the threat level here is low," she added.

Charlie stood up and opened his mouth to protest.

She waved him back down, but her expression softened. "You want her safe. We want her safe. That's our job and we intend to do it. If you don't feel comfortable with the level of security here—and believe me, it's high—you can hire your own man. Some of the other players go that route. I'm happy to give you names."

"Can't afford it." I pushed out of my chair. "Thanks for your time."

"I'll pay if you want someone," said Charlie.

"Not necessary. I feel better already and I'm glad we

came." I shook hands with both of the women. "I'll keep you posted if anything else comes up." I paused at the door. "Any word on Amber Clancy?"

The women exchanged a glance. "Nothing yet," said Sarah.

I charged out of the clubhouse ahead of Charlie. The wind had kicked up, heavy again with the greasy smell of grilled meat. After this week it might be a while before I had the urge for a sausage sandwich.

Charlie caught up and grabbed my wrist. "Are you okay with this?"

I took both of his hands in mine. "Really, big brother, I feel fine. I think I overreacted. These things happen when you're a 'celebrity.' It wasn't love letters or hate mail, it was *The Rules of Golf,* for God's sake." I rolled my eyes and laughed.

He frowned. "What's Dr. Baxter saying about this anxiety-attack business?"

We passed a bench under a large maple near the media tent. I dropped down and patted the seat next to me. "We're working on a few theories. Fear of success has been mentioned. As has fear of failure."

"All bases covered there," Charlie said.

"Yeah. Of course, it all goes back to Dad and how he left in my formative teenage years and how my subconscious equates succeeding in golf with bailing out on your family."

Charlie looked puzzled. "But he didn't succeed in golf."

"The subconscious is not always up on the facts," I explained. "Dad left because teaching at a golf course jammed with inept tourists was not his dream. Whether he succeeded after he bailed out is moot."

"And then you add in the pressure of the PGA opportunity and this US Open, and suddenly you have a lot on your plate."

I nodded.

"But what actually set the attack off? Why did you freak out at the golf course?" Charlie's dark eyes searched my face.

I would have taken offense at the wording, except for his obvious concern. "I was waiting to find out if I made the cut or was there going to be a play-off." I shrugged. "It was hot. I was worried. I don't know. The doc in the ER says it's like hot flashes in menopause. The feelings are riding just below the surface, so any subtle shift in the environment can set off an attack." I shivered. "That's the worst thing—the first attack sneaks up on you and you're always terrified about another one coming. It's awful. You feel like you're dying. I was starting to feel the same way earlier tonight."

"Outside that little restaurant on the way to the golf store?"

I nodded. "Can I be honest? I'm also worried about you and Dad getting along this weekend. I'm pretty sure I can't count on Maureen and Mom to make nice, but will you promise you'll make an effort?"

He raised one hand and placed the other on an imaginary Bible. "On my word. I won't let that cheap cheating bastard get to . . . oops! I mean, yes, Cassie, I will act the angel with our father."

I checked my phone messages on the short ride home. Joe was arriving midday tomorrow and looking forward to offering whatever support I needed. Laura was still camped out in the ICU. She'd try me again in the morning.

Too late to phone her now, though a wave of guilt washed over me.

After sliding my key card into the slot by the dormitory door, I vaulted up three flights of stairs. Julie was already in bed, snoring gently. I snuck across the room to get my pajamas and travel kit and headed down the hall for a fast shower.

I hated to admit this, even privately: It appeared that my anxiety about the rules e-mails was directly related to the recent panic attack. A normal person would have shrugged them off.

Once in bed, I pulled on Bose earphones and spun the iPod forward to a relaxing meditation. The speaker instructed me to watch a large white seagull drifting over an expanse of azure sea.

I, too, was going to learn to fly. . . .

Chapter 12

I met my father and Charlie at the range at seven A.M. With my bag stashed protectively between his legs, Charlie was scrubbing the club heads with a wet towel.

I hadn't seen the two of them together in ages. There were some changes—my brother was now taller by half a foot, and Dad's brown hair was a little thinner and edged with gray. Both of them had stayed in great shape, though Charlie had a muscular bicyclist's build and a more pronounced bow to his legs. Dad's stomach barely showed the beginning of a basketball paunch. He'd pushed himself to get in top form for his run at the Champions Tour last year. Even before that, I suspected that Maureen the aerobics freak focused at least fifty percent of her nagging on keeping her husband buff.

A picture popped into my head of the two men circling me, the preliminary round of a catfight. *Try for breezy, Cassie,* I told myself. *They are supposed to be here for you.*

"Remember what you promised," I whispered to Charlie as I bussed his cheek.

I gave Dad a quick hug. "Thanks for coming so fast."

"I'm thrilled you called." He was beaming. "I'd had enough of the art museums in New York City anyway. Maureen's idea of what's a dose of culture, and what's an overdose, just don't match mine." He grinned again and nodded at my golf bag. "Am I taking over this morning?"

"Yup." I glared at Charlie, who passed the bag to my father. "Let's all work together, okay, boys?"

I started into my regular warm-up, beginning with easy shots using my sand wedge, saving the unreliable driver for last. I'd been determined to master the big dog ever since Laura commented that I treated drivers like men: I didn't give any of them a reasonable chance to see if a relationship would take. My current Callaway Fusion Big Head Pro worked pretty well if I spent enough time warming up. I flushed, thinking of Joe and how quickly I'd shut him down. Mike, on the other hand, had been given more chances than were actually needed to determine that our relationship was a fiasco.

I might have the driver mastered, but the man thing was still a puzzle.

"Ready for the seven-wood?" asked Dad.

Having spent his entire adult life in the golf world, my father knew the ropes: He passed me each club at just the right moment and cleaned the grooves as I finished.

Twenty minutes later I teed a ball up, waggled four

times, and swung my driver. Dad's eyes followed the ball's curve to the right.

"Have you changed your grip? It looks like the right hand has slipped a little. Try moving the club into your fingers."

I shifted the shaft slightly and admired the next ball as it shot straight out over the range. "Thanks."

Charlie watched, sulking, a couple of yards away.

"Would you mind awfully running over to pick me up a granola bar and a bottle of water?" I asked him. My stomach was leaden with the Mount Holyoke dormitory special—eggs, hash browns, bacon, and toast—but one Burdette man on the bag at a time was all I could handle.

"You look pretty calm," Dad said. "How are you feeling?"

"Not too bad. Trying to enjoy the moment." I knew he wanted the lowdown on my mental status, but I didn't trust that he'd keep it to himself—Maureen would worm it out of him before night fell. Not that it was a good idea to review problems before my tee time anyway.

Fifteen minutes later Charlie charged down the hill toward us with Mike Callahan, Joe Lancaster, and Lloyd on his heels. A tidal wave of testosterone powering toward my hitting station.

My stomach flip-flopped at the sight of Joe. And that meant what? I had no idea. I offered up a virginal pucker. "Gosh, it's good to have you here."

Joe gripped me in a hard hug and then stepped back with a wistful smile. "It was tough to stay away."

My brother grabbed my hand and pulled me aside. "Listen to this," he whispered. "There's a rumor that Amber Clancy was poisoned yesterday. Julie told me."

"Oh, my God." I dropped my club and pressed both hands to my temples. "She was poisoned? Shit. Is she okay?"

"That's all I heard." Charlie swallowed. "It's just a rumor, Cassie. I shouldn't have said anything before your round."

"You got that right." I frowned. Charlie seemed to be struggling with my father's presence. Maybe insider gossip was a way of demonstrating his special connection to me. Why the hell else would he report news that would upset me right before I teed off? He knew better than that.

"Morning," said Mike, stepping around Charlie to greet my father. Dad pumped his hand. They'd developed a truce of sorts after our joint tournament last fall. Neither one of them had played worth a damn in the Pine Straw Tri-Tour Classic, and in some strange way they had bonded over that. Besides, Dad was positively ebullient about Mike's removal from the boyfriend category.

I introduced Lloyd to my father and Joe, and nudged my brother a couple feet away.

"Tell me again what you heard. Amber was poisoned? With what? By whom?" I whispered.

Charlie shrugged. "I didn't hear any details. Listen, we'll find out later, okay? I shouldn't have said anything— I didn't have time to follow up. I ran into this bozo"—he gave Mike a friendly shove—"and I knew you'd be anxious for your snacks."

"Jesus."

"Whatever's going on up there with the rest of the girls in the field," said Joe, moving in to massage my shoulders, "most important, is how are you? Gosh, your muscles feel a little tense."

I shrugged his hands off. "Great," I muttered, still reeling from the gossip. And then I remembered Amber asking me whether my detective skills were for hire two days ago in the locker room.

"Can you go up to the clubhouse and find Sarah Washington?" I asked Charlie. "Tell her I have something she needs to know."

Whether the rumor was true or whether it wasn't, I planned to unload everything I knew about Amber to security. Sarah Washington was in the position to sort it out. I certainly was not.

In the distance Julie and Jason began to make their way across the range, stopping to chat with several other players. "Back in a jiffy," I said to the guys, and trotted over to Julie's station.

"What did you hear about Amber?"

Julie grimaced. "Everyone's saying she was poisoned. The USGA is holding a press conference this afternoon. I didn't stay around—the crowd was intense and my irons are leaking to the right." She patted her forehead with a Kleenex. "I can't think about it right now."

Then Julie unfastened her ponytail, smoothed the loose strands from her forehead, and snapped the elastic band back into place. "I wouldn't say this to anyone else, but that girl has made some enemies around here. And dragging Lucien Beccia through a practice round probably didn't help her popularity."

"And that's a reason to poison her?" I flashed again on my truncated locker room conversation with Amber. "I think she was feeling me out the other day about a problem. What if she thought someone was threatening her? I should have talked her into asking for official help—maybe she wouldn't have gotten sick."

Jason stepped in between us. "You've got to let it go, Cassie. I'm sure the cops and the USGA are all over it now. It's not your worry. I'm telling this one the same thing." He prodded Julie in the butt with her pitching wedge and she slapped him away. "Let's get warmed up, babe. The stars await you."

"Who are you playing with?" I remembered her saying she'd arranged her final practice round with a couple of the "big girls."

"Laura Davies and Grace Park," she said. "I hate to play like a goon in front of them."

"They won't be watching you," Jason said, smiling in my direction. "Right, Cassie?"

"Right." Neither will anyone else, I almost added. But that would have been harsh. My nerves were eating me alive. "Gotta get back to the boys."

Julie winked. "You have quite a fan club this morning."

"Feast or famine."

I walked slowly back to my station, unable to get the image of Amber convulsing on the driving range out of my head. Suppose she had intended to ask me for help and I'd blown her off?

Charlie was still there, gabbing with Lloyd and Joe. I squeezed his arm and frowned. "I told you—I need to talk to Sarah Washington right away." I pointed up the hill. "See if you can find her for me. Please?"

At quarter to ten I finished at the range and started toward the chipping practice area, trailed by my father with the golf bag, Mike, Lloyd, and Joe.

"Did you have a good breakfast?" Lloyd asked. "You shouldn't be relying on Power Bars."

I nodded curtly.

"When do we tee off?" asked Mike. "Have you left enough time to putt?"

I pulled a lob wedge out of my bag and moved away from the men. "Ten-thirty. We're going off the tenth hole. I'll be fine." When do *we* tee off?

My first chip barely cleared the rough. I rolled my cement-hard shoulders in circles, desperate to relax.

"What's your target?" Joe called from behind the ropes.

I sculled my next shot across the green. On my way to collect it, I saw Sarah Washington talking with several USGA officials just below the putting green and the first tee. She should have the straight dope about Amber. Even if she didn't, I was prepared to spill what little I knew. Getting that off my chest might help settle me into a productive round. Lord knew my personal gallery of overinvested men would make things tough enough. I waited to approach until Sarah finished her conversation.

"Cassie," she said with a tight smile. "How's it going? No more mysterious notes?"

"Everything's fine. I was just wondering . . . we're hearing rumors about Amber. Is she all right?"

Her face darkened, though she flashed another smile. "We're sorting things out. Not to worry."

"There's something I thought you'd want to know." I described the brief conversation I'd had on Monday with Amber. "Looking back on it, I wonder if she was having trouble with someone. Or something." I sighed. "Maybe she was planning to ask me for help, but she couldn't get over the hump."

"We'll take it from here," said Sarah. "Glad you told me. Now let me do my job and you go out there and do yours. And have some fun!" Her pat on the back felt more like a shove, propelling me down the hill in the direction of the tenth tee.

I passed the grilled-meat tent and waded through the fans clogging the paths to the tee. My father had already introduced himself to the marshal and the two girls we'd be playing with. Joe, Mike, Lloyd, and Charlie stood by the tee in an anxious cluster. Time to take charge.

"Listen up, guys." I waited until I had their attention. "I'm touched that all of you came out to support me. But I've got one caddie today—he's inside the ropes." I clapped my father's back. "If I want advice, tips, or information from the rest of you, please be sure I'll ask. Clear enough?"

I forced a smile and turned away.

"This is a hell of a hard hole to start out on," I told my father. "I overclubbed myself yesterday because of that damn stream. It's the same one that gave me fits on the first hole. Tricky chip coming back; I rolled right off the green and into the creek—which was what I was trying to avoid in the first place."

"Let's see," said Dad. "The book says one hundred and sixty-three yards. One hundred and forty of them look like carry. If I remember right, you should be on the green with a five-iron. Yes?"

"Yes."

He handed me the club. "Put a nice, easy swing on it." He smiled and pulled the Birdie Girl bag out of range.

I swung, landed the ball just in front of the pin and watched it roll up close. The crowd gathering by the tee box applauded.

Dad grinned and shifted the bag to his shoulder. "Easy game," he said.

* * *

We completed the round in record time. Even Charlie had to admit that Dad was a dream—positive, inquisitive about the right problems, and meticulous in note taking and club cleanup. I shook hands with the other girls, feeling tired but hopeful.

"Don't forget we have dinner with Mom and Dave tonight," Charlie said. "I'm going to pick them up now."

"No way," I moaned.

Months ago I'd promised them a night out during the tournament. Back then, it seemed like getting it over with early in the week would be the least painful alternative. Everyone knows the pressure gets more intense as the week goes on.

"Can we eat at the place right behind the bookstore? Fedora's, I think it is. That way I can beg off early and get home."

"She'll want a couple of drinks," Charlie warned. "You know how she hates to fly."

"Good luck." Dad rolled his eyes and hugged me. "I'll see you tomorrow. Sleep well."

I turned to Joe, a professional trained to manage dysfunctional families—maybe he could handle mine. I felt bad about blowing hot and cold. But it would be worse to face Mom and Dave without him.

"Will you come? Please?"

Joe beamed. "Of course I'll come."

I started up the hill to the clubhouse. A crowd had gathered around the outdoor stage where press conferences would be held during the tournament. Sarah Washington stood on alert behind three USGA officials dressed in regulation tan and blue. A trio of uniformed cops hovered farther in the background. In front of the stage, TV cameras jostled for position with golf writers and a smattering of players.

Looking tense and almost angry, Alice Maxwell stepped up to the microphone and cleared her throat. "I'm sorry to have to report the death of Amber Clancy early this morning at the Holyoke Hospital. There will be an autopsy, of course, and we will pass on any new information as it becomes available. We extend our deepest sympathy to her family and friends."

Good God. Amber was dead? I wormed back out of the crowd and crouched down, breathing hard, my back resting against a large oak. A sea of hands began to wave in front of the officials. Alice pointed to a man in the front row.

"What was the cause of death?"

"There will be an autopsy," said Alice. "We will inform you as new information becomes available. Right now there is no reason to suspect anything other than natural causes." I watched her thin lips form other words, but my mind was spinning too fast to take them in.

Natural causes? They had to be joking. What was natural about the sudden death of an eighteen-year-old athlete at the top of her game?

"What effect will this have on the tournament?" shouted out another reporter.

Alice turned to a man I recognized as the president of the USGA. She had to break the hard news, but he would take the hardballs.

"As you can imagine, we have had considerable discussion on this point. Mr. and Mrs. Clancy are one hundred percent behind our decision to continue with the tournament as planned. Amber was a fierce competitor"—his voice wavered—"she would have wanted the game to go on."

Alice moved back to the mike. "There will be a prayer vigil tomorrow evening in the chapel on the Mount Holyoke campus. Friends, fans, press—you are all cordially invited to attend. We will keep you apprised of other plans as they unfold."

"Miss Maxwell! Miss Maxwell!" called several voices in the crowd.

"We heard that Lucien Beccia was also taken to the hospital. Can you comment on that?"

"We will keep you apprised of any new developments." The cops moved forward as the officials retreated from the stage. Still wearing my golf shoes, I staggered over to the shuttle and headed home.

Chapter 13

Julie had left a note on my bed: She hoped my round went splendidly. She'd outdriven Laura Davies on the twelfth hole and just missed an eagle. She was on her way to Northampton for dinner with Jason and a couple of the other players.

Her note was so chipper—they must have gotten off before the shocking news about Amber hit the scene. I wondered again if she and Jason had hooked up. But mostly I was glad to unwind in the room alone. I was stunned by Amber's death—filled with a swirl of guilt, fear, and anger. At the same time, it all felt oddly distant.

I opened my computer and clicked on the tournament Web site. A small box rimmed in black had been added to the home page. "We are deeply saddened to report the death of one of the members of our golf family, Miss Amber Clancy. Although the funeral will be private, there will be a short prayer vigil at the Mount Holyoke campus chapel tomorrow evening. Details about memorial contributions will be announced at a later date."

My skin felt simultaneously sticky and clammy and my stomach churned. Could I cancel out of tonight's dinner? I tried to imagine my mother's response and how far a last-minute cancellation would set us back.

Not a chance in hell.

I skimmed through my e-mail before showering. There were offers for low-priced Xanax (how did they know?), sex partners of various persuasions (abstinence was my current line of thinking), and pirated software for a computer golf game. The oddest thing about a tragedy was how life moved on all around you even if your own reality was crumbling. Garbage would still jam the Internet bandwidth even though a young star was dead.

The last message in my account was from Ruleswhiz.

"Rule 8-1. Advice. During a *stipulated round,* a player must not: (a) give *advice* to anyone in the competition playing on the *course* other than his *partner,* or (b) ask for *advice* from anyone other than his *partner* or either of their *caddies.*

"The swing looks good and I like the skirt. But I saw you tie your shoe on the sixth tee. Be careful what you show the world."

My heart pounding furiously, I glanced down. At the last minute this morning, I'd thrown on a new skort. I liked the no-wrinkle fabric and the dark tan color, but I wasn't sure the pockets were large enough or that I'd feel comfortable wearing it in front of a crowd. The style suited the younger players, but it was more girlish than my usual look. I felt a quick flush of heat, then my teeth chattered lightly.

Who had been watching me and why? I thought back to the sixth tee. Had I tied my shoes? I couldn't remember. Even if I had, nothing would have been exposed—that's why I bought a skort, not a skirt.

Suddenly I wondered if Amber had been receiving creepy e-mails before she died. One unkind part of me thought a girl who was willing to pose naked deserved whatever comments she got. But why me? I pushed the thought away before a true panic could roll in. Goddammit, whose business was it anyway?

I had to pull myself together. Mom has always had a direct line to my anxiety. Show up at the restaurant tonight with the jitters and she'd be all over me. And if I wouldn't spill the beans, she'd manage her own matching anxiety by ordering more drinks. I needed to consult Charlie, alone. Meanwhile, a hot shower might help.

My feet slapped softly on the hall's bare linoleum on the way to the bathroom. I squatted down to peer under the doors of the shower stalls—empty. Then I threw the dead-bolt on the shower room door and begin to sing loudly as the hot water pounded my back—snatches of old hymns, my favorite Beatle songs, country music ditties with wacky words. Anything to push the latest e-mail out of my conscious mind.

I towel-dried my hair and dressed in khaki flairs, a faded rose polo, and sandals, and walked across the college campus. The sun beat down strongly, highlighting the thin edges of the storm clouds gathering in the distance. Small brown birds rustled the ivy climbing the stone walls of the buildings. At the first sign of a threat, they could dart into the foliage and disappear from the world. I sighed and looked at my watch. Twenty minutes before I was due to face Mom and company.

I crossed the highway and stopped in front of the Odyssey Bookshop. An extensive display of golf books spilled out from the window to a set of shelves and a table inside the door. There were how-to books by every golf teacher and celebrity who'd ever intersected with the game, books on obscure moments and figures in golf history, golf fiction, golfer profiles—every possible golf angle appeared to be covered. I thumbed through a biography of Freddie Couples.

How did a player that famous manage his popularity with so much grace? People went crazy for Freddie. They wanted to share the most intimate details of his life. They followed him in unruly hordes at golf tournaments, screaming "You da man!" before his tee shots and "Fred-die, Fred-die!" after, until their throats were hoarse. He wasn't the only super-star golfer, either. Fans would kill to get close to John Daly, Tiger Woods, Annika Sorenstam, Nancy Lopez. . . . I shivered, realizing what I'd just thought. Had Amber Clancy been a direct casualty of her celebrity?

Notwithstanding sour grapes, from what I'd seen so far, fame would not agree with me. The first time a reporter pressed me about my failing marriage or my latest trip to the rehab facility or the ten pounds I appeared to have put on or why I slipped twenty places in the world rankings, I'd be a goner. I'd had a taste of this with the Buick Championship invitation—the spotlight illuminated my cobwebby corners rather than my best features. The true stars managed to give a friendly inside look into their lives without allowing the public to become intrusive. I put Freddie's bio

back on the shelf, muttered a quick thanks to the girl behind the cash register, and headed next door to meet my
family. Deep breath in, and out. I was determined to face
them with a blank mind.

Fedora's Bistro was casual, full of serviceable wooden
furniture and hanging plants. Rock n' roll blared from the
wall speakers and ESPN news from the flat screen TV in
the corner. My party had already been seated at a table in
the middle of the room. I took the chair next to Mom and
kissed her and then my stepfather, Dave. I waved across
the table to Charlie and Joe. If things got rough, at least I
had a full view of the television. Dave seemed supremely
uncomfortable—I realized I'd never seen him outside of
South Carolina. He wore stiff new blue jeans and a Ralph
Lauren polo shirt. The horse and rider had been sewn on a
little crooked—they looked as though they were cantering
down hill. Mom must have blitzed the outlet malls before
their trip.

My mother sported a yellow cotton dress—though the
shirtdresses of the seventies were coming back into style, I
suspected this was a vintage sample direct from the hinter-
lands of her closet. I listened to her complain to Charlie
about the motel room view, trying to assess her mental status. She desperately hates to fly. I could be certain she'd
managed the trip from Myrtle Beach to Springfield with as
many little bottles of Tanqueray gin as the flight attendant
would allow. She was likely to be riding out an alcohol
trough—on the way down from her airplane high and not
yet on her evening cocktail upswing. Charlie would have
discouraged her from hitting the mini-bar before he escorted them here.

The arrival of our waitress with a tray of drinks brought instant cheer.

"Where's the town?" Mom asked me, her voice on the shrill side. "I thought you were staying right in town?"

"This is it," I said. "Isn't the college gorgeous? Wish I'd applied here."

Mom relaxed into her gin and tonic. "You did just fine. If you had only taken a couple of math classes, you could have gotten a decent job in the business field."

"A bunch of snotty rich girls go to this school." Dave tore off a hunk of Italian bread. "What would you need with that? They're not your kind."

Which was the sort of comment you were always tempted to take him up on. But thirteen years into the relationship, I knew it would be a waste of time. Besides, I'd pretty much said the same thing to Julie as we first rode into South Hadley. Like me, Dave probably just felt out of his league.

He looked around the table. "Where's the butter?"

Joe handed him a vial of olive oil infused with a sprig of rosemary and a garlic clove. "Pour a little of this on your plate and dip." He demonstrated, using his bread to blot the spreading pool of oil on his own plate.

Dave grabbed the arm of a passing bus boy. "I need some damn butter. Who ever heard of oiling your bread?"

I ordered a Buffalo chicken tender salad and half-listened to Charlie spar with Mom. Joe was working hard to draw Dave into a conversation, with marginal success. Awareness of Joe's psychological credentials led to a powerful clamming-up mechanism on Dave's side. Later he'd tell me all about what a waste of money it is to spend money on having someone explain you to yourself, but for now, he was busy dodging Joe's friendly questions. So far, all he'd admitted was that he was the breakfast cook at Littles' Restaurant in Myrtle Beach. And that they served up to 200 units a morning, depending on the season.

"I waited on tables to put myself through college," said Joe. "It's a bear of a job. One night the chef actually walked out in the middle of the dinner rush and I had to take over. We only served burgers and salads the rest of the night, but my hat's off to anyone who can juggle all those orders."

I noticed a flash of movement out of the corner of my eye. I grabbed the edge of the table, hands trembling. It was our waitress, delivering dinner salads to Charlie and Mom.

"What the hell's the matter with you tonight?" Dave asked. "You're nervous as a cat."

Was there anyone *less* likely to have noticed? "I'm playing in the US Open tomorrow," I said with as much dignity as I could manage. "It's a big f—" I caught Mom's disapproving frown. "It's a big damn deal."

"We know it is, dear," Mom said, touching my cheek. "That's why we came up, right, Dave?"

Why had they come up? I sure hadn't pushed them. In theory, their visit was heartwarming—all of my family supporting me through the biggest moment in my career so far. The reality was much more complex. And this was only one side of the family tree. Just wait till Maureen hit town.

"Excuse me, I'm going to run to the ladies' room and wash up before we eat," I said.

I patted my face with wet paper towels and peered into the mirror over the sink in the pink tiled rest room. My eyes were puffy and ringed with dark circles. The blood pounded in my ears so loudly I thought the woman in the stall could probably hear it. Hard to know if it was the weird e-mail, Amber's death, or the close encounter with my parents that accounted for the heavy heartbeat. Or some combination thereof.

I banged into Charlie in the darkened hallway on my way out. He rubbed my back.

"Is something wrong? Besides the obvious," he added, tipping his head toward our table with a snort of laughter. His face creased into lines of concern. "You shouldn't take this thing with Amber so hard. You're not a detective. Or a cop. Or a private investigator. Hell, we don't even really know why she died."

"We think she was poisoned. Besides, I'm scared someone's watching me now." I whispered the contents of the latest message and told Charlie about trying out the new skort. "It's probably nothing." I wasn't convinced and neither, from the expression on his face, was he.

"What's up?" Joe hurried down the hallway and draped an arm across my shoulders. His hand felt moist as it skimmed my bicep. "Are you okay?"

I paused a beat, blinked, and smiled. "Good, good, good. Just taking a small respite from the family fun." I grinned again.

Joe squeezed my neck. "You're doing great. See you in a sec."

Charlie looked puzzled as the door to the men's room thumped shut. "You don't want him to know?"

I shook my head. "He gets too worried. Do you mind calling Sarah Washington for me? See if she can round up one of those private security guys for us. It's probably nothing."

"But this way you can focus on your golf game," Charlie agreed. "You go back to the table, I'll call her right now."

Dinner had been served when I reached my parents, a welcome distraction and a sop for Mom's infusion of gin. I'd stopped at one beer. I needed all my wits about me tomorrow. Besides, watching Mom head toward sloppy drunk knocked the appeal of alcohol down a couple of notches. Dr. Baxter would be proud.

Charlie returned and showed me a quick thumbs-up. I shoveled in my salad and stood to leave as soon as the plates had been cleared. "Sorry to be rude, but I'm too antsy to sit any longer. I'll see you guys tomorrow."

"When's your tee time?" Charlie asked.

"I'm meeting Dad at the range at nine-thirty. We tee off at twelve-fifteen." My stomach fluttered. "I'll see you guys after the round." I kissed Mom on the top of the head and patted Dave's shoulder. "It means a lot to me that you came up for this."

"I'll walk you out," said Joe.

"I'll run you over to the dorm," said Charlie at the same time, jumping up as Joe got to his feet. "Go ahead and order dessert," he told our parents. "I'll be back in ten minutes."

They both followed me to the door. It was an awkward moment. Why would Charlie take me home and leave my parents with Joe? But I didn't care how he explained it.

"You know what's really neat?" Joe reached over to smooth a curl off my forehead. "You're not calling your father Chuck anymore, you're calling him Dad. It's really nice to see your relationship with him grow and change." He had another wistful expression on his face.

He was right. My father and I were getting closer as Joe and I drifted apart. It wasn't the kind of thing that anyone else would spot. And only Joe would feel he had to say something about it.

Charlie rolled his eyes. His relationship with Dad was not growing or changing, not for the better anyway. Not yet.

"See you tomorrow, old boy," he told Joe. "Hope you don't mind sitting with the folks for a couple of minutes. We have a little family business to discuss."

Joe stood still for a moment, his arms dangling loosely, then gave a small nod. "Happy to help."

"Washington says she'll have a security man meet us first thing in the morning," Charlie said as we got into his car.

I nodded and we drove the three blocks in silence.

"Are you sure you'll be all right?" he asked when he'd pulled up in front of the dorm. "I have another bed in my motel room."

"I'll be fine. The security is top notch and there's no one staying over here anyway."

I pecked him on the cheek and got out of the car. I could feel Charlie's eyes following me as I walked up the cement path to the main door and slid my key card in the card reader. I vaulted up the stairs and flashed my room lights to tell him I'd arrived safely.

One if by land, two if by sea . . .

Chapter 14

By the time I reached the golf course, I had almost talked myself into believing we'd overreacted the night before. I hadn't been wearing a skirt yesterday—some fruitcake was taking a bet that he could rattle me with that e-mail. Probably half the girls in the field had received the same thing. I would call the cavalry off.

Sarah Washington was waiting outside the USGA hospitality tent with a short man dressed, like her, in all black. They were talking with Charlie. Damn.

"Greg Merrill. You're Cassie." It was a statement, not a question, punctuated by a firm handshake and a quick smile. Up close, I could see that his small stature belied a powerful build. His eyes darted like lasers, seeming to take in everything.

"Greg's the best security consultant in the business," said Sarah. "We were lucky to be able to put our hands on him for the weekend. He flew in from Dallas last night."

"Thanks," I said. "I'm not sure—"

"Now's not the time to talk," said Greg. "You need to put your energy into your golf round. I'm going to free you up to do just that."

"We've already ridden around the course, so he has a feel for the layout. Why don't you tell him who you've got in the gallery today?"

"You'll need to draw up a family tree to keep track of the Burdettes," Charlie said with a laugh. "Lots of monkeys . . ."

I listed off Mom, Dave, Dad, Charlie, Joe, Mike, Michelle, Maureen, Lloyd, and my half brothers David and Zack. Greg scribbled notes into a Palm Pilot.

"Perfect," said Greg. "We'll go over everything later in more detail, okay?" He patted me on the shoulder, nodded at Sarah and Charlie, and slid on a pair of sunglasses. Show time.

I began to warm up at the range with my father. When my swing felt as good as it could, considering the occasion, we walked up the hill to the short game practice area. I circled the edge, chipping three balls from each vantage point. Greg shadowed my progress, about twenty yards away. I never caught him staring directly at me—he seemed to watch the spaces around me. I started to relax. Maybe calling him hadn't been such a horrible idea. My father flipped a ball up from the grass onto the face of my wedge and began to bounce it into the air.

"A couple more years on tour with me on the bag, and maybe you'll master this," he said, grinning.

A laundry truck drove up the driveway next to the chipping area, its gears grinding loudly. Two men hopped out of the front seats and moved around to the rear doors. Supposing a madman, a killer, was hiding in the truck? My heart lurched and my muscles clenched. The men exited from the truck carrying piles of yellow, white, and blue caddie bibs, and delivered them to the caddie shack.

The receding rush of adrenalin left me momentarily weak. I would be wrung out if I let myself imagine danger everywhere. I had to believe that my newly hired "security consultant" would take care of any problems that arose.

Greg trailed me past the caddie shack to the caged-in green. This morning half a dozen uniformed policemen had been stationed by the opening in the fence.

Ordinarily there would be a lot of chatter between the players and caddies on the putting green—who'd eaten where, who'd discovered the best happy hour, who'd stayed out to what time, who was changing putters. Or partners. But today felt different—we all wore black ribbons in memory of the starlet who had died.

Besides that, this was the first day of the US Open. We were approaching Our Lady of the Fairways, heads bent in prayerful supplication. You could hear relief when balls rattled into the practice holes, and soft curses when they did not.

I wasn't supposed to think this way.

"Tell yourself it's just another day," Joe had emphasized during one of my mini-meltdowns the week after I'd qualified and then ended up in the ER. "Tell yourself to do nothing special, nothing extra. If you're having trouble, try focusing on something concrete in your physical surroundings."

So I studied the logos decorating other players' clothing—MasterCard, Toyota, Cleveland, Taylormade— golfers sold as much of the square footage of their attire as their agents could manage.

I leaned over the fence to whisper to my brother. "I feel naked," I moaned, pointing to my unadorned shirtsleeves and baseball cap.

"They look like walking billboards," said Charlie. "Just remember what an honor it is to be here. And how hard you've worked to make it this far."

"We're very proud of you," my father added, smiling at Charlie. Even if I blew this opportunity to hell, maybe the forced togetherness would mend some fences for my divided family.

At twelve noon my father and I walked to the first tee. Two young volunteers fidgeted nervously by the standard that listed the names of the golfers in my group. At this moment all our scores were even.

I could hardly feel my legs. How the hell would I remain standing long enough to swing a golf club?

We greeted the other two women I'd be playing with, So Won Lee and Lindsay Hanson, the amateur I'd practiced with yesterday. Marquee players get some special treatment when it comes to tournament pairings, often grouped together into crowd- and prime-time-TV-pleasing trios. And they aren't assigned the dewsweeper or bottom-of-the-barrel tee times, either. For the rest of us, it's potluck.

We three weren't likely to be a big draw. Okay by me. I could use some extra time and space to adjust to this occasion. The meaning of the day had begun to settle in my chest like a heavy weight. Besides, a smaller crowd would make for less chaos for Greg Merrill.

Lindsay appeared to have a little gallery of hometown fans, and I imagined she'd draw a few more as we went, just because of the cute outfit and the sunny smile. So Won Lee might attract some serious golf addicts—I hated to be mean, but if you were looking for entertaining reactions to golf shots, interaction with the crowd, and an upbeat personality, you wouldn't follow So Won Lee. And I'd have my own strange gallery. Charlie had gone to fetch Mom and Dave. My stepmother and the boys had showed, too, though not in time to officially say hello. Maureen hovered below the tee, dressed in the latest golf fashion designed for Annika, and glowering. Dad would get an earful later. His face was split with a wide grin—I didn't think he'd care.

My lips and throat felt parched and swollen. *You're about to tee off in the US Open,* whispered the devilish part of my brain. *This is such a big deal.*

"Nothing special, nothing extra," I told myself sternly, and walked to the cooler to pull out a bottle of springwater. I stared down the long green sweep to the first putting green, trying to see only shapes and colors.

The marshal, an elfin, sixtyish woman in khaki pants, a blue blazer, and a jungle hat, stepped out of a small white tent onto the tee and held up her hand for quiet. Her amplified voice crackled across the crowd. "Ladies and gentlemen, this is the twelve-fifteen starting time. Please welcome from Seoul, Korea, So Won Lee."

So Won Lee, in short white shorts and a lime green shell, approached the tee markers, clutching her driver. She had her father caddying, too—a tiny Korean man with birdlike movements and not much English. Her drive zinged down the middle of the fairway. The fans crammed into the bleacher behind us applauded with enthusiasm.

The marshal moved out from under the tent again. "From Stillwater, Oklahoma, please welcome Lindsay Hanson."

Lindsay's caddie/father patted her on the butt and pushed her toward front stage, a nervous grin flickering. She waved at the crowd and blew a kiss to her mother. Her drive sailed down the fairway and bounded into the rough just in front of the stream. Huge.

"Please welcome, from Myrtle Beach, South Carolina, Cassie Burdette."

I pulled my three-wood from the bag and edged out onto the tee box, my heart pounding. Feeling like Gumby Girl, I gulped a deep breath and swung. A few hands clapped.

"Good shot!" called my father.

It wasn't a great shot. I'd paid for the lack of confidence by popping up my three-wood and landing twenty yards short of the other two players. And a downhill lie to boot. I could feel my shoulders knotting with tension. This was not how the tournament started in my dreams.

I snatched the seven-wood from the bag, marched down the hill to my miserable lie, and swung again. The ball didn't make it to the green. Meanwhile, Lindsay plucked an iron from her father's hand and sent her ball flying to the putting surface. So Won Lee's second shot joined Lindsay's.

Dad put his hand on my shoulder. "You're playing the golf course here, not just these girls. Go on up and look at the break on the green. You'll chip it close and we'll get the heck out of here with a par."

I rolled my chip fifteen feet by the cup, but sank the putt coming back. The other two girls two-putted for their pars—one hole completed and we were still even. Lindsay Hanson looked disgusted. Who knew what was on So Won Lee's mind. The standard bearers, scorekeeper, and our rules official marched ahead of us to the second tee.

"This hole marshaled by Easy Mountain Country Club," read a sign on the tee box.

My fellow competitors launched monster tee shots.

"I'm going with the driver," I told my father. He handed me the club without comment, and I yanked the shot into the left rough.

"Not to worry, I'm in my office," I told Dad.

That was Laura's joke, whenever I made a familiar error—meaning I'd been there lots of times before and knew just what to do next. Dad hadn't said a word, but he wasn't smiling now. I missed Laura something awful. It made sense for the other two girls to have their daddies on the bag. Lindsay couldn't be more than eighteen and So Won Lee, probably twenty-one. I, on the other hand, was edging up on thirty. People probably thought it weird as hell that my father was caddying—a case of arrested development, maybe.

This line of thinking was not helping my confidence.

I muscled my ball out of the rough and up the hill to the second green. The main road ran by thirty feet beyond the hole. Two police cruisers were stationed among the trees just off the shoulder. The cops faced the road, hands poised near the guns at their hips. I wondered if the cars passing had any idea what was at stake on the green below. Or whether they cared.

I chipped past the hole, marked and cleaned my ball, and sank the putt coming back down.

"That's my banty rooster," said Dad, his face lit up with a broad grin. It was hard to be annoyed with the silly name.

By the time we reached the fourth fairway, I felt like I'd played an entire round. Lindsay had loosened up and gotten down to the work of charming the volunteers and the gallery, including my brothers and Joe. So Won Lee and her father stayed quiet and apart. We waited by our tee shots for the green ahead to clear.

Lindsay turned to look back at me. "Awful news about Amber Clancy."

I nodded. Was it my imagination or did she not quite sound sincere?

"Did you hear about Mr. Beccia?"

"Someone said he felt ill after Amber got sick yesterday. That's all I know," I said.

She arched her brows. "I don't believe that for a minute."

"Why? What did you hear?"

"They say he was making a lot of money off Amber Clancy," Lindsay's father said. "I heard he's the one who set up her PGA appearances. Losing that kind of cash cow could make you feel nauseated, all right."

"But she was an amateur. No one was supposed to be making money. Not yet anyway."

Lindsay winked. "By the way, how did you get invited to the Buick Championship? I'd love to do something like that."

"The tournament is supposed to honor Ollie Crum. They wanted someone with experience as a PGA caddie," I said, teeth gritted but trying to smile pleasantly. "It certainly wasn't my money-list ranking." I thought back to my conversation with Amber in the locker room. There were lots of ways to interpret her curiosity about detective services. I was beginning to see more possibilities here.

"Weren't you playing with Amber yesterday?" Lindsay asked So Won suddenly.

So Won swiveled around to stare at us. "I'm not interested in talking about this now."

I gulped. She sounded as angry as her subdued, polite demeanor would allow. I hated to have her think that besides our trouble back at Q-school, I'd torpedoed her US Open chances, too.

"Green's clear," said my father.

Chapter 15

I walked off the eighteenth green, stopping to scratch my name on the ball caps of several excited girls holding out Sharpie pens. My half brothers hovered just behind them. I hugged one boy, then the other, a little surprised that their enthusiasm about greeting me had overridden the natural teenage reserve.

"Thank you guys so much for coming! I have to sign my card and give a couple of interviews"—I winked—"but I'm really looking forward to having dinner tonight."

Zack winked back. "ESPN or NBC?"

"That Lindsay is hot," David whispered, his gaze following her boisterous exit from the green. The small crowd who had gathered for my signature rushed toward Lindsay, hats, programs, and pennants in their outstretched hands. "Do you think you could introduce us later?"

I reached over to rub my knuckles against his brush cut, beginning to see what the enthusiastic welcome was all about. "I'll try." I glanced up at the leaderboard that loomed behind the bleachers. "She shot the lowest score in the tournament so far. I have a feeling she's going to be very popular this evening. Haven't you grown half a foot since I saw you last?"

I blew a kiss to Mom and Maureen—thirty feet apart and not acknowledging each other—ducked under the security ropes, and headed through a temporary green fabric tunnel that ran beneath the grandstand surrounding the eighteenth green—a fan-free shortcut to the scoring tent and the clubhouse. Behind me, Alice Maxwell and two other USGA officials met Lindsay to lead her to the outdoor interview stage where they'd broken the news about Amber just yesterday. A cluster of reporters and TV cameramen were jostling for front-row positions. I didn't need to stay and listen—I'd been a first-pew observer already. After an ordinary start, she'd gone on a birdie binge midround, punctuated by a chip-in eagle on the fifteenth hole. I paused on the outskirts of the crowd anyway, drawn in like a rubbernecking bystander.

"Ladies and gentlemen," Alice began, "this is Lindsay Hanson. She shot seven under par, breaking the amateur record for low round in the US Open by two shots." The reporters clapped and whistled. "Lindsay, could you start by giving us your impressions of the golf course today, and of course, your round?"

"Oh gosh," said Lindsay, with a girlish giggle. "This is so awesome! You know I started out just saving par. I was a little nervous, you know, it being my first Open and all. And my first putt was so short, I was just lucky that second one broke in the way my dad told me it would. And that I listened to him," she added, flashing a big smile in his direction. Her dad waved back, looking proud to the bursting point and completely exhausted.

The reporters laughed. In my experience, they were a hardened bunch. They'd seen every golf shot invented and every kind of golfer. They'd take dirt over fluff any day. But this girl had them nibbling out of her palm. Besides, after yesterday's tragedy, brilliant golf might bring some much-needed cheer. I edged around the perimeter of the gathering and started over to the clubhouse, Lindsay's amplified voice trailing after me.

"The course is so awesome and everyone has been so sweet! You should see all the free stuff we got this week."

Another laugh from the crowd.

Alice steered her back to golf. "Take us through your birdies today and tell us which clubs you used and how long were your putts?"

I showed my badge to the security guard and headed up the back stairs to Sarah Washington's borrowed office. My round had been disappointing in the end—four over par. But assuming I could stay in the right moment tomorrow, I still had the chance to make the cut and play the weekend.

Even so, next to Lindsay's radiant play, my game definitely lacked luster.

How would it feel to burst out of the blocks by posting the lowest score in the tournament field? What were the chances of keeping up a pace like that over four days? I told myself I'd be better off creeping up through the ranks than putting on an early dog and pony show.

Greg Merrill and Charlie had arrived in the office before me. "Congratulations on your first round," said Greg.

"Wasn't she awesome?" Charlie grinned.

"Four over par is awesome? You sound like David and
Zack. I suppose you want to meet Lindsay, too?"

Charlie laughed. "She's a little young for my taste."

"Do you want your brother to stay for our discussion?"
Greg asked, tapping on his teeth with the tip of his sunglasses. "Your choice."

I weighed the pros and cons. If he stayed, Charlie would
be privy to everything I said. On the other hand, I wouldn't
be alone. "I'd rather he stayed."

Greg nodded, leaning back to balance his chair on
two legs. "Let's talk about the messages you've been getting."

I reviewed everything—the e-mails featuring *The Rules
of Golf,* the handwritten note at Kripalu, and yesterday's
"I'm watching you" message.

"I feel stupid about this whole thing. Someone's probably just goofing around. Who would bother watching me?
The cops could probably use you on the Amber Clancy situation. Everybody's nerves are shot over that."

"Did you notice anything out there today? How can you
tell if someone is watching in an abnormal way?" Charlie
asked, ignoring my protest.

"Most of the spectators are interested in golf. When a
player tees off, the fans are absorbed in the results. Just
like a TV camera, their eyes follow the trajectory of the
ball." Greg drummed the table leg lightly with one black
Reebok. "If I notice that someone is observing the player,
not the golf shot, I pay attention."

"I guess even your most dedicated fan would take his

eyes off you long enough to follow the ball," Charlie said to me.

Greg's chair thumped to the floor. "A golf fan has a certain look, you know? Though it's gotten more complicated in the past couple of years. Your professional organizations have been reaching out for a wider audience—and those new fans don't necessarily fit our profiles."

I knew what he meant. There'd been an influx of rabble-rousing golf nuts over the last five years—attention deficit-disordered transplants from football and baseball and basketball. They didn't always understand or appreciate the strict etiquette and decorum that we live by in golf.

"The guys chugging beers and screaming 'you da man!'" I said.

He nodded and shifted his sunglasses to the top of his head. His hair was thick and wiry, with one white streak wandering off his left temple. Crinkles radiated from the corners of his eyes—smile lines, or maybe just a lot of time spent in the sun.

"Let's start with your ideas about the messages."

"Hmm. My first thought was the rules were coming from the USGA, but Alice Maxwell said no, definitely not. It didn't really make sense anyway, because of the stuff tacked onto the ends of the e-mails. And I did wonder whether my sponsor, Lloyd, was sending me suggestions about points I should brush up on. Same problem—the extra comments don't fit him, either." I frowned. "The note at Kripalu? I figured it was from a fan. Celebrity worship and the yoga institute don't really mix—unless you're talking Dalai Lama—so I figured it had to be a closet golf lover just laying low. It all made me a little nervous, but then I've been nervous lately anyway."

"Tell me more about that."

Geez. He was beginning to sound like Dr. Baxter. *What are your thoughts about that? Tell me more? Spell it out? How do you feel about that?* A headshrinker is never satisfied with what you've told him. He always, always thinks there's more.

I took a deep breath and then let it out slowly, like a leaking balloon. "I had a little panic attack just before I qualified for the Open," I said, waving my hand. "No biggie. I thought I might be having a premature heart attack, but they checked me out and everything was fine." I fought back the tears and tried to smile. "Besides the Open, I'd been issued this invitation to play in the Buick Championship. I'd be honoring professional caddies, Ollie Crum in particular."

"She'd be playing with PGA professionals in Cromwell—the men," Charlie added. "She's gotten a lot of publicity for that, and fan mail, too."

"But you're not a caddie," said Greg.

"But she used to be," said Charlie. "And the idea was to honor this Ollie fellow who recently died."

"It's basically a publicity stunt," I said. "The good news is that money would go to a cancer charity. Bad news? It doesn't really make any sense for me or my game. But people want me to carry the standard for them. Total strangers." I pulled Mom's forwarded letters out of my backpack and tossed them on the desk. "Here are a couple of examples."

"Tell him about the newspaper articles."

So I summarized the ongoing debate about whether or not I should play, and what it would mean for my gender if I played and played badly. The more I talked about it, the clearer I got: When this week was over—if it ever ended—I would be calling the Buick tournament committee with my regrets. Ever since the offer had arrived, I'd been feeling like an emotional cripple. Enough was more than enough.

"There are strong opinions on each side," I finished. "As if I need all that now. There's a ton of pressure this week just because it's the Open." I ran my fingers through my curls and pulled the hair back into a tight ponytail. "It all boils down to this: I can't imagine that someone who's never met me is out to get me. That just doesn't compute."

"What about your reputation as the detective golfer? Maybe he should know about that," Charlie suggested.

Greg raised one eyebrow and tipped his head to the side.

I described my unfortunate tendency to show up in the aftermath of murders and explained that I'd been curious and distressed enough about them to get in deeper than maybe I should have. "A nosy reporter caught wind of all this and wrote a piece about it at the end of last week. That could have ruffled some feathers."

Amber's scornful face flickered to mind. Where was she now? Ready to be sawed open on some coroner's table? I shivered.

"It's good to have all that background. But most often a stalker is not a stranger," said Greg. "So let's talk about who you might have had personal trouble with lately. Any kind of problems at all."

Stalker? I went cold and numb. I licked my dry lips. "I don't think I'm being stalked." Up to this moment, I had refused to recognize that possibility. Amber Clancy might be stalked. And murdered. Cassie Burdette, not a chance.

"Maybe, maybe not," said Greg. "But it's my job to fig-ure that out. Once you fill me in, you go play golf and I make sure you're safe." He laughed. "I can't help with your game—you'd know that if you saw me hack around. But it should certainly be easier to play without all this on your mind."

"My friends wouldn't send me this shit," I said, and crossed my arms over my chest. "I haven't had trouble with anyone."

"After today's e-mail, I think we should assume the sender is here at the tournament." Greg pulled his Palm Pilot out of his pocket and flicked it on. "Let's just review the list you gave me this morning. 'Mom, Dave, Dad, Charlie, Joe, Mike, Michelle, Maureen, Lloyd, and half brothers David and Zack.'" He looked up. "Chuck's your dad."

"Maureen's his wife, Mom's my mom, Dave's my stepfather, Charlie's my brother. David and Zack are brothers, too. It's my family and friends," I said flatly.

"What about Mike?" Greg asked.

"What about Mike?"

"Mike's her ex," Charlie explained.

"Ex-boyfriend," I put in quickly.

"He's here watching," Charlie went on. "They've had a difficult relationship for years."

"Difficult relationship?" asked Greg.

"Hold on just a damn minute." I felt a hard rush of blood flood my face. The way Charlie made it sound, we'd been immersed in cutting-edge S&M.

"Don't get pissed," said Greg. "The more I know, the easier it is to help you."

I took a deep breath, eyes closed. My shoulders, chest, and neck muscles had drawn into painful knots. "Mike and I went together for a while, even though we were a train wreck in the romance department. Before that, I caddied for him his rookie year—that's how I landed the Buick Championship invitation."

Greg made a note in his PDA.

"Mike would never hurt me," I said firmly.

He gave a minute nod. "Who else?"

He didn't believe a word I'd said.

"Michelle?" Greg prodded.

"Mike's current girlfriend," I explained. "They were dating the year I was his caddie. I don't like her and she doesn't like me. But look, she has what she wanted— Mike. What would be the point of her going after me now? That's ridiculous."

This conversation was making me crazy.

"Lloyd," Greg prompted.

I rested my forehead on my fists and tried to keep the mounting frustration out of my voice. "Lloyd's the only reason I'm here." I lifted my head. "If it wasn't for Lloyd and his deep pockets, I'd be asking 'Paper or plastic?' at the local supermarket."

"Tell me about Lloyd," said Greg.

"He's my sponsor. He was a fan and he had some extra money to spend and he offered to stake me for this year. He's a royal pain, but he's not dangerous. He's never come on to me or anything. . . ."

Had he come on to me? Maybe he'd been so clumsy or I'd been so dense that I hadn't recognized it.

"How did you meet Lloyd?"

"He contacted the LPGA office." Hadn't I told him this yesterday? This was no chat, it was a full-scale inquisition. "They forwarded his query and I decided to call him. I wasn't making enough to pay my expenses. My mother doesn't have any money to spare, and Dad doesn't have a whole lot and it comes with strings. He means well, but I needed to be able to make my own decisions. Play my own game."

"How's it working out with Lloyd?"

I wrinkled my nose. "He has a lot to say, but I just nod and then let it wash over me."

"Do you get the sense he's trying to control you?" Greg leaned forward a little, his eyes searching mine.

"No!"

He glanced back at his Palm Pilot. "And Joe?"

"He's a golf psychologist. And a good friend." I blushed and looked away.

"What exactly are you going to do for her?" Charlie asked. "Will you be following her after her rounds? And shouldn't we be talking money?"

"My fee is a thousand a day. That's for the golf grounds only. I'll be checking everything out before she arrives and following her during the round and while she's on the golf course premises." He smiled at me. "While you're here, I'm here. If you think you need more than that, we'll have to talk."

I gulped. A thousand dollars a day? It was almost enough to make me hope I'd miss the cut. "That sounds like plenty."

"Don't worry about it, I've got you covered," said Charlie. "If you decide you want him around more, you let me know." He reached for my hand and squeezed. "What should we be looking for? What do you think's going on?"

"It's my job to watch," said Greg. "But there's one thing I tell all my clients: trust your intuition. Most of us—you women especially—don't want to be rude. To anyone. If your intuition is telling you something's wrong, you're reacting to important information. Your intuition is always working in your best interest, even in the cases where you misinterpret the cues. Got it?"

I nodded, stood up, and thrust out my hand. "I tee off at seven A.M. tomorrow. Dewsweepers." I grimaced. "So I'll get here before six." I glanced at my watch and then over at Charlie. "We've got dinner with Dad in forty-five minutes. I'd like to eat fast and then stop in at the service for Amber."

"Have a good night," said Greg. "I'll be here as soon as it gets light."

A loud crack echoed from the dark sky as I stepped out of the building. Then I heard the horn signaling that play on the golf course had been suspended. Too dangerous with lightening flashing nearby. Damn, if the golfers out there didn't complete their rounds, they'd have to finish in the morning, making a hash of the scheduled tee times. Another loud crack and the skies opened to a torrent of warm rain.

Chapter 16

I had just enough time to shower before Charlie picked me up for dinner. A sweet Holyoke alum with white hair greeted me in the dorm bathroom. She inquired politely about my round but seemed really more interested in describing her annual reunions with ten women from her graduating class. Which suited me just fine—her reminiscences might keep the conversation with Greg from grinding through my mind again.

Back in the room, I ran a comb through my wet hair and pulled on a pair of black jeans. Then I rustled through my drawers and found a black spandex top that wasn't too tight to pass for funeral-appropriate attire. One of the silver and turquoise earrings that I thought resembled miniature golf balls seemed to be missing in action. Hard to stay organized on the road.

Outside the window, I could hear Charlie tapping his car horn in the courtyard. I buttoned up a pink oxford shirt over the spandex and dashed down the three flights of stairs. The thunderstorm had blown by, leaving the ground saturated and the air heavy. Kids from summer camp had churned the square in front of the dormitory into a muddy soup.

"Sorry I'm late. Where are we headed?"

"Your father made a reservation in Amherst at the Lord Jeffrey Inn."

My father? Wasn't he Charlie's father, too?

I'd been looking forward to seeing Northampton—a couple of the golfers at the range this morning had described it as vibrant and colorful, jammed with fabulous restaurants and cute shops. But what did it really matter—this dinner was all about survival and escape, as far as I was concerned.

"How did you think it went with Greg—"

I cut Charlie off before he could finish. "Can we not talk about it tonight? My intuition tells me I'm on the edge of losing my mind." I chuckled grimly. "It's bad enough I'm going to owe you my life's earnings after this weekend. Reviewing the whole mess is not likely to improve the situation. Okay?"

He glanced over at me. "Okay. Are you all right?"

"Just exhausted and tense. I want to try to relax, if that's possible."

We retraced the ten miles up Route 116, passing the staid brick campuses of Hampshire and Amherst Colleges. Neither one could match the regal beauty of Mount

Holyoke. We rode in silence until we reached the wide rectangle of the Amherst green. A foursome of mothers was pushing their young children in fancy strollers across the sidewalk that split the green.

Would I ever get to the point where I wanted kids? I couldn't imagine knowing what to do with them—I'd be frozen just trying to avoid mistakes. And who the hell would I have them with? I'd heard players talk about how their families keep them sane. Kids and a husband make up an alternate reality that draws them out of the brutal pressure to perform on the Tour. Sounded nice.

But there was not much sanity in my own splintered family. And at this moment, it was hard to imagine handling anything but my nerves. Of course, those women were not dealing with a stalker as well as the tournament.

The skin over my cheeks tingled and I started to breathe harder.

"Here we are," said Charlie, pulling the car into a space along the green. "It's pretty, isn't it? This town's got a little more to offer than South Hadley."

I sucked in some air, forced my mind back into the present, and stepped out onto the grass.

"Hellooo!" called Maureen.

Independent of how glad she actually was to see you, she always got in the first word. And the last, of course. I was curious to see how she and Charlie would make out—he'd spent very little time with her in the years since she married Dad. And the feedback hadn't been all that positive from either direction. On her side, Maureen took my father's disappointment with Charlie's estrangement personally. From Charlie's point of view, Maureen had blown the gust of fetid air that toppled the precarious Burdette house of cards.

My younger brothers pushed ahead into the vestibule of the inn, a traditional New England brick building that claimed to serve "Classic Tavern and Family Fare." Dad, with Maureen clamped firmly on his arm, came close behind.

"The boys wanted a burger," said my father. "Hope this is okay with you guys."

"Looks fine," I said. The place met my criteria: (1) Budweiser on tap and (2) an empty dining room that would allow for a quick meal and a fast exit.

The waitress glanced at my brothers and led us to a back table. Above the bar a brick wall melded into a dark green painted ceiling that slanted down to the windows. The wall was studded with old-fashioned lanterns and hanging green plants. All very New England quaint.

Maureen flipped through her menu. "I don't think there's a thing here on my diet." She dropped her glittery half-glasses onto her chest and glared at my father. "Or yours."

He offered a pained smile. "It's only one night. And look, they have baked scrod and grilled salmon."

"Scrod! What the hell is that?" Zack said. "It sounds disgusting."

Maureen tapped his wrist. "Language, please."

Joe appeared, slightly breathless, just inside the bar entrance. The hostess pointed him toward our table.

"You look wonderful." He took the empty seat between Charlie and Maureen and kissed her on the cheek. "Don't tell me you lost more weight? What is your secret?" He patted his gently rounded stomach and winked at the rest of us. "Can I get you to take me on as your next project?"

She ran a hand down the length of her sculpted bicep and smiled. "You don't need me for that. How is that sweet girl we met last summer in Connecticut? What was her name? Rachel? Wasn't she a doctor, too?"

I knew she was referring to Joe's former girlfriend, Dr. Butterman. She and I had never hit it off—oil and water, fire and gasoline, falling bodies and concrete sidewalks. She fit into the dreaded perky category, too, besides being smart, and well dressed, and never having a mean thought. That she let show anyway.

"Rebecca," I said. "Her name was Rebecca. And she's not a doctor, she's a shrink." I sounded bitter, confusing even to me. After all, Joe had supposedly dropped her to try a relationship with me. Would I ever figure myself out?

"I haven't seen her in a while," said Joe. "Last I heard she was just fine." He leaned across the table and touched my hand. "Nice job out on the course today. You hung in there. You have a chance to really turn it on tomorrow. And when you used too much club on the twelfth hole, you recovered nicely."

"That was Dad's fault," said David. "He told her it was uphill and she'd never get there with the seven. Listen, if you don't like the way he's handling your bag, I'm your guy."

I gave him a quick hug. "You'll be the first to know. You were a godsend at the Pine Straw tournament." My youngest brother had taken over my bag at a tournament last fall and managed the pressure well enough. But the Open was something else. The pressure at the Open could eat a green caddie alive.

The waitress delivered our dinners, grilled salmon with steamed vegetables for Joe and Maureen, burgers dripping with cheese, bacon, and onions, spicy fries on the side, for the rest of us. And one tall glass of cold beer for me.

"That little girl you played with today was a whiz-bang, wasn't she?" asked Dad.

"She was special," said Joe, delicately dissecting the gray skin off his fish. "It remains to be seen whether she can repeat the same kind of performance tomorrow. You can just imagine how wired she is. From what I've read, she's certainly never been in a situation like this before, so she's hardly prepared for handling it."

"Unless she has an outstanding coach to consult with," said my father, winking at Joe.

"Speaking of coaches," said Charlie, "did you hear any more about Lucien Beccia? Is it true that he got sick after Amber was taken to the hospital?"

"What did happen to that girl?" demanded Maureen. Her eyes narrowed as she looked at me.

"She was poisoned. That's all we've heard," I said. "And that's not the official word." Maureen fancied herself an amateur expert in true crime. If we discussed Amber's death any further, I was certain she'd get the idea of attending the memorial service to look for clues.

"Her dying is just so sad," said Maureen. "Her father was African-American, wasn't he? We watched them on TV in the men's tournament. Even Johnny Miller liked her."

Johnny Miller, former PGA player, current golf commentator, and ego extraordinaire, could and did shred any performance with his zingers.

"She was hot, too," said Zachary.

"I like Lindsay better," said David.

The waitress came by to clear our empty plates. The Burdettes left nothing but streaks of ketchup and hamburger grease. Joe left a small pile of fish skin and bones.

Maureen had neatly divided all her portions into two sections and consumed only one of them.

"It's my secret weapon," she said to Joe, touching her flat belly with one manicured hand. And to the waitress: "Could you wrap this please?"

The waitress returned with a white foam container and Maureen scraped in the leftovers. If the fish had been unappealing fresh, it was roadkill now.

"Dessert and coffee?"

"Dessert," said both boys.

"Hope you don't mind, but I need to get back to the dorm," I said.

"I'll take you," Joe said.

I cringed, wishing he hadn't offered. I just plain didn't want to be alone with him. He knew me too well. Somehow I'd end up confessing about my new security guard. And then we'd move onto the topic of trust—not the legal kind, either. The kind where I should know by now that I could tell him anything. And the expression on his face would tell me how hurt he was that I hadn't. If I got really unlucky, he'd start on Hawaii.

"I've got her," said Charlie quickly. "My hotel's right on the way." It wasn't, but it was a graceful enough white lie. I flashed him a grateful smile.

"I'll take her," Joe repeated firmly. "We need a chance to catch up anyway."

"See you all tomorrow," I told the family as I got to my feet. "I'm really, really glad you're here." The tears that filled my eyes surprised me. I *was* glad they were here— every last one of them. I followed Joe out to his Honda.

"I get a kick out of your folks," he said, unlocking and opening the passenger side door for me.

"Maureen sure keeps Dad on a short leash," I said.

"But he seems happy. You never know what goes on with a couple behind closed doors."

I covered my eyes and laughed. "I'd rather not think about that."

He started the car and turned to look at me. "Are you all right? I'm getting the strong sense that something's wrong."

"I'm okay." I swallowed and focused on rolling up my shirtsleeves. "You kept telling me to expect a tough week. Everything's been hard—the competition, the press, missing Laura, my family baggage—and then Amber dying. That's got all of the players upset."

He leaned against the headrest. "Knowing you, it's bothering you a lot."

I nodded. "Have you heard any more about what really happened to her?"

"Something she ate or drank during her practice round—that's the scuttlebutt anyway." He gripped the wheel with both hands. "Listen, I'm not asking you to talk about this now, Cassie. But I don't know what's happening with our friendship."

I opened my mouth, ready to repeat the litany of stressors that might explain why I needed to shut him out. He held his hand up, palm facing me.

"I want you to know that I'm not going to allow you to just fade out of my life. You're too important to me."

My mouth was starting to water, the way it does before you throw up. "Maybe we can have dinner next week in Ohio."

He shifted into gear and started down the road. "Sounds good."

We talked about my first round for the rest of the ride,

with Joe pointing out times I'd taken a tough moment and turned it into something good. "You're starting to look more poised—not easy in a setting like this."

He pulled into the cul-de-sac in front of Abbey Hall. "Sure you'll be okay? Want me to walk you in?"

"I'm going to make an appearance at Amber's service. It's only two doors away. And Julie's got the light on." I pointed to our third-floor window and then leaned over to peck his cheek. "Thanks for the ride and the pep talk. I'm good."

Chapter 17

Some of the people packed into the chapel were already crying. The lights were dim, the altar was loaded with flowers and a photograph of Amber, and the organ ground out a grim march. I couldn't swear to it from a distance, but it looked as though they'd chosen a photo of Amber posed with her driver. She'd been so proud of that club—Callaway made it special to suit her game. It was an investment—they were willing to wait out the time until she turned professional. Then they could reap the rewards of her endorsement. Would the nude calendar have changed their minds?

I moved to the side aisle and leaned into a sliver of wall space next to a golfer who played on the Futures tour. Her face glinted wet under the faint light from the sconce just above us.

A woman with short gray hair and round gold-rimmed glasses stepped up to the pulpit and smoothed her robe. She looked around the room, visiting each quadrant of onlookers with her attention. I wondered if any of the members of Amber's family had come. Up toward the front, I recognized several USGA officials and LPGA players—mostly those who'd been elected to positions within our organization. Another reason to keep a low profile. God, how I hate funerals.

"We are gathered tonight to celebrate the life of Amber Tamika Clancy." The minister sighed and adjusted her purple stole. "I have had divinity students ask me, how will I ever handle a funeral for a child? How will I ever thank God for a life that has been so clearly ended before its rightful time? And I have answered this way: It is through remembering the joys of their lives that we mourn their loss." She pushed her glasses farther up the bridge of her nose and looked out into the crowd again. "I'm told that Amber loved to play and to compete. And we have much to learn from this. She embraced her life with its many challenges. She did not fear them. And still, we ask our frightened questions: How can we possibly live on, shadowed as we are by the tragedy of her death?"

A wave of sniffling swept through the audience.

"We shall find a clue in Psalm 122," the minister said. She opened an enormous Bible and leafed through its thin pages. "Verses one and two."

The glasses slid down her nose.

> "I will lift up my eyes to the hills—
> From whence comes my help?
> My help comes from the Lord,
> Who made heaven and earth."

She cleared her throat.

"And verses seven and eight:

> "The Lord shall preserve you from all evil;
> He shall preserve your soul.
> The Lord shall preserve your going out and
>   your coming in
> From this time forth, and even forevermore."

She held her arms out to the congregation. "Will you pray with me?"

I zoned out as she launched into her prayer, focusing on the architectural details of the chapel instead: an intensely blue stained-glass rose window at the back of the church, stone walls, red-and-blue beams supporting a Gothic-looking ceiling.

The president of our women's golf association made her way to the podium, and voice cracking, began to talk about Amber's astonishing talent—how she had taken the golf world by surprise and the tragedy of the matches we would now never have the opportunity to witness. It was dark in the chapel, light coming only from the flickering candles on the altar, a small focused beam illuminating the papers on the pulpit, and dim wall sconces. I began to count mourners to try to block out the pain in the room. Over three hundred people—golfers, caddies, reporters, employees of the USGA and the LPGA. And many more I didn't know—some still dressed in their volunteer uniforms or casual clothes of the fans.

How many of these had really known Amber? And how many of them really cared about her personally? In my opinion, the minister danced around a crucial point—when a kid dies, half the agony is all about the unfairness, the terror, the lack of control that exists in our own fragile lives. This girl had most likely been murdered. I shuddered, suddenly missing Laura something awful.

"Jesus told his disciples," said the minister, "come to Me, all you who labor and are heavy laden, and I will give you rest."

As the organ music surged, the woman made her way slowly down the center aisle and positioned herself just yards from where I stood. "May the Lord bless you and keep you, the Lord make his face to shine upon you, and give you peace. Amen."

Escaping the crush of mourners spilling onto the front steps of the chapel, I slipped out the side door and trotted over to my dormitory.

I slid my key card into the lock, then paused in the formal parlor just inside the entrance. Upholstered chairs, table lamps, paintings of important historical figures from the college—the room could have been plucked from the home of a maiden aunt, right down to the slightly musty smell. I felt like I had a bad case of indigestion, but it had to be the aftereffects of the funeral. I pulled out my cell phone and hit the button to speed-dial Laura.

"Oh my God, am I glad to hear from you," she said when she answered. "I've been trying to reach you ever since I read about Amber Clancy. What the hell's going on up there?"

A little tension drained from my shoulders, just hearing her voice.

"I just got back from her memorial service. They wrung us out like wet towels."

"What did she die from?"

"Unofficially, poison."

"You mean someone killed her?" she asked in a shocked voice.

"The authorities haven't been that specific, but everyone thinks so." Then I told her about Amber approaching me in the locker room.

"Don't you dare start feeling guilty about that," said Laura. "Did she ask you for help?"

"No. But now I'm wondering—"

"If she'd told you someone had threatened her and you did nothing, that would be a different story," she said sternly. "Tell me about your round. How did it go today?"

"Went okay. But first, how's your dad?"

"Believe it or not," said Laura, "they're letting us go home tomorrow."

"That's great!" I felt a whoosh of relief. This meant everything to Laura. Besides, my father had done just fine on the bag, but Laura fit like a favorite old sweatshirt. And I meant that in only the nicest way.

"He still has a long road, but apparently we've survived the worst. And they say the hospital's a terrible place to be unless you're really sick. Germs everywhere and they don't let you get a wink of sleep." She sighed. "And I've been catnapping in a plastic armchair most of the nights."

"You must be exhausted."

"I'm fine. Now you. Tell me everything."

So I gave her the eighteen holes shot by shot, glad to shuttle the mournful prayer vigil from my mind. No one else in the world could have listened without glazing over. No one else in the world would have cared.

"Dad did okay," I said. "But I sure missed you. Are you going to be able to make it tomorrow?"

"I have to get a caregiver lined up and then I'm yours. A couple weeks, tops. I'm just bummed I'm missing the Open."

Deep down, I knew she wasn't coming for the weekend, but hearing it felt like a punch to the gut.

"There'll be other years," I said after a small pause.

"Is there something else going on with you?" Laura asked. "You don't sound right."

I got up out of my wing-back chair to peer down the hallway in both directions. The floor was deserted. So I told her about the e-mails I'd received and hiring Greg.

"No way! I'm coming up there tomorrow. I'll find someone to stay with Dad."

"Absolutely not. I only mentioned it because it's under control. And I need someone to talk to. I don't need you to be here, I just need you to listen."

"I feel terrible—"

"You're right where you should be. I've got plenty of help. Too much, really. And I'll keep you posted every step of the way." I pressed End, promising to call her back after round two.

I trudged up the three flights of stairs to my room. A wedge of light spilled out onto the hallway's weathered linoleum tiles. I slid my key into the lock and pushed open the door. Julie was sitting up on her bed in pink sweats, reading. On the cover of her book, a man on a large horse had thrown a struggling woman across the saddle in front of him. I wondered suddenly why she hadn't gone to Amber's service.

"Hey, stranger. How's it going?" I almost hated to ask— I'd seen her 80 posted on the scoreboard at the golf course.

She grimaced. "Disappointing, to put it mildly. Shot myself in the foot with too many three-putts."

I tried to think of something reassuring to say that wouldn't come off patronizing or false. Truth was, with that kind of start, her chances of making it to the weekend looked bleak. I perched beside her and patted her leg.

"I'm sorry. I wasn't exactly brilliant, either."

"Seventy-three, right?"

I nodded.

"Did you have a good dinner?"

"Indigestion, family-style." I laughed. "I suppose I should be flattered that every one of my living blood relatives insisted on making the trek, but it feels worse than it sounds. Did your folks make it?"

"Nah." She waved her hand. "They're not golfers."

Mom and Maureen and Charlie weren't golfers, either, but they were here. Julie's face had closed down, though. Subject over.

"How did it go with Jason?" I asked.

"He's a good guy, I can't blame the 80 on him, if that's what you're asking."

"Are you guys"—I tilted my head—"involved?"

Julie laughed and snapped her book closed. "Oh no. He feels just like a brother to me." She paused. "Why? Are you interested?"

"Just nosy," I said, wishing I could learn to keep my mouth shut. I didn't like people probing into my personal business; why did I think she wanted to talk about hers?

Julie turned off her bedside lamp, dropped the book on the floor, and slid under the top sheet. "Nighty-night. Sweet birdies in your dreams."

"Mind if I use the computer for a few?"

"Be my guest." Her voice drifted sleepily through the half-dark. "Nothing's going to keep me awake tonight."

I turned on my laptop and padded down the hallway to brush my teeth. It felt eerie living here in the dorm, away from all the other players. Lonely. I'd never thought of Julie as a lonely person. Maybe that explained why she was so eager to rescue me.

Back in bed, I typed in the US Open Web site address and scrolled through the first round scores. Lindsay Hanson still held the lead with her record-breaking eight under par. Annika Sorenstam was breathing down her neck, whether she realized it or not, just eight shots behind. My name was there, two thirds of the way down the list: Cassie Burdette, 73. That's all I wanted to see—me, staying alive in the US Open. The present moment . . .

I shut the computer down and the light off and stretched out, feeling every wire in the skeleton of the mattress press into my back. I got up, doubled the blanket, and spread it over the top of the mattress. When pigs could fly, I would sleep.

Chapter 18

Yesterday's thunderstorm and a second deluge in the early hours of the morning delayed my seven A.M. tee time an hour. I refused to let myself get rattled. There were girls out there who had yet to finish their first round—girls who had to tee off in the dawn light this morning, play five or six or seven holes, and then start right in on the new round. If they'd had a good thing going when the skies opened up yesterday, chances were, that rhythm was gone today.

Extra time warming up would not hurt.

The path to the practice area was rutted and muddy, partly matted with slippery grass. I headed over to the far end of the range, hoping to duck early morning fans and distracting chitchat. My father was already there, giving a last minute polish to my clubs. So was Greg. He stood about thirty yards away from my father, facing the bleachers. Even dressed in all black and deadly serious, he blended in with the surroundings. I barely smiled and passed by him without speaking. Dad might have to know about Greg sooner or later, but right now I preferred to keep my "problem" to myself. I picked up my wedge and swung it slowly around my body, loosening small cricks of tension in my back and neck.

"Mind if I run up and grab a cup of coffee?" Dad asked. "I got here a little on the early side."

"Not at all. I take mine light, no sugar." I looked at him. He was jumpy already, fingers snapping and eyebrows twitching.

"Sure you need more caffeine?" I asked.

He grinned and started up the hill.

Rolling the first ball off the neat stack in front of me, I gazed out over the range. I'd spent half an hour stretching in the dorm room, but I hadn't felt like taking the twenty-minute jog that had become part of my preround routine. Hope it wouldn't come back to haunt me.

I pushed the thought aside as two men in suit-coats approached. Fifteen yards behind them, Greg tensed and took several steps closer.

The first man, heavyset with a neat part in his gray hair, reached into his jacket, took out a small leather case, and showed me his badge. "Cassie Burdette?"

Damn. I nodded.

"We're with the South Hadley Police Department. I'm Detective Boyd. This is Detective Zimmerman. Can we have a couple minutes of your time?"

"Of course." I dropped my wedge back into the Birdie

Girl bag and wiped my hands on a damp towel. It had to be Amber. "What can I do for you?"

"Amber Clancy," said the second man, a redhead with a carpet of freckles who looked like he shouldn't spend much time in the sun. "You've probably heard about her death?"

I nodded, pulling the wedge back out of its slot, and scraping minute specks of dirt from the grooves with a white tee. My father hadn't left much to keep me busy. My hands felt suddenly clammy and the wedge slipped to the ground. "Did you guys figure out what happened to her?"

Neither man responded.

"Tell us about your practice round on Wednesday. Apparently your group was some of the last folks to see her alive." Detective Boyd shoved his hands in his pockets and waited.

"Not much to say, really. We were behind them half a hole for a couple hours. We had to wait some because of Amber's fans." I crouched down beside my bag, stuffed my wallet into the bottom pocket, extracted a new glove, and retrieved the wedge. "There was a little talk about why was Mr. Beccia following her practice round, how much it must have cost, her being an amateur and all that. But I didn't hear anything someone would have killed her over."

The detectives exchanged a glance. Me and my big mouth. So far, no one but me had mentioned murder.

"You didn't notice anything unusual ahead of you? Someone in the gallery acting funny maybe?" asked Detective Zimmerman.

I paused. I had to say something about my locker room conversation with Amber—but what? It would sound stupid no matter what words I used.

"Not really, but I did see Amber the day before that round. Maybe she looked a little worried. Like she was concerned about something. I don't know what, though. She didn't tell me any details. You know what teenagers are like—not the greatest communicators. It was just an impression. There was an article published last week about me getting involved in another mur—um, in a . . . murder case. She seemed sort of interested in that, I guess."

The cops didn't look at all satisfied.

"What exactly did she say?"

"That's just it. She didn't tell me anything really."

My father approached carrying two steaming foam cups, Charlie on his heels.

"This is my father—he's caddying for me," I told the cops. "And my brother. They're asking questions about Amber Clancy," I explained to the guys.

The redheaded cop raised his massive shoulders. "You were also in the group following Amber Clancy and Mr. Beccia on Tuesday, then?"

My father shook his head and touched Charlie's arm.

"I was there," Charlie said.

"We're investigating Ms. Clancy's murder," said Detective Boyd, throwing me a hard look. "You people were following her right before she was taken to the hospital. We're hoping one of you noticed something helpful."

"Can't really think what that would be. Nothing seemed amiss." Charlie scratched his chin.

"She looked fine on the golf course. She was hitting the ball like an animal," I offered. "As far as we knew, she wasn't sick. But on the range, it looked like she was having epileptic seizures."

"But it sounds like these guys want to know about suspects and motives," said my father.

The cops nodded.

"After the round, a couple of the caddies were talking about how much Amber might be worth when she turns pro. And whether Beccia would get a cut or was he just on retainer," Charlie said. "I'm reaching here, fellas."

Dad sipped his coffee and shrugged. "I've been involved in a lot of tournaments, seen a lot of crowds. These people are among the friendliest and the best behaved, in my experience. That's no help at all, either, is it?"

The detectives handed cards to each of us. "Let us know if you think of something."

"Will do." My father slid the card into his shirt pocket. "There're a lot of rumors out here. Can you tell us how she really died?"

"Strychnine. In her sports drink," said Detective Zimmerman. He glared at us and turned away.

"Damn," said Dad.

"Damn is right," I said, looking at my coffee and then setting it down on the grass next to my bag.

"Who the hell would do a sick thing like that?" asked my father.

"That's why we're here," said the redhead, then followed his partner up the range.

Dad let out a long sigh. "That young lady had game." He smiled weakly at me. "I know you feel bad about this, honey, but we have to put it aside for a couple hours, right?"

"Gotta put it aside," Charlie echoed and kissed my cheek. "Hit 'em straight."

"Right." I took my driver from Dad and teed up a ball. Too many thoughts crowded my mind, plus I felt faint and queasy. It would take an ocean of sports psychology tips to get me through this round.

At eight-thirty we finally started up the hill to the golf course. My entire family lined the path toward the first tee. Mom and Maureen were separated only by their men— Dave, Charlie, Zachary, and David. Joe hovered just behind them. Knowing him, the poor guy was exhausted from distributing strained chitchat fairly to both sets of relatives.

Maureen and my mother hadn't been this close in proximity for fifteen years—the night Mom stormed over to Maureen's apartment and, by all reports, told her she could have the cheating bastard, he wasn't worth keeping anyway.

I was overwhelmed with a wash of sadness. Not for me this time. For my mother, whose worst fears had come alive: Hard as she tried to hold on, she'd lost her husband to another woman. And she'd stood sentinel ever since, waiting for her children to follow him out the door. Sharing this day with Maureen would challenge every molecule of politeness and good grace in her body. And she was no student of Emily Post.

Maureen would be struggling, too—especially with my father so focused on me. I understood her better after we'd spent the week together last fall in Pinehurst. She knew men could be stolen—hell, she'd stolen one herself. At any point, he could be discovered and pilfered by the next woman in line. And the first two children in her husband's life would always sap more of Dad's attention than she liked. She managed her anxiety by squawking fearfully if her husband or her own sons stepped outside the protective circle she'd drawn.

I hugged and kissed my way down the family gauntlet, suddenly feeling freer than I had in years. These were their problems, not mine.

I slapped my thigh. *Come on, Cassie, you can play better golf than what you've been showing.* I grabbed the driver from my father and strode the last yards toward the tee box.

Feeling mighty fine.

So Won Lee had a bright orange shirt on today, replacing yesterday's lime green. She'd also replaced her father with her mother on the bag. Was this equal opportunity caddying or had the father made a fatal miscalculation? Mrs. Lee was even smaller than her daughter. She had covered herself against the sun from head to toe including a wide straw hat and two large blue leather golf gloves.

Lindsay Hanson, decked out in a short flowered skirt and a delirious expression, floated through the crowd last, accepting congratulations for yesterday's round. In my opinion, her father should have reined her in: It was too close to tee time to be fooling with fans. But what did I know? Everybody handles pressure differently, Joe liked to tell me.

"But you can only play one shot at a time," I imagined him saying. I turned, searched the crowd until I found his face, and flashed him a thumbs-up.

The marshal introduced us in the same order as yesterday. But this time I had nothing to lose. Either I played lights out and made the cut, or tensed up and took a fast train home. Lindsay had a different story. You could tell she was thinking too hard about holding her lead. She was practically in tears after double bogeying the first hole; even with a par on my card, I was starting to feel bad by proxy.

"How's it going with your mother?" asked my father as we walked down the second fairway. An odd question now, but I supposed he'd do anything to keep my mind off the score.

"Not bad," I said. "She's the least of my worries, really. How about you two?" We never had talked about my mother in any depth. Unless you wanted to count the screaming matches we'd held when I was a teenager after he left home.

"She's ignoring me," he said. "And that big lunk of a husband is hanging around glowering like he'd take my head off given the slightest opportunity."

I laughed. "That's just Dave. He always looks like that."

"I never did figure out what she saw in him."

"Let's not go there," I said stiffly. "You gave up the right to criticize her choices when you walked out the door."

"Sorry, sorry," he said, both hands up in surrender. "Just trying to get your mind on something other than golf."

"You succeeded." I took the putter and wedge he handed me, lined up my chip shot, and knocked it in for birdie. The fans cheered.

"Now you're talking!" Dad yelled.

The birdie put me into a different mental world—a space where great golf felt possible and even easy. Lindsay, on the other hand, moped through most of the round, hitting massive drives and then struggling with her second shots and putting. The gallery that had swelled to see the unheralded amateur who led the tournament yesterday had to be disappointed. So Won Lee was quiet and tense, and her golf uninspired. We reached the sixteenth hole with only me under par.

Donald Ross had designed this hole as a par five, but the USGA had seen fit to change that to four. Girls with big tee shots—Lindsay in our group—had a decent chance of getting on the green in two. The rest of us laid up and prayed for an up-and-down par.

"I'm at a big disadvantage here," I complained to Dad.

"You've got to play your own game, Cassie," he said. "It's sure working well so far."

So Won and I placed our second shots in front of the creek. As predicted, Lindsay's second hit the green, but high above the pin with a slippery downhill putt. Technically a birdie chance, but in reality, she'd run happily to the next hole with a par.

I chipped close and made another four-foot putt for par. The gallery cheered. They'd come to see the amateur sparkle, but they were willing to get behind me, too. Lindsay and So Won Lee two- and three-putted for bogies. We stumped to the par-three seventeenth hole.

"You were a little short here yesterday," said Dad. "Let's take an extra club."

"What about the marsh on the right—"

"Don't even think about it. Your ball's going in the middle of the green, right?"

"Right." I visualized a perfect arc, a soft landing, and a lucky roll to within inches of the flagstick. I swung hard and looked up in time to see the ball hit the green and shoot forward, just as I'd imagined. This was starting to feel like fun.

Another par on the scorecard, and we made our way around the final bleachers to the eighteenth tee. A beast of an ending hole: Just when you were running out of gas and dying to coast in, you faced an uphill fairway, into the wind, bisected by the creek that had dogged you all the way around.

My brother Zachary's voice hollered from the crowd. "Cassie, you da man!"

I cracked out a final drive and breathed a sigh of relief—almost home.

When the ball clattered into the hole, I scooped it up and threw it into the gallery. My father squeezed me into a bear hug, and I shook hands with the other players, dialing my grin down a few notches to mirror Lindsay's crestfallen face. In the scoring trailer, I checked my card three times, signed it, and turned it in. Alice Maxwell waited for me outside.

"Press would like to talk to you."

"To me?" I looked around for a likelier candidate.

She smiled. "One under par. That's news at the US Open."

Lindsay slunk by toward the clubhouse as my questions began.

"Good round, Cassie. You were pretty consistent. How did the course play out there today?"

"Fabulous, really. The greens are softening up real nice for us after the rain yesterday."

"Does this round affect your thinking about the Buick Championship?"

I squinted to read the name on this reporter's media pass. "I'm sure you've heard the same advice I have, Kiel," I said with a smile. "One shot at a time."

Chapter 19

I finished the interview and headed to the clubhouse, blinking in the bright sun. What was that odd croaking noise? I giggled, feeling slightly giddy. It was me— humming "Oh what a beautiful morning"—a sign of rare and welcome optimism even if I did have the time of day wrong. Unless my luck ran terribly thin, I, Cassie Burdette, would be playing in the US Women's Open this weekend. Never mind a healthy lunch—for that, I deserved a grilled sausage. Patting my pocket for my wallet, I remembered that I'd stuffed it into the Birdie Girl bag this morning. I hadn't wanted to risk being even one ounce off balance during my swing.

I walked quickly up past the clubhouse and around the putting green toward the caddie shack. A crowd jammed the periphery of the entire first hole, watching the tee shots of Annika Sorenstam, Christie Kerr, and a player I didn't know who looked stunned by the attention. Annika waved to the people, the sleeve of her black shirt retracting to reveal an impressive muscle that my guy friends would have salivated over—for themselves. She's a superstar now, and she draws masses of fans, especially since her groundbreaking performance in a PGA tournament a couple summers ago. She would never have skipped part of her workout routine before her morning round, no matter what kind of flimsy excuse she dreamed up. Nor would she gobble down a greasy sausage sandwich when she finished.

What fun was that?

The gallery roared as she completed her backswing. I grinned. At this moment, I wouldn't trade my round in the clubhouse for anything, even a day in Annika's skin.

"Excuse me," I said to the caddie master, "I believe I left my wallet in my golf bag. Burdette?"

"I'll need to see some ID."

I showed him my LPGA badge and tried not to sound snotty: "My license is in my wallet. My wallet is in my bag."

He scowled, stomped off to the rear of the trailer, and returned with the bag.

"Thanks. Sorry to bother you."

I rustled through the zippered compartments and found the wallet, which was nestled behind a white plastic sack printed with the red-and-green Stop and Shop supermarket logo. My name had been scrawled across it in black marker.

"What's this?" I held the white sack up.

The caddie master shrugged and turned away. "I have no idea. I'm not a bellhop."

"Sorry." Either he was pathologically grumpy, annoyed that I'd rejected his pathetic caddie candidates in favor of my family, or just exhausted by the tournament. He had a lot of responsibility after all—storing the expensive equipment of a big field of golf divas whose nerves were already jangled by the Open and who were poised to flip out if he misplaced so much as a lucky ball marker. I smiled, trying to move into the percentage of players who weren't giving him extra work or a hard time.

"Thanks again," I added. My father must have tucked snacks in my bag. I reached into the sack and pulled out a snow globe.

This was no ordinary winter scene. A picture of a lady golfer on a golf green, her putter in hand, had been inserted into the waterproof capsule inside the liquid. Palm trees stood sentinel beside her. It reminded me of the table decorations my friend Jeanine had used for one of her wedding events last fall. Except the woman's head rolled on the green next to her silver and turquoise golf ball. Red splotches had been painted on her neck. And the golfer was me. My hand's involuntary jerk dislodged hundreds of tiny red glittering flakes that drifted through the clear liquid contained in the globe.

I barely stifled a scream.

Twenty paces up the hill, I spotted Greg's blocky figure as he chatted with one of the policemen stationed near the practice green. What the hell—wasn't he supposed to be watching me? A flush of warmth spread from my chest to neck to cheeks. I steamed through the crowd and grasped Greg's arm, registering the heft of his forearm and the heat of my skin meeting his.

"Can we go somewhere and talk? Right now?"

Charlie's head bobbed up beside Greg. "What's the matter?"

"Let's go." Greg pushed Charlie ahead of me, their two bodies cutting a wedge through the fans so that I could slip safely behind. We showed our badges to the guard at the front door of the clubhouse.

Rosie Jones was on her way out. "Nice round today, Cassie," she said.

"Thanks." Any other day I would have thrilled to have a golfer like that notice. But now I was just focused on reaching the end of the striped hallway and plunging into Sarah Washington's office.

"What the hell is going on?" Charlie's voice broke the silence, sharp with concern.

I took a shuddering breath and set the white plastic sack on Sarah's desk. "Someone left this in my golf bag. I don't have any idea who," I said, cutting off what I figured would be Greg's first question.

I dumped the globe out of the bag onto the calendar blotter covering the desktop. Red particles sifted down onto the photograph.

"Good God almighty! What the hell is that?" Charlie asked, moving closer. "Is that supposed to be you?"

"Don't touch it," said Greg.

"I know, I know." Charlie raised his hands and backed away two steps. "What the hell is it?" he said again.

I shook my head. "Honestly, I have no clue."

"Tell me again where you got it." Greg gestured for Charlie and me to sit.

I collapsed into one of Sarah's side chairs and described my visit to the caddie shack: how I'd forgotten my wallet, the grouchy caddie master's warning, the urge for a sausage sandwich, Annika's gallery—every meaningless detail I could retrieve.

Greg leaned back in his chair and watched me.

"It's got to be some kind of a practical joke," I said finally. "A sick one, I'll grant you that."

Greg slammed his fist on the desktop, startling both Charlie and me. Tears filled my eyes.

"This is bullshit," he said. "This is about your life. If you don't tell me everything, you're wasting my time." He looked at Charlie. "And his money." Then trained his brown eyes back on me. "And quite possibly risking your life."

I was suddenly filled with a hot rage. "What would possibly be the point of hiring you and then holding back?"

He waited, tenting his fingers. They were slender and strong, with smooth nails trimmed precisely to the edges of his fingertips.

"Let's start again," he said. "Anything like this ever happen to you before?"

Charlie cleared his throat. "Tell him about Gary."

"It wasn't like this," I protested, balling my hands into fists.

Greg stretched his arms out, palms open. "Tell me."

"Besides, Gary's in jail. Murdered his own sister and had it in for me next."

"It was like you said," Charlie added, nodding at Greg. "He had a thing for her in high school."

"The most common form of stalking involves men stalking formerly sexually intimate partners," said Greg.

"We weren't intimate," I moaned. "We never even went on one date. Can't you believe me? The guy was wacko and now he's in jail. Unless they sprang him for parole twenty years early."

"Thirty-eight percent of stalkers are former boyfriends or husbands," said Greg.

"What about those tennis stars?" I was almost shouting now. "Serena Williams, Monica Seles, Steffie Graf—they didn't have any connection with their stalkers. You're blaming the victim. With Gary and me, just like those women, any *relationship*"—I made quotation marks in the air with my fingers—"was strictly in that guy's head."

I crossed my arms over my chest and pushed my chair back six inches. Big freaking mistake to hire this little Napoleon, who thought he could make up for his short stature by bullying his female clients.

Greg's voice broke through my angry thoughts, softer now and sounding kind. "As I said earlier, the majority of women killed by stalkers had been in intimate relationships with their perpetrators. A woman is most vulnerable in the period just after she breaks up with her husband or boyfriend."

He was a persistent bastard, too. Then I really heard what he'd said: women *killed* by stalkers.

"So the asshole decides he'd rather kill her than live without her?" Charlie asked.

"But no one's tried to kill me," I argued. My hands felt slippery with sweat. Saliva gathered in my mouth and my stomach churned.

"Not directly," said Greg, pushing his sunglasses through his hair to the top of his head. The white streak bisected one arm of the glasses exactly. "Let's go back to the names you mentioned earlier." He pulled his Palm Pilot out of his pocket, switched it on, and read the list we'd made yesterday: Mom, Dave, Dad, Charlie, Joe, Mike, Michelle, Maureen, Lloyd, and my half brothers, David and Zack.

"You can cross the family off that list right now," I said loudly. "It's just not possible." I took a deep breath, pushing the hint of bile back down my throat.

Greg sighed. "Let's try this. Who's the person you'd be least likely to suspect?"

"Get real," I said. "You can't talk me into being afraid of my own friends."

Greg's expression softened. "I know it's hard to think this way, but try for me—who's the least likely?"

"Charlie," I snapped.

Charlie's face broke into a lopsided grin. "Right. I'm paying this clown a thousand a day to figure out who's sending *my* e-mails. And then I held arts and crafts hour in my hotel last night and came up with this." He waved at the snow globe.

"Come on, Cassie," Greg said, not even cracking a smile. "Who else?"

I met Charlie's eyes and shrugged. "Joe, I guess. Joe's crazy about me."

"And?"

"Mike. Mike would never hurt me. He's so excited that I'm finally playing well."

Stalking formerly sexually intimate partners. I couldn't get the phrase out of my mind. Couldn't be Mike. I knew Mike. If he felt any lingering resentment, it was locked away in some part of his heart or brain so distant, no one would ever discover it. He certainly wouldn't act on it. He was reserved, polite, and kind to women. His mother had taught him well. Laura might argue that last point, but he was not a stalking kind of a guy. He was not the kind of guy who'd doctor up a snow globe to scare the pants off me.

"Tell me what you're thinking." Greg rolled the computer

chair from behind the desk and up beside mine. He patted my thigh. I looked down at the spot his hand had touched.

"Mike and I broke up last fall. He's here with his girl-friend, Michelle. We had dinner with them the other night. They seem head over heels. Wouldn't you say?" I asked Charlie. "As much as Mike Callahan can show anything. Let me put it this way, he did hold her hand in public."

Charlie shrugged. "Who really knows with Mike? Why is he here anyway?"

"He's excited for me to play in the Open," I said, scowling.

"Do you have a boyfriend now?" Greg asked.

I flinched. "Not really. I started to go out with Joe, but we've put it on hold for the time being." I shifted in my chair, aware that I'd blushed right up over my scalp. I wouldn't be surprised if the back of my neck was red.

"And who exactly is Joe?"

"He's a psychologist," I said, tapping my forehead, "specializing in the mental golf game. He's a sweetheart. He adores me. He would never do anything to hurt me." Pretty much the same thing I'd said about Mike and it was sounding lame, even to my ears. Greg would think I thought that every guy I knew was in love with me.

"And you've been dating Joe?" Greg asked evenly.

"We went to Hawaii together with another couple. Our good friends Jeanine and Rick were getting married. You've probably heard of Rick Justice—he does real well on the PGA tour."

"Hawaii? That's some first date," said Greg. "Hard for the rest of us guys to compete with something like that." He and Charlie laughed.

"Ha, ha." This felt entirely wrong, even talking about

Joe with a man I'd barely known for twenty-four hours. No way the messages and the snow globe could have come from Joe. He wanted me to succeed at the tournament, not get so screwed up and frightened that I couldn't play.

"Okay, so we don't think it's Joe," said Greg. He glanced down at his list. "What about Lloyd?"

"Oh Jesus, Lloyd again." I sighed. "We certainly don't have a relationship, except in financial terms."

"Do you think he wants one?"

"Honestly, no. And if I flip out and my game collapses, he gets nothing."

"Who else do you have a connection with here at the tournament?"

"I know a lot of the girls, of course, the golfers. And some of their caddies. I see them all the time at the other tournaments on the circuit. Nobody's acted funny, nobody's mad at me, nobody's lost their marbles—as far as I can tell."

"How about that girl who got kicked out of Q-school when you were there?" asked Charlie.

"So Won Lee," I said impatiently. "She was in my group the last two days. You watched her play, for God's sake. She doesn't care for me, but believe me, she's been way too focused on her own golf to be designing snow globes."

"What do you really know about Lloyd?" Charlie asked.

I sighed. My brother was trying to be helpful, I knew that. But I wanted to wring his neck all the same. "God knows he's a pain in the ass, but a stalker? I can't picture it. He's invested in me. Financially, I mean," I added quickly. "When he offered to sponsor me, I looked him up on the Internet. He had a real job at a real law firm—nothing looked suspicious. He's certainly never made a pass at me."

Both men stared.

The questions I'd considered briefly yesterday reared up again. Had Lloyd made a pass at me and I was too pre-occupied to notice? Or was he so clumsy that his moves were unrecognizable?

"You looked him up on the Internet?" Charlie asked. "Did you get references?"

I was very close to tears. Greg patted me again.

"We need to report this incident to the cops."

"Can't we—"

"Sorry, but they need to know. For the sake of the other players, too, not just you."

He called Sarah Washington on his walkie-talkie and asked her to bring the cops to her office.

I dropped my chin to my throat and closed my eyes. "I can't believe this. This was one of the top-ten days of my life. Now it stinks just like the others." I took a deep breath. I had to shake off the whiney girl-baby routine to have any chance of playing decent golf this weekend.

Fifteen minutes later Sarah escorted the two detectives who had interviewed me on the range into the office. With Greg's prompting, I described the package and the messages that had preceded it. All three leaned in to study the snow globe.

"What's with the weird golf ball?" Greg asked suddenly.

I looked again. Damn. "It's my earring," I said slowly. "I noticed it missing yesterday."

"Who has access to your room?" asked Detective Zimmerman.

"Just my roommate, Julie Nothstine," I said. "But the other day we came back to the dorm and our door was cracked open." Dammit, dammit, dammit. I dropped my head into my hands and tried to massage away the press of frightened tears.

"Unfortunately, just about anyone could enter the dorm if they follow someone staying there. We'll have a talk with the college security department," said Sarah.

"Best thing we can do is recommend that you withdraw," said Detective Boyd.

"What?" For a moment all I could do was glare at them, rigid with anger. "How would that help?" I demanded. "Then he—whoever he is—follows me to the next stop and we start all over again. So I pull out there, too? Or shall I go home to my mother's and lock myself in the bathroom?"

The detective and Greg exchanged a look. "She's losing it" I was pretty sure was the translation.

"You can handle this all right?" Sarah asked Greg. "I have a press conference in five minutes. The media's going wild about Amber."

"Did you find out how her drink got poisoned?" I asked.

Sarah grimaced. "She must have brought it in with her. We don't have anything like that on the grounds. But we've replaced all the snacks and water bottles and locked them up at night just to be sure." She started out the door, then paused and looked at me and then back at the cops. "Can we keep this snow globe business under wraps?"

"For the time being, yes," said Detective Boyd. And to Greg: "You'll be watching Miss Burdette?"

"During the tournament hours," he said.

"I'll keep a close eye on her tonight," said Charlie. "She's moving over to share my motel room."

I glowered. I'd agreed to no such thing. But what was the alternative?

"We'll interview the caddie master," said Detective

Zimmerman. "Maybe he saw someone put this object in Miss Burdette's bag."

As we stepped out of the clubhouse into the humid afternoon air, Joe and Lloyd were waiting. Both faces lit up when they spotted me. I felt instantly guilty about suspecting either one of them of anything sinister, especially Joe. Lloyd rushed over, gripped my shoulders, then grabbed me into a hug.

"I made reservations at the Del Raye Bar and Grill in Northampton. Seven-thirty." He held up one finger, as I opened my mouth to turn him down. "You have to eat somewhere. Filet mignon's on me."

"Sounds nice, Lloyd, but I'm bushed."

"You have to come." He paused and grinned. "The Titleist rep is eating with us. They're interested in a possible sponsorship."

"That's fantastic," said Joe. "Wonderful! I came by to see if you wanted to grab a bite, but Lloyd's definitely got a better offer!"

Under ordinary circumstances, I would die for a chance to have dinner with someone from Titleist. Only all the best golfers in the world, male and female, are paid handsomely to use their golf balls and equipment. But tonight I just wanted to bury myself somewhere dark and safe, away from everyone's prying eyes and Greg's painful questions.

"Let's go," said Charlie, rubbing comforting circles on the knots of my back. "We do have to eat. And this sounds like a fantastic opportunity."

"We'll meet you up there," I told Lloyd.

"Good luck," said Joe, looking forlorn as we started down the hill to the shuttle.

"What if Lloyd's the one who left the stupid snow globe?" I muttered, for Charlie's ears only.

"We can both keep an eye on him, and at the same time delve into his background a little more thoroughly." He raised his eyebrows.

The way you should have before you got involved, was what he didn't say.

Chapter 20

Charlie waited for me in the car while I went into the dorm to retrieve my stuff. Julie was lying facedown on her bed, her breathing soft and rhythmic. I tiptoed across the room to my closet, scooped up an armload of dirty clothes, and fumbled to open my suitcase. It clattered loudly to the floor. Julie rolled over and rested her head on her outstretched arm—her face was lined with the imprint of rumpled sheets and she looked like she'd been crying.

"I'm sorry. I can be so damn clumsy."

"Don't worry, I wasn't sleeping. Just feeling a little blue. I'll get over it. Eventually."

"Lots more tournaments down the line. Next time, right?" I was the one who was supposed to have washed out of the Open, not Julie, with her intense connection to Mount Holyoke. I felt like a jerk. After all she'd done for me . . . this was worst side of competing against women you liked. You might be ecstatic about your big day, but someone else's high hopes had drained off into the sewer.

"I can't decide whether to stay around and watch this weekend. I'd kind of like to clear out, but Jason's going to try to get another bag and I'm his wheels." She ran her hands through her hair and stretched out the length of the bed, fingers and toes pointed ballerina-style.

"You should do what feels right to you." I'd be out of here so fast . . . "For God's sake, he's a big boy. He can surely get himself a ride home. Or take a Greyhound bus: Leave the driving to us."

She grinned, then seemed to notice that I was packing. "You're moving out?"

"Charlie wants to spend more time with me." Joe hadn't bought this thin cover story and Julie didn't appear to, either. She'd stuck close by me when I was at a low point, and now here I was, bailing the hell out on her. I swept the toiletries from the top of the battered bureau into my travel kit. My heart started pounding when I spotted the single turquoise golf ball earring. Who had broken into our room? Was it fair to leave Julie by herself?

"I feel bad deserting you," I said. "Do you have a friend you could stay with? What if someone breaks in here while you're alone?"

"Don't be silly," she said. "I probably won't stay anyway. If I get into trouble, I'll sing the college fight song and bring every alum in the building to the rescue." She grinned. "How did you like your accommodations?"

"I do have a confession," I said, smiling. "I don't know

how these Mount Holyoke students get any sleep. This could be the worst mattress I ever slept on."

"Sorry about that."

I'd hurt her feelings. "I'm not blaming you. It was a joke. I wouldn't sleep on a dial-a-dream mattress this weekend. Too much at stake."

There I went again. She no longer had a damn thing at stake. I had to get out before I ruined our new friendship completely.

"We're having dinner with a rep from Titleist tonight. Lloyd set it up," I said, sliding into the least-rumpled khakis in my wardrobe. I had to tug the zipper—they seemed to have gotten a little snug. "I'm pretty nervous."

She blinked. "Good for you! Boy, things are really looking up, Cassie. And you deserve it." Her eyes pooled with tears. I hurried across the room and hugged her.

"Thanks for all your help. I wouldn't be here except for you." I could feel my own eyes well up.

The *toot-toot* of Charlie's horn sounded in the courtyard.

"That's my brother. Gotta go." I grabbed my backpack and my suitcase. "See you in a week or two. Take care." I dropped my key on the desk by the door and started down the stairs without looking at her again.

I dumped my luggage in the trunk, slammed it shut, and slid into the front seat. "This is a brutal way to make a living," I told Charlie. "It's hell to be competing against your friends all the time."

"Julie had a rough day?"

I nodded. "Hey, maybe she's the girl of your dreams. She's cute, athletic, and sweet—"

"I don't need my kid sister setting me up, thank you very much."

I shook my hand. "Touchy."

I called Laura on the way to Northampton and filled her in on the latest—good round, potential sponsor dinner, creepy snow globe.

"That's sick," she said. "What did it look like?"

"They inserted a photograph of me inside, but the head was cut off and then pasted so it was lying on the putting green with a palm tree in the background. And one of my earrings had been made into a golf ball."

"Cassie, that's awful," Laura said.

"Tell her about the snow," said Charlie.

I described the red glitter floating in the globe's liquid.

"Good God! That's really scary. What do the cops think?"

"Greg, that's my bodyguard, he wonders if someone I know is stalking me."

"Oh my God, Cassie! What are you going to do about it? How can you concentrate with all this going on?"

"The cops are on the snow globe thing. And Greg's with me every minute on the course. And I'm staying with Charlie tonight." My voice trembled. "The truth is, I don't know how the hell I'm going to concentrate. I'm looking over my shoulder every minute and imagining the worst."

Silence on the other end of the line, then: "Have you thought about whether you should just come home?" Laura said. "Just get away and spend some time with your family?"

"What home?" I asked. "And everyone I know except you is here. And besides, I'm about to make the cut in the US Open."

"Good point."

"Tell her Greg seems suspicious of Mike," said Charlie loudly.

"He's suspicious of everybody," I snapped back. "Listen," I told Laura, "I can't have a reasonable conversation with this big lug butting in, so I'll give you a buzz later, okay? I'm going to be fine. Give my love to your dad."

I wouldn't have any privacy later either, I realized, sharing a room with Charlie. I could lock myself in the bathroom and turn on the shower for background noise. God help him if he snored.

The hostess at the Del Raye Bar and Grill led us to a round table, half-circled with an upholstered bench seat. Lloyd was already bending the ear of our man from Titleist. Aaron, the rep, was tall, dark, and impeccably polished—no rumpled khakis here. On the other hand, he probably had cut-rate access to top-line golf clothes. He waved me and Charlie onto the couch. Bad news, being small relative to the average American diner, the table would be a little too far away to reach comfortably—and my feet dangled above the floor. I could already picture the food stains down the front of my shirt.

"Shall we order a couple of bottles of red?" Aaron asked as soon as we'd been seated. "Or would you prefer white?"

From the tone of voice, he obviously wanted red. I never touched the stuff, but if it made the difference between an equipment sponsor or not, I'd drink Ipecac. Well, maybe not. But I could certainly pretend to enjoy a glass of vino. Even if it wasn't made with hops.

Aaron waved over the waitress. "While we're getting settled, could you bring us a couple of bottles of Frog's Leap Cabernet and some appetizers for the table?" He peered through half-glasses and ran his finger down the menu. "We'll have a dozen oysters on the half shell, an order of venison carpaccio, a couple of duck spring rolls, and the grilled squid." He smiled at me. "Something for everyone. Sound good?"

Not really—he had a lot to learn about the Burdette palate. We don't go for anything that has the texture of a car tire or that might not be dead when it arrives at the table.

"Fabulous," I said, trying to sound like a successful and worldly golfer. Annika probably loves squid.

I studied the menu quickly, hoping to head off any chance of Aaron ordering the main course for me. The chef had added one, two, or three ingredients too many in most of the dishes for my simple tastes. Braised short ribs looked safe enough. At least there should be no question about them getting served raw.

Wine was poured, a toast drunk to my performance at the Open, and then Lloyd and Aaron launched into a discussion of the technology behind the newest line of Titleist balls. I pulled my legs up to sit Indian-style on the bench and took a sip of the wine. Not bad, though it would never make the cut next to a cold stein of beer. I looked around the room, wondering if the pompous tone these men shared had something to do with the double letters in their first names. Maybe their mothers had expected them to grow up knowing everything and they were simply following through. I zoned back out and resumed casing the dining area.

Rose-colored walls and cherry-wood trim warmed the appearance of the restaurant. At the back of the room, I noticed So Won Lee sitting at a table with both her parents. From what I could see, they weren't talking at all. I wondered which of them was taking the fall for So Won's missed cut. She got up and headed to the rest room.

"Excuse me. I'm going to make a pit stop." Sheesh, what class. I grinned. "Don't finish all those oysters before I get back." Damn. Now I'd have to really try one.

I wandered off to the ladies' room. This making a good impression business was not that easy. I waited by the sinks until So Won Lee emerged from her stall.

"Hi!" I said brightly. "Fancy meeting you here."

"Hello," she said without the slightest trace of warmth or interest. She filled her palm with antibacterial soap and began to scrub with a surgeon's precision.

I leaned against the sink, not noticing the large pool of water on the counter. It began to seep rapidly into my pants. "Oh crap." I stepped back and brushed at the wet spot on my butt. "I enjoyed playing with you the last couple of days. Hope we get a chance to do it again. You have a super swing. And your mom's a doll."

So Won didn't say anything, didn't even look at me.

"I'm sorry you won't be playing this weekend."

She continued to wash.

"Julie Nothstine—I've been staying with her the last couple of days—she didn't make the cut, either," I babbled, "so I'm going to move into my brother Charlie's hotel room. I was thinking they might make a good pair."

She looked up from her hand washing. "Julie and your brother? She's gay."

Julie was gay? No way! How had I missed that? I missed it because she was infamous on the tour last year for her short-shorts and attractive girlish looks that brought comparisons to tennis star Anna Kornikova. And I was blinded by stereotypes. Not to mention that we'd officially met last fall when she asked my advice about dating Mike. Maybe So Won Lee was pulling my leg.

She dried her hands on a paper towel and turned to leave. "Good luck this weekend."

"Just one thing." I shifted three steps over to block her easy escape. "The cops were asking me questions at the range this morning about Amber's death. The tournament honchos think she brought the poisoned drink onto the grounds with her, but I'm not sure I'm buying it."

So Won Lee just stared.

"They must have approached you, too. I remember you played with them during the practice round before the tournament started. Did you notice anything unusual that day?"

"This isn't any of your business. Or mine." She started around me.

"Please. I know it looks like I'm just being nosy, but I have some reason to think the person who killed her might be after me, too." A gross exaggeration, but I needed her to talk.

So Won Lee looked skeptical. "I don't know anything about it. Amber was Amber. She hit the ball a ton and argued with her father all the way around."

"Argued about what?"

"It was none of my business, so I tried not to listen."

"But you heard something? So Won, please, I'm being *stalked*."

So Won blinked. "She wanted to fire the coach and her father wouldn't hear of it."

"She wanted to fire Beccia?" That was breaking news. So Won Lee nodded, curtly.

"So what were things like between her and Beccia?" Silence. "Please, So Won," I begged. "Anything you can remember might help."

"She barely spoke to him the entire round."

"They were mad at each other?"

She took a step toward the door, combing her bangs with her fingers. "Amber wouldn't give him the time of day."

"Anything else? Anything at all?"

She licked her finger and smoothed her eyebrows, already perfectly orderly. "He made a few minor suggestions, but she paid no attention to him. Her father was angry with her—that was easy to see. Then Beccia started complaining that his stomach was upset on the ninth hole. So they left."

"His stomach was upset, not hers?"

So Won Lee nodded.

"What kinds of suggestions did he make?"

"Nutrition, hydration, all the usual. And he had *The Rules of Golf* with him and he kept quizzing her about obscure situations. Smart, really. You can cost yourself shots if you don't know how to take advantage when the rules could turn things your way."

My heart beat a little faster. *The Rules of Golf* again.

"Were there any incidents with fans?"

She shook her head. "Lots of kids wanted her autograph and all, but there weren't any problems that I noticed."

"Doesn't sound like the day was a lot of fun," I offered.

"Fun?" she said, her expression snapping back to its customary sour cast. "I'm not out here to have fun. I've got to get back to my parents."

I stepped aside and the heavy door of the ladies' room whooshed shut behind her.

Back at our table, the conversation had shifted to baseball.

"If the Yankees can't win a series with that whopping payroll . . ." said Charlie.

"You have to land a great pitcher," said Lloyd, winking at me.

I wondered if they'd discussed my professional prospects while I was out of sight. At Aaron's insistence, I choked down the one oyster remaining on the plate. Then I gobbled half a spring roll to clear out the slime.

"Those players aren't hungry anymore, that's part of the problem," said Charlie.

Was he implying I'd play better if I could only afford baloney? Not the best tack to take in front of my potential sponsor. I took a sip of wine and leaned back into the bench.

What had I learned from So Won Lee? That Amber was an annoying teenager—I already knew that. And that she was having a problem with her coach—at least on that particular day. And that maybe she'd had enough of the guy. But no big blowouts or screaming matches—certainly nothing in So Won's report highlighted anyone who hated Amber enough to poison her.

Which was a dumb theory anyway. In truth, I didn't really know what I hoped to find. Some connection between her problems and mine. Some incident that might suggest that with Amber dead, the sick bastard who was bothering me might be satisfied to move on. So far, Beccia's fondness for *The Rules of Golf* was the only slender thread. And it seemed foolish to pin too much on that coincidence. After all, most of the players in the field carried a copy of the same booklet in their bag.

My short ribs arrived, swimming in a sauce that featured strange-shaped mushrooms. "Delicious," I said to Lloyd after scraping off the topping. "Thanks for setting this up." I smiled at Aaron. "Thanks so much for the invitation tonight. I'd be thrilled to be associated with your organization." Why not put my money on the table?

Lloyd frowned. Apparently I'd jumped the gun.

"Great. Let's see how the weekend goes. We're quite impressed with your round today, young lady."

Ugh.

"Tell us how you got interested in the LPGA. Are you a golfer yourself?" Charlie asked Lloyd. "Where did you meet Cassie?"

"Hacker," said Lloyd. "That's why I love watching someone who knows what she's doing." He winked at me. "I saw your sister play at the ShopRite Classic, and I said, there's a girl with a lot of potential. A couple of rough edges, but nothing the right backing can't file down." He patted my hand. "We've done some good work already, haven't we?"

"Mmrph," I answered. My mouth was full and I had no polite response to that comment anyway.

"So you got in touch with the LPGA office?" Charlie prodded.

"Correct," said Lloyd. "I wanted to do this the right way, not have her thinking I was some creep." He winked again. Did he have something wrong with his eyes? "Strictly business between us. Though I do have suggestions about aspects of her preparation and play that might make a difference for both of us." He cleared his throat. "Short ribs, for example, are not what I would have chosen for you. There's a lot of fat in them there bones. . . ." He chuckled, as did representative Aaron.

"She's a Burdette," said Charlie. "Some battles just aren't worth fighting, and food is where we draw the line. Right, Sis?"

I nodded, thinking that the chocolate fudge cake with chocolate sauce might not be worth the comments. On the other hand, I felt out of control right now. And chocolate cake could only help with that.

Chapter 21

The Burdettes had ensconced themselves in the Best Western in Northampton. Charlie reported that the motel was plain, clean, and included a free buffet continental breakfast, a feature my mother particularly enjoyed. She was not so happy with the views—a bowling alley on one side and a strip mall on the other.

"I told her she could get nature and atmosphere at the tournament," my brother said, heading into the bathroom with his towel.

I stretched out on one of the beds. The coverlet was a slippery synthetic in an abstract print, and the walls, bare. Still, the mattress lacked obvious lumps and wires. And I felt safe.

By the time I'd taken my turn getting ready for bed,

Charlie had launched into bone-rattling snores. How would I ever sleep? The events of the last two days loped through my mind like hungry wolves. Without Laura's sensible input, I was wandering in a wilderness of confusing suspicions and theories. I got up, dressed in sweats, and went down to the lobby. Sinking into one of the couches next to the breakfast area, I punched in Laura's number. She wouldn't care what time it was.

"It's crazy here," I told her when she answered. "I really miss you."

"Tell me everything," she said, sounding sleepy. "Dad's starting to feel human again, but you—I'm just worried sick."

So I started from this evening's dinner and worked back. "First off, So Won Lee told me Julie's a lesbian. Which I'm finding hard to believe—in fact, I don't really trust anything So Won Lee says. That girl still doesn't like me. Remember how hot Julie was for Mike?"

"Yeah," Laura answered slowly. "But she's been very attentive to you over the past couple of months. I wonder if she was using Mike to get close to you?"

"Oh great, this is what I called you for. More kooky theories." I didn't care what Julie's sexual persuasion was, but I had zero interest in getting more involved with her. And I didn't like being surprised. Apparently my intuition could use a little fine-tuning.

Next I described the evening out with Mr. Titleist. "If having his company as a sponsor means eating raw oysters on a regular basis, I'm not sure it's for me."

She laughed. "He was probably showing off for the potential clients. Did you make a good impression?"

"It all depends on how I play the weekend. We're not a

perfect match in terms of wardrobe or tastebuds, that's for sure." I sighed. "And get this—I asked So Won Lee about her practice round with Amber Clancy and Lucien Beccia. She said he quizzed Amber about *The Rules of Golf* all the way around. Amber ignored him, of course. And Amber tried to convince her father to fire the guy, but he wouldn't go along with it."

This sounded silly to me now. A clue to nothing other than the inner workings of a top-level golf coach and a pouting teen. What was I thinking? That Beccia had poisoned his pupil rather than lose her? Made no sense at all.

"Tell me more about the bodyguard. What does he think's going on with the snow globe? I'm worried about you," Laura repeated.

I was worried about me, too. I described Greg's theory about stalkers most often coming out of formerly intimate relationships. "Charlic almost makes it sound like he thinks it could be Mike. But that's crazy, in my opinion."

"Insane," she agreed. "What about Michelle?"

"We've hardly spoken since they got here. She doesn't seem at all interested in me."

"What does Joe think?" she asked.

I clicked my tongue against the roof of my mouth. "I haven't said anything to him."

"You haven't told him? But this is his strong point, figuring out crazy people."

I was quiet for a minute. "Greg's got him on the suspect list."

"Come on! Joe?"

"I know, I know, it's nuts." An uncomfortable spurt of suspicion pushed its way back into my mind. "But what if he was truly angry? He thought we were going to get together in Hawaii and I blew him off." Laura was one of the few I'd told about that night in Maui. And even she didn't know all the excruciating details.

"But, Cassie—*Joe?*"

"I know." Several seconds of dead air ticked by.

"Anyone else?"

"Lloyd, of course, but we had dinner with him tonight. Charlie and I were both watching for signs of something creepy and we saw nothing. He's intensely interested in the money aspect of my career, and I think he'd enjoy basking in the reflected glory of my fame"—I laughed—"but I don't feel anything personal."

"What about the content of the e-mail messages? Any clues there?"

"I hadn't really thought of looking at it that way." A tear started down my cheek. I dashed it away. "I miss you and Joe. Between the three of us, we could tackle anything. How the hell am I going to play golf tomorrow with all this going on?"

"We have to take charge, Cassie," Laura said briskly. "Let me think a minute."

I waited.

"Here's a plan. First, I'll look over the rules that were in those e-mails. Maybe I can pick out a pattern in the messages. Meanwhile, you call up each of the guys on your list, just to chat. Then maybe you get an idea of who sounds uncomfortable or weird. At least you're not just sitting on your hands waiting for his next move—whoever he is."

Reluctantly I hung up with Laura. She was right—I couldn't just hang out waiting for another message. I hated the way this made me feel—anxious, helpless, and distracted. I punched in Mike's cell phone number.

"Hey, buddy, I can't sleep. Can you talk? Figured you might have some advice on playing the weekend in my first US Open."

"Sure. Michelle's in the tub—that could take hours." Mike laughed. "As for my first Open, you were right there when I played Bethpage, remember? I was a wreck. You kept telling me I could only control what was right in front of me and I should focus on one shot at a time. Good advice then and still is now."

We chatted a few more minutes, about the golf course, my family, and the rounds of some of the other players. He sounded completely normal. Well, as normal as Mike gets.

"I guess this is as good a time as any to tell you," he said. Then he paused. "Michelle and I are getting married. We got engaged last weekend."

As good a time as any? He had to be kidding. He and I had struggled for years to make things work between us, then six months after calling it quits, he's ready to marry someone else? In the middle of my debut US Open? Jesus. It wasn't the first time this had happened to me, either. When I had the time and energy to really think this news bomb over, I'd look forward to developing a full-scale relationship complex. Laura's plan wasn't going too well, so far.

"Congratulations," I said finally. "Just please don't ask me to be in the wedding party. Jeanine's shindig did me in."

"Done." Mike sounded relieved. "I was a little afraid you'd take it badly."

Part of me did feel like pitching a full-size hysterical fit. But I knew it was based on pride—not a true burning urge to be with Mike.

"Are you really happy with her?" I asked. "She was"— how did I put this delicately without insulting them both—"a

little bit high maintenance when you were going out before."
A raving lunatic was closer to the truth.

Mike chuckled. "Oddly enough, it's really good between us now. Even my father likes her."

Another blow. George Callahan had never warmed up
to me, try as I might to grovel pleasantly every time I was
in his presence. He wasn't a fantastic golfer himself, but
that didn't stop him from having strong opinions about
Mike's career. One of the strongest was that a man should
not hire a girl to caddie—and if he made that mistake, he
should certainly not take her advice while playing a round.
Not in public anyway, where everyone in the world would
witness his weakness.

"That's great," I said. "Happily ever after, et cetera, et
cetera."

"Try to have fun tomorrow," said Mike. "God knows
that was never my strong point."

The only good news about calling Mike was that I could
now cross him and Michelle off my list of suspects. No one
that recently engaged would be lurking around an old girlfriend trying to scare the bejesus out of her. Besides, for
Mike, he sounded deliriously happy.

I felt inexplicably sad—certainly in no mood to call
Joe. What kind of breaking news would he spring on me—
married to Dr. Rebecca Butterman this afternoon by an
Elvis impersonator? I wasn't willing to risk it.

In the old days I would have gone directly to the hotel
bar and ordered a beer, possibly accompanied by a shot of
something stronger to ease down the news. That option still
sounded pretty damn good. Except this hotel didn't have a
bar. And I was on this annoying maturity kick.

The elevator doors slid open and my mother stepped

out, blinking like Mr. Magoo in the lobby's fluorescent lighting. She had belted her faded tartan plaid flannel robe over an aqua sweat suit. Three curlers stuck out above her forehead, wound tightly with gray hair. I sank a little lower into the couch. What was she doing down here? And more important, was she drunk?

She shuffled across the room through the maze of breakfast tables and rummaged on the counter, coming up with a teabag. Then she glanced over and noticed me. Her face brightened. I felt instantly bad that my first impulse had been to hide.

"Cassie!"

"Hi, Mom."

"Would you like a cup of tea?"

I nodded. "Okay."

"I couldn't sleep," she said. She poured hot water from a glass carafe into two foam cups and then added packets of sugar. "It feels so strange to be here. You know how long it's been since we spent a night away from home?"

I tried to remember her and Dave taking a vacation. Maybe never.

She carried the tea over and sat next to me on the couch. "You look so sad," she said, touching my cheek. "Aren't you happy, baby? Isn't this what you've always wanted?"

I nodded, my voice choked with tears. There were a million things wrong, but last in, first out. "It's Mike," I blurted. "He's getting married."

She leaned back into the plaid cushions. "Man trouble. Can't live with 'em . . ."

"It's not that I want him," I added quickly.

"I know. I felt just like that when your father left. You and me, we have the same problems."

Wait a damn a minute. I was sitting here calmly having a reasonable discussion with my voice barely raised just after hearing Mike's news. Whereas she'd been a total basket case for years after Dad left. She still couldn't say his given name out loud without tacking "that no-good-cheating-cheap-bastard" onto the end.

I counted to ten, watching goldfish the size of small flounders blunder through a murky tank. This week, life felt a little like that for me, too.

"You get used to a man in a certain way," my mother went on. "He may be a royal pain, but he's woven into your life for better or worse. Then he says he doesn't want to be there anymore and he rips out all the threads. It hurts, that's all, whether you really want the no-good-cheating-cheap-bastard or not."

I laughed out loud and gave her a hug. "I'll be okay, Mom. Once you got past the golf, Mike and I weren't a very good match anyway."

She tucked a strand of hair into one of the curlers. "I'll say."

Chapter 22

I escorted Mom to her room and walked down the hall to mine. Charlie rolled over and mumbled something about getting the deposition ready. He pulled the comforter up over his ears and lapsed back into snores. I couldn't face lying in bed in the dark, eyes wide open, waiting for sleep that wouldn't come.

I switched on the TV, muted the sound, and surfed to the Golf Channel. They were running a short segment I'd seen once before—Lucien Beccia demonstrating his patented twelve positions of the golf swing, using who else but Amber Clancy as his model. I couldn't hear the words, just watched him manipulate her into perfect positions with just a touch. Her swing had been textbook gorgeous. She was young, flexible, and buff. She'd dressed—for her—conservatively for this shoot, and if pressed, I couldn't have said there was anything sexy about the sequence. His body language was proprietary, but definitely not sexual. Had there been more between them than just business? The frames flashed by silently.

So I powered up my iBook. If I could understand why Amber Clancy died, maybe I'd find clues to my own problems. By noon tomorrow I needed to have enough of a grip on my nerves to stay in the present and give myself a shot at enjoying what should be the highlight of my career to date, if not my life.

I clicked onto the message board featuring Amber that I'd seen earlier in the week. Now the posts were filled with sappy eulogies, bad poems, and memories of fans who'd experienced "special moments" with their girl golfer. Mostly, Amber had signed a hat or poster. In one case, the fan had gone into a bathroom stall recently vacated by Amber. Someone needed a little more excitement in her own life.

Farther down, I read a post titled "USGA conspiracy." The author insisted that the authorities were covering up the fact that Amber had been murdered. A respondee with EMT training talked about the symptoms described in newspaper articles about Amber's death.

"This sounds like strychnine poisoning."

This pronouncement was followed by a string of hysterical reactions.

Where the hell was Lucien Beccia after all this? So Won Lee said he'd had an upset stomach during the practice round. I'd seen him on the range when Amber was first taken ill, looking terribly concerned. And then he'd dropped clean off the map.

I thought back to Amber's new calendar. Why the hell

would a young girl poised at the top of her game pose nude? Why was she willing to open herself up literally and figuratively to the lust, disgust, rage, and envy of total strangers? There was one simple answer: She truly believed what she'd said on the Web site about how proud she was of her body and how women's golf needed a sexier image. And she was looking forward to the cash windfall the calendar might produce. But would her parents have endorsed this?

There was another possibility—one that seemed more believable to me—someone had the goods on her and had coerced her into the public display of nudity. A likely candidate? Lucien Beccia, who'd disappeared like a snake into a stone wall just after his star pupil died.

I typed "Lucien Beccia golf academy conflicts" into the Google toolbar. Only a few listings came up—parents had been interviewed for an article about Beccia's policy of encouraging his young and phenomenal protégées to skip the college thing and go directly to qualifying school.

"The professional golf tour is too much pressure," said the mother of one player. "She's exposed to things she shouldn't have to face yet—drugs, sex, lesbians." (Did she think these didn't exist on a college campus?)

"Martha only wants to play golf," said another girl's father, when asked about a player's reported six-figure sponsorship deal directly from high school. (Six figures? Good God. Where were these people when I needed them?) "She will always be able to continue her education, but in terms of the opportunity and the ability to compete professionally, we feel that her time is now."

I skimmed through several other articles, finally landing on one describing a lawsuit against Beccia and his academy. This student, Jim Polonski of Salinas, California, had been dismissed for an alleged "lack of commitment to the program." Polonski was suing for breach of contract.

"Beccia has his favorites—the ones he feels will bring in the most money with the least effort and the rest of us can go to hell," the disgruntled golfer was quoted as saying. "This guy picks off the top prospects as young as he can get them and passes them off like hot potatoes to his underlings if they don't develop quickly enough."

To me this had the ring of sour grapes. Yes, Beccia wanted stars and the chance for big bucks when one of his pupils hit the big time. But wouldn't he also want a steady stream of wannabe's populating his clinics and filling his bank account?

I closeted myself in the bathroom, found Jim Polonski's California phone number in the Yahoo Internet directory, and dialed. I was going to figure this out before it killed me.

"This is Cassandra Leiner from *The New Haven Register*." He'd never track me down using my stepfather's last name. "We're doing a follow-up story on Amber Clancy's death and her relationship with Lucien Beccia. I noticed online that you had also been one of her coach's students."

"Is this one of those sappy 'he's a great guy and he did so much for her' deals?" he asked. "Because frankly, I've got nothing positive to add."

"I'm an investigative reporter," I said. It was so easy to fib.

"Off the record?"

There was no record. "Sure."

"He's not interested in taking on students that need work. He only stays with the hottest talents—golfers who bring attention to his academy without much investment on his part. Have you seen his Web site?"

"Yes."

"He finds the stars and then he uses them. What better advertising than to be able to say Lucien Beccia made the next wunderkind of the LPGA or the PGA tour?" He lowered his voice so I could barely hear. "You push a little on those kids, you're going to hear other stories, too. Mental abuse at the least. There's a lot more than meets the public eye. And no one calls him on it because he has all the power. He's the great white hope for players dying to make it onto the professional golf circuit. Do you have any idea how difficult it is to succeed at that level? Most players don't have a chance in hell."

My heart was sinking lower and lower. I did not need to start thinking about my slim odds of success on the tour. "As far as you know, was there any strain between Beccia and Amber Clancy?"

"Like I said before, you push a little harder and you'll find the truth."

Not all that illuminating. This guy sounded like a crackpot. "Thanks for your input."

"When will this article be out?" he asked.

"Next week some time, depending on space." Once the lies started, they just tumbled out. I pressed End and moved back to my bed, feeling cold and shaky. The room air conditioner lurched on. I pulled the covers back and slid in, grateful for the warmth of the iBook on my lap.

I shifted to the USGA Web site and read the transcript of the press conference about Amber's death. By official report, Amber had brought a sports drink onto the grounds on Tuesday morning and stashed it in her bag. She consumed the tainted drink after her round, succumbed to seizures on the driving range, and died at the hospital. The USGA was deeply saddened by this loss of a young star to the golf community. Funeral arrangements were to be private, but a memorial service would be conducted later in the summer. Details to be announced.

What was the real story? What was the relationship like between Amber and her coach? Who hated her enough to kill her? Was the drink really meant for Amber? The USGA insisted that she'd brought the stuff in from outside the golf course premises—important to avoid a lawsuit later, I assumed. But who had access to Amber's golf bag?

I remembered suddenly the snow globe stuffed into mine—it wasn't so hard after all for a stranger to get closer to one of us than he belonged. I flashed on the men who'd carried in the clean caddie bibs earlier in the week. And all those volunteers. You couldn't have the FBI do a background check on everyone involved. Though in Amber's case, the killer would have had to know her well enough to choose the drink she'd expect to find in her bag. I wondered if I could get hold of Amber's father tomorrow. And whether he'd be willing to talk to me if I did.

What did Amber and I have in common? Obviously we played golf. And we'd both been invited to compete in a men's tournament.

I started an e-mail to Laura, summarizing the messages I'd received so far from Ruleswhiz. My college statistics teacher would have called this meta-analysis. Laura would call it looking things over.

"Rule 6-4. The player may be assisted by only one *caddie*." Followed by "Cassie, don't play where you don't belong. You could get hurt." This seemed frighteningly transparent.

"Rule 19-1. If a ball is deflected by an *outside agency,* it's a *rub of the green* and you play it as it lies." Nothing personal after.

"Rule 28. The player may deem his ball unplayable at any place on the *course* except when the ball is in a *water hazard,*" followed by "Who's your daddy, Cassie? Who's your caddie?"

The phrase "Who's your daddy?" had been made famous by a pitcher on the Boston Red Sox, capitulating to his archenemy, the New York Yankees, after a particularly bad loss. What did this have to do with me? I didn't have a rival or enemy—that I knew of.

Certainly I'd had more than one caddie this week, one I didn't know and two relatives. The kid who carried my bag the first day was a complete stranger. He could not have known in advance who I was, my e-mail, or that he would be assigned to me that day. Charlie and Dad? Out of the question. Dead end.

"Rule 8-2. Except on the *putting green,* a player may have the *line of play* indicated to him by anyone, but no one may be positioned by the player on or close to the line or an extension of the line beyond the *hole* while the *stroke* is being made."

And added below the rule: "Remember what happens to girls who don't play by the rules. Girls just want to have fun."

I added an asterisk here: This note had been sent in hard copy to Mom's Myrtle Beach address. Which meant it could actually have been sent earlier than Rule 19. Might it also mean something about showing the line to my mother's home? I could make paranoid projections about any detail at this point.

Next I jotted down "Snow globe: headless golfer, putting green, red snow, palm tree, earring." I tried to remember the photo that had been used in the globe. Where had the picture been taken? Hawaii maybe? I'd been too rattled earlier to pay close attention.

The rub of the green—if a ball is deflected by an outside agency . . . rubbed out on the green? The golfer girl in the snow globe? I was getting nowhere.

The third rule only emphasized golf's bottom line: You are basically in this game alone. You can scramble for help ahead of time and beg, borrow, or steal feedback after, but when you go to hit the shot, you're alone.

I sent the message off to Laura and typed "Lloyd Pompano" into the Google toolbar. As I remembered from last time I looked, he was a partner in Pompano, Falcone, and Warm, LLC—a law firm that specialized in personal injury and medical malpractice. I wrinkled my nose. There were headlines about particular cases, but none of them suggested that Lloyd had been involved in anything worse than legal sleaze. His bio reported him to be happily married with two kids in college and a 3-handicap. That last point I doubted, based on the swing I'd seen him pantomime while he was offering tips.

Next I typed in "Julie Nothstine." As I waited for the hits to come up, the computer dinged and a small box hopped in the bottom right corner of the screen: a message from Ruleswhiz, but nothing in the subject line. My shoulders tightened and I began to breathe fast and shallow.

Sticks and stones can break your bones, but an e-mail cannot hurt you, I chanted inanely.

I clicked on the box. There was no written message this time but a tinny tune danced out from the speakers and filled the room—high little voices singing about how it was a small world after all.

"What the hell?" Charlie rolled over and pushed himself up onto one elbow, his hair and eyes half-wild with sleep. "What is that racket?"

I passed over the laptop. "Ruleswhiz."

The song started up again. My teeth were chattering now and my chest hurt.

"Call Greg," said Charlie. "We're paying him a lot of money to handle this. Meanwhile, I'm shutting the damn thing off."

Feeling sick to my stomach, I dialed Greg's cell phone. He sounded wide awake.

"Bring the computer with you in the morning. I'll take care of it. Are you with Charlie?"

"Yes."

"Do you want me to come over now?"

I thought of his compact, muscular frame and the look of serious menace in his eyes when he followed me on the course, when the sunglasses were off, of course. No one, nothing, would get by him. He made me feel safe. But what could he do for me tonight? Camp out on the hallway carpet outside our door? Set up a chair just inside? I'd never sleep. Neither would he.

I got up to check the locks.

"I'll be okay with Charlie."

"Then get some rest and I'll see you first thing tomorrow."

Easier said than done. I put my headphones on and squeezed and relaxed the muscles of my body according to the instructions on the CD. A huge knot of tension had built gradually over the day and crescendoed with Ruleswhiz's theme song.

When the meditation wound down and I was still not sleepy, I played through the golf course in my mind. Each of my imaginary drives centered perfectly on the fairway, irons were hit with crisp authority, and putts sank without a thought of running by. I even made it across the stream on sixteen with a fairway wood second shot.

What would it feel like to win a tournament? How would a Cassie Burdette victory go over with the other girls? I'd studied the ways of the winners—how some of them pumped their fists and made guttural animal noises and how others dissolved into girl tears. And I'd watched the other players react, too—was it a popular win? I dreamed of going the way of first-time winner Kate Golden, drenched in beer and mobbed by congratulatory friends.

The small world song pushed back into my mind. There was absolutely nothing smaller than the Ladies Professional Golf Association. This tournament was a little different, with sixteen amateurs in, plus players from the Futures Tour, and sponsors' exemptions. That added up to who-knows-how-many professionals squeezed out of the field—all no doubt very disappointed. Maybe pissed off, too. It would be hard for the losers not to feel cheated—this was our livelihood after all.

Then I wondered if they'd admitted an alternate to the field after Amber died.

In the morning, I decided just before I drifted off to sleep, I'd call Dr. Baxter. Maybe a couple minutes on the phone with his deadpan calm would clear some of this clutter and fear out of my mind and show me the right path home.

Chapter 23

⏻ **Saturday** morning, the clubhouse felt like a wake. Not the Boston Catholic drink-a-lot-and-tell-bawdy-stories-about-the-deceased kind of wake, either. Half the golfers had already been sent packing and the rest of us were waiting for the axe. Today, the pressure of the US Open weekend felt like a wet shroud. Not to mention all my other anxieties, which I'd pressed down just below surface level, promising myself I could call Baxter after the round and fall apart after that.

Geez, enough with the morbid thoughts, Cassie.

After a quick breakfast, Charlie and I turned my laptop over to Greg in Sarah Washington's office. "I had some ideas about the e-mails last night," I told him. "But can we talk later? I need to get to work."

He stepped closer and I imagined for a moment that he might hug me.

"Fine. I'm going to have someone trace the Ruleswhiz address. Long shot, but worth a try." His hair was wet and slicked down to his scalp. I thought I could smell Irish Spring.

I grabbed a to-go coffee from the dining room and headed to the driving range to loosen up, Charlie and Greg just steps behind. Jason Palmer was working with an amateur from New Mexico—I could hear his steady patter of reassurance from twenty feet away.

"It's just another day, like any other," he told the girl, whose chubby face appeared frozen with fear. Her swing looked wooden and choppy, too.

"Morning. New gig?" I asked, smiling at his golfer.

"Monica's caddie caught the stomach flu. You're only thinking tempo and target today," he reminded her, and stepped back to chat with me.

"You're lucky to have this guy," I told Monica. "He knows just what he's doing."

"And believe me, Cassie and I were just as nervous when we were amateurs playing in big events."

"Possibly worse," I said.

"Only our friend Jack Daniel's calmed us down."

"Not recommended," I added, wishing he'd drop that line. Besides, I'd hardly ever drunk whiskey. And never before or during a tournament, for Christ's sake. Maybe a few too many beers after, but I was getting a handle on that.

"Sorry about how things turned out for Julie," I said to Jason, my voice low. "I felt bad for her."

"There's a lesson there for all of us." He shook his head. "You can want something too badly. She's a sweet girl with a lot going for her. She'll grow into it." He tapped the tip of my golf shoe with his amateur player's wedge. "Actually, I think she spent too much time worrying about you this week."

Not what I wanted to hear. "Hope my problems didn't bring her down."

Jason shrugged. "Good luck out there today. We're playing in the group ahead of you."

I laughed. "For God's sake, don't hold us up."

He winked and turned back to Monica. "Looks excellent. Now all you have to do is relax and enjoy." His golfer grimaced.

"Say listen." I turned back to Jason. "Do you have any idea why Julie's family didn't come out for this?" I raised my chin to indicate the course, the day, the *Open*.

"Family? Her parents divorced when she was a kid. She never heard from her father again and her mother's a witch. Nothing's ever been good enough for that woman, and her daughter playing in the US Open didn't qualify, either. That's why she gets so attached to people—she's looking for the family she doesn't have—if you want my amateur analysis, that is."

A sad story, but it wasn't necessarily the recipe for a stalker. "Have you heard anything more about Amber? I'm pretty sure there was more of a connection between her and Lucien Beccia than what we've heard so far. I think it has to do with that calendar," I whispered. "Why has the guy disappeared completely?"

"Oh Cassie" —he draped his arm across my shoulders and squeezed—"let the cops unravel all that. You've got a championship to play!" He grinned a lopsided smile and shifted his attention to Monica.

My father was waiting by my name marker with a neat pile of new Titleist balls. For once, I felt grateful for my own family. They might be crazy as loons, but in full, powerful, overwhelming force, they had turned out to support me.

"Morning," said my father. "Sleep okay? Charlie said you moved over to his room."

"Not too bad, considering he snores like a wood chipper."

Dad pulled the pitching wedge out of the bag and handed it over. I rolled a ball off the top of the pyramid. If I could play well today, I might never have to buy another ball. I slapped my leg. *The present moment* . . .

"Not for nothing, but who's the little monkey on steroids who's been following us for two days now?"

I giggled. Greg wouldn't be too crazy about that description. Now how much to say?

"With all the concern about Amber and her coach, Charlie talked me into hiring a security guy." I glanced in Greg's direction. "Nothing to worry about—just a little extra precaution so I can concentrate on my game." My gaze shifted back to Dad. "Charlie insisted."

"Fine. I think it's a good idea. Just wondered, that's all."

He looked hurt. Wasn't he my caddie and shouldn't he be consulted on these things? More important, wasn't he my father?

We practiced longer than I wanted to. Thirty players had been caught in the fierce thunderstorms yesterday and had to finish their second rounds. I tried to stay calm by reminding myself how bad it would have felt to wait through another night to see whether I'd made the cut. I was damn lucky not to have hovered so close to the bubble that a couple good rounds this morning would have knocked me out of the game.

A little after nine-thirty we took the short walk from the practice putting green to the first tee. The crowd blurred into patches of color and noise. I knew my family was there, but I kept my head down, muttering my mantra. Mantras. *Nothing special, nothing extra. Just another day. The present moment . . .* A hand reached out to grab my shirt and I jerked away in alarm. Joe.

"Good luck," his lips mouthed through the din. "Knock 'em dead. You're the best."

Without thinking, I blew him a kiss. Oh sweet Jesus, how would he take that?

Today, we were playing in twosomes; me with Joan Lambert, a veteran tour player who'd ground out a steady but unremarkable career over the last eighteen years. She'd never contended for a tournament title. I wondered if she was satisfied with that history, or if, when she stood on the first tee, she still really believed she might win. She was a solidly packed woman with short black hair, slender ankles, and bulging calves. Her caddie was a knockout blonde, as willowy as Joan was thick. We shook hands and faced the announcer.

"Ladies and gentlemen, this is the third round of the US Women's Open, the nine forty-five starting time. First on the tee, from Desert Palms, California, please welcome Joan Lambert." The crowd buzzed and clapped.

Joan waggled her driver once, twice, three . . . I counted eleven times. I could feel my shoulders tighten as her nickname suddenly popped into my mind: Slo-Mo Joan. She finally hit the ball.

"Same old routine." My father smiled and fit the driver into my shaking hands. The ball sailed out and rolled to a stop ten yards short of the creek.

"Gotta love that adrenalin rush," I told Dad.

By the fifth hole we were all moving in slow motion. Joan gave new meaning to the word *deliberate,* pacing out every distance, conferring endlessly with the willowy blonde, and stacking up golf club waggles like bankable commodities. A USGA official had already warned us once about not slowing up play. Ahead of us, Jason's golfer and her playing companion had receded into distant pinpricks of color.

My father tried to distract me by describing the students he was currently teaching, including a feeder tour player he thought might make it to the PGA tour this year. As Joan's waggles accumulated, he moved on to the politics at his Santa Monica club. He'd mellowed, my father. And he was trying really hard. But I missed the rude comments that Laura would have made. Comments that would have gotten me laughing and possibly helped me shake off the sense of impending collapse. I three-putted the fifth hole and penciled my first bogie on the scorecard.

When my turn came on the sixth tee, I slashed at the ball and watched it drift out to the right of the small pond and nestle into the USGA's pride, the rough. A few fans cheered—obviously they hadn't watched a round of professional golf in their lives. I chucked the driver next to my bag and stumped down the hill ahead of my father.

"This looks like a drainage ditch to me," I told him when he caught up, panting slightly. "Don't you think I get a drop here?"

He set the golf bag down, walked around the ball, and shook his head. "I think you have to play it as it lies."

Onlookers had begun to cluster several yards away. I thought about what So Won Lee said yesterday in the restaurant—you need to use the rules to your advantage.

"Just hit it, Cassie!" shouted a man with a big belly, khaki shorts, and black socks. And I would consider advice from him?

I beckoned to the official who waited in her cart fifty yards from my position in the rough. Her cart skidded to a stop next to me.

"This looks like ground under repair," I said.

"I don't believe it is, but let's have a look." She stepped out of the cart and approached my ball, barely visible in the tall grass. She pointed. "There's definitely a depression in the turf, but it's not a drainage ditch."

"It's a French drain," I insisted, "an abnormal ground condition."

I'd reviewed the local rules for the tournament each night before bed—players are entitled to take a one-club drop to get relief from problems that interfere with their stance or swing. Besides, I'd benefited from the extra study while trying to understand the messages from Ruleswhiz. I'd managed to keep all that out of my mind over the first five holes, but now my anxiety rushed back in full force.

She shook her head again.

"Can we call someone else?"

She pursed her lips. It's always a player's option to ask for a second opinion, but her face told me she thought I was being a pain in the ass. She'd never say so, of course. We waited several minutes for a second official to arrive—a thin man this time who left his cart on the path and scurried across the fairway like a worried rodent.

He confirmed the first official's opinion. So now I had a

lousy lie, two irritated officials, and the fellow-competitor from hell to contend with.

"Let's get a move on, Cassie," said Joan, "we've got to catch up with the group ahead."

As if I'd been the one to hold things up. I hacked my ball out of the long grass, banged it up onto the green, and three-putted for a double-bogey.

"Take a deep breath and shake that one off," said my father, holding my driver out with a tentative smile.

By the time we reached the tenth hole, we were officially on the clock. And I was five shots over par. I knew exactly what the problem was: hard not to rush your swing when your group is slow. You're desperate not to be marked as the player who's taking more than her allotted time to play a stroke. It's not just reputation at stake either—penalty strokes and even disqualification lie just behind the first official warning.

My tee shot hit the short side of the tenth green, spun backward, and dove into the creek. The crowd moaned in sympathy. I pinched the inside of my forearm, willing myself not to cry.

"We're going to scramble back," said my father, "one shot at a time." His face was beet red and perspiring. All we needed was a minor heart attack to make the day complete.

As we walked down the short length of fairway to retrieve my ball (not a Titleist and probably never would be) from the creek, I noticed my entourage. Mike was there. Michelle, too, with her hand perched on her waist to show off a diamond ring that winked ostentatiously, even from a distance. Maureen stood close to her, with my three brothers twenty yards up the path. And then Mom. And Dave, appearing hot and grumpy in his heavy jeans. And Lloyd, trying not to look like his meal ticket had lost her engines and was screaming in a free fall toward the earth. He'd been walking with Aaron the Titleist rep earlier in the round, but was now alone. And Greg, facing sideways toward the crowd, probably wondering what the hell I was doing out here and why someone in this crowd would bother with me.

I hated disappointing them all. I hated the feeling of spiraling out of control. Joe would say—where was Joe? I scanned the gallery for his tall frame and the blue Mount Holyoke cap I'd seen him wearing earlier. In the last row of the gallery ringing the green, I thought I saw Julie. She had apparently decided to torture herself by staying on. My stomach muscles tightened—I hoped the decision had nothing to do with me.

I fished the ball out of the creek with my sand wedge and popped it onto the green. Two putts later, my score climbed to seven over par. I trudged through the next five holes, eking out more workmanlike pars. The meaning of the day hung over me like a blanket of smog. Each swing felt awkward. My mind whirled in a hundred unhelpful directions.

We finally reached sixteen, the devilish par four that I'd imagined reaching in two shots last night. I popped up my drive—there would be no dream performance today. My chip skittered across the green, leaving a long second putt for another bogey. The way things were going, I'd be lucky to break eighty.

Between Dad's cajoling and sheer force of will, I carded two pars on the final holes. I shook hands with Slo-Mo Joan, teeth gritted, praying I'd never be paired with her in another tournament.

"We can't blame her," said my father in a low voice.

"We have to learn to block out all the annoying distractions and play our own game."

Kind of him to use the royal "we," but it wasn't him who'd allowed her deliberate shotmaking to ruin my round. I ducked under the ropes and headed up the hill through the green tunnel.

A reporter waited on the other side. Couldn't he find someone more interesting and successful—and less crabby—to harass?

"Given today's round, Miss Burdette"—the young man thrust a small tape recorder toward my mouth—"how are you feeling about your invitation to play in the Buick Championship?"

Translation: You fell flat on your face today. Do you really want to repeat that performance while playing with the guys in a front of a bigger audience?

"No comment," I snapped. "I'm playing one shot at a time."

Yeah right.

•

Chapter 24

On my way to the clubhouse, it occurred to me that I definitely did not want my father to leave my golf bag at the caddie shack. One grisly surprise was quite enough. I changed directions and hustled past the putting green toward the caddie shack.

A man stumbled into my path. My nose registered powerful alcohol fumes and sour body odor. I stuck my arm out to keep him from falling into me—it was Tony, the caddie I'd rejected earlier in the week. On his butt drunk.

"How shdid you play today?" He wobbled and staggered, almost falling a second time.

"Just okay," I answered, stepping away from him. "I'm sure it'll go better tomorrow."

He belched, blasting loose a cloud of halitosis. "I shaw

that other caddie you like. . . ." He lurched to the left, and mumbled, his eyes rolling backward and arms waving. "You shouldn't let him mesh with your bag."

Last thing I wanted was to get into an argument with a drunk about why I'd chosen a kid over him three days ago. For once, my intuition had been on target.

"My father's on my bag," I said stiffly.

The caddie master approached with a uniformed policeman. "Time to go, Tony." He grasped the man's forearm. The cop took the other side and they marched him down the hill to a waiting taxi. Apparently the rehab program hadn't gone so well.

"Dad!" I waved across the path to my father and hurried over to where he chatted with two other caddies. "Do you mind taking my bag home with you tonight? I'm feeling a little superstitious."

"Sure, I'll take care of it." He smiled and pulled me close for a quick hug. "Listen, you did okay out there today. Everyone has one of those days from time to time, and the secret is plugging through and then leaving it behind."

"I know. I just wish I could have had my lousy day at a smaller tournament." I patted his back. "I'm lucky to have a great cheerleader. Catch you later. I'll be ready to practice in about an hour."

I returned to the clubhouse and looked for a quiet corner to phone Dr. Baxter. Not so easy—the place teemed with golfers and their families famished after their rounds. I stuck my head into Sarah Washington's office but she was nowhere to be seen. I'd practically lived in her office so far this week, I hoped she wouldn't mind if I borrowed it for a few more minutes.

Baxter picked up on the first ring. I felt a rush of relief and then an urge to hang up, which pretty well sums up our relationship. Too late now. "It's Cassie Burdette. I wondered if you had a couple minutes free?"

"I do have five minutes," he said, with just a slight emphasis on the five. "How is everything going?"

"Okay, I'm just feeling stressed out," I said, tears sliding down both cheeks. At least he couldn't see me cry. On the other hand, his basket case antennae had probably rolled right up.

"Two sides of the family?" he suggested helpfully while I struggled for words.

I blew my nose and cleared my throat. "They're actually behaving pretty well." I described Laura's absence, Amber's death, the e-mails, the snow globe, hiring Greg, Mike's engagement, and today's god-awful, rotten round in front of a record crowd at the US Open.

"That's a lot all at once. How are you feeling?" he asked, shrink shorthand for "are you flipping out yet?"

"A few panic symptoms, but I managed to handle them." I paused. "The worst is trying to figure out who might be stalking me. I'm suspicious of everyone." I told him what Greg had said about previously intimate partners. "He doesn't think it's a stranger—he thinks it's someone I know."

"Someone you know?"

I thought Dr. Baxter's voice sounded incredulous. His eyes were probably bugging out, too. I had that effect on him.

"Tell me about that," he prodded.

"Greg said to pay attention to my intuition. He said most women don't want to hurt someone's feelings or be rude and that's how they get into trouble."

Why did I have to defend myself with my own shrink? I was beginning to wish I'd never called. Or told this guy anything. Wasn't he supposed to keep an open mind and stay planted on my side?

"My golf was awful today," I said just to fill the silence. "Julie's caddie, Jason, said something about how she washed out of the tournament because she just wanted it too badly."

"It's a lot of pressure," Baxter agreed. "You had all your loved ones watching."

All my loved ones? He made it sound like a eulogy.

"Oh by the way, Julie turns out to be a lesbian, or so I've been told. And Jason said she's very attached to me." Which reminded me that I'd seen her in the crowd on the tenth green. "Charlie and I had dinner with Lloyd and a representative from Titleist last night. I doubt they'll be rushing to sign a contract with me after today."

"They'd reject you because of one round?"

"First of all, I barely broke eighty. Second, it doesn't take much. Remember how fast Birdie Girl dropped me?" I chuckled. Baxter didn't seem to know a thing about golf before I stumbled into his office two years ago—or care. He'd come a long way, baby.

"Probably the best thing you can do is go back to basics— try to keep your focus limited by using your breathing and your positive thoughts. We'll have plenty of time to sort all this out when you're back in South Carolina. We'll have a lot to talk about."

Apparently my five minutes were up.

"Thanks for your time." I pressed End and leaned back in the desk chair. Though Baxter hadn't come through with any brilliant interpretations, I did feel a little better. The world hadn't ended after all. Then I noticed a page of scribbled notes on the blotter. Lucien Beccia's cell phone number was at the bottom of the sheet. I wrote it on the inside of my wrist with a red pen.

Sarah Washington buzzed into the room. She startled, obviously surprised to see me. And not all that pleased, either.

"Were you looking for me? Everything going okay? Greg working out all right?"

"He's great," I said, horrified to find myself blushing. I hoped she hadn't seen me steal the phone number. "I'm sorry to bust in like this. I had to make a personal call and there was nowhere else I could think to go."

She held the door open and waved me out into the hall. "Gotta run," she said. "They're holding another press conference about Amber Clancy."

I stiffened. "Is there news?"

"No. But the media are badgering us with questions. The timing is awkward as hell, but we can't just pretend nothing happened."

She held the door open for me, and we walked back into the sticky brightness of the late afternoon. Might as well go listen to what people had to say about the girl when they had a microphone in front of their faces. I was in no hurry—other than spending an hour practicing my chipping, I had no plans for the night. Time spent waiting for the final round would crawl by.

A medium-sized crowd had gathered in front of the makeshift stage. It looked to be mostly reporters and officials, with a sprinkling of players and their caddies.

Alice Maxwell took the mike. "We didn't want this tournament to conclude without noting that we lost an important member of our golf community this week. Amber

Clancy had a remarkable talent—and we were all so looking forward to watching the arc of her career. She was fearless. Nothing gave her pause—not even making the cut at a PGA tournament—the first woman to ever break that barrier." She hesitated. "We will miss her energy and we will miss watching her blossom. Now I'll take a few questions." She glanced at her wristwatch. A few questions . . . like Dr. Baxter, she'd be counting.

Lately, I'd been to other press conferences after someone died. By listening carefully to the reporters' questions, you could tell whether the dead person was considered to be a nice person. You had to stay tuned for what the speakers didn't say.

A sportswriter from *Golf Magazine* rambled through a story about a pro-am event where he'd been paired with Amber. The recitation devolved into a description of his own personal golf game and how he'd lost a hundred dollars on a recent outing. Apparently he could hit the ball a long way but couldn't putt to save his life.

Mercifully, Alice cut him off. "Thanks for your comments. I'll take a few *questions*." She called on a man I didn't recognize, burr-headed with intense gray eyes.

"You reported yesterday that Amber had been poisoned by a sports drink. Have the police made any progress understanding how that drink got into her bag? Can you tell us the brand of the drink?"

"We have very little new information on that," said Alice. She turned to confer with the officials behind her, then back to the microphone. "The drink was called Aqua Surge. It was transported in from outside the venue and had been laced with strychnine." She pointed to a woman in the middle of the crowd, who asked about increased security and the safety of the other players in the field. Alice insisted that every possible resource was being focused on those very concerns, and moved on to a reporter at the front, balding with thick glasses and a reedy voice.

"I don't have a question really, just a comment about Miss Clancy. She was the most remarkable golfer I have seen, Tiger Woods included. We all wondered how such a young girl could perform at that level. She never paid attention to scores; she didn't care about the numbers," the man continued. "She had the swing path, she had the work ethic, and she always, always played by the rules. And she had nerves of iron."

They were going to have to pass out hip boots so we could wade through all this shit if the testimonials continued.

Alice Maxwell stepped up to the podium again and gave a half-smile. "She did know the rules of golf. Lucien Beccia made sure of that."

I felt suddenly cold—I nearly screamed when Charlie touched my elbow.

"Hey, I've been looking for you all over," he whispered. "About tonight. Everyone wants to spend time with you."

I groaned. "Who's everyone?"

"Mom, Dad, the boys, Lloyd . . ."

"Jesus, Charlie. Did you explain that I need some downtime?"

He shrugged helplessly and grinned. "I suggested bowling."

"Bowling," I squeaked. "You have to be kidding."

"It was that, or a hot tub. Apparently that's the biggest attraction in the happy valley."

I closed my eyes. "I don't even want that image in my mind."

"Chinese food, first, just you and me. We can't go back to the room and twiddle our thumbs until bedtime." He lifted his wrist to check his watch. "It's not even five o'clock. You can't spend the night at a bar before the final round of the US Open."

"Sounds good to me," I muttered.

Greg materialized from the crowd and Charlie clapped him on the back. "Do you like Chinese?"

I scowled. Greg nodded.

"How about we meet you at Taipei and Tokyo in Northampton at six-thirty?"

"He has to eat somewhere, too," said Charlie, as Greg walked away. "Besides, we'll both feel better with him nearby. But this way, he's not on the clock, right?"

"Always thinking like a lawyer," I said.

Chapter 25

Charlie ushered me into a small Asian restaurant near the center of Northampton. Greg was already seated at a wood table in the front window. If he'd been taller, red fringe from the lanterns hanging from the ceiling would have brushed the top of his head. He wore blue jeans and a salmon-colored polo. It was the first time I'd seen him out of black. Be still my cheating heart.

"Thank God you didn't go for the sushi counter," I said, sliding into the chair across from him and pantomiming a gagging motion. "We did the raw oyster bit last night."

"I'm not big on raw fish, either," said Greg, pushing a placemat printed with the Chinese zodiac across the polished surface of the table. "What are your signs?"

"The dragon," I said.

"Robust and passionate, your life is filled with complexity," he read.

"Ain't that the truth," said Charlie. "The robust part anyway."

I kicked him under the table.

"Compatible with the monkey and the rat, your opposite is the dog," Greg continued. "I'm a monkey, myself."

"No comment," said Charlie.

Time for a new topic. "Did you bring my computer?" I asked Greg.

"The FBI's got it."

I stiffened. "The FBI?"

Greg shrugged. "They have the resources to track this kind of e-mail."

What could I say? I was the one who'd called in the red alert. "How the hell am I supposed to check my messages?"

"Everyone you know is here at the tournament," said Charlie. "You can just talk to them."

"Is there any news about that stupid song?"

Greg shook his head. "Nothing yet."

"The worst thing is I can't get the damn melody out of my head."

A small Asian woman in a brocade dress arrived with a pad. As we finished ordering, my cell phone rang.

"Is this the famous US Open golfer, Miss Burdette?"

"Joe!" I said. "How are you? I had my eye out for you during the round."

"I didn't want to be a distraction," he said. "You had enough going on."

"You got that right. The flow wasn't flowing today. Besides, Slo-Mo Joan nearly cost me my sanity." We chatted for a minute about my struggle to get our group off the clock.

"Did you learn anything you can use for tomorrow?" he asked.

I knew he had some definite ideas about what I *should* have learned. "Patience," I guessed. "Isn't that what Annika always says? Maybe I tried too hard to hit the ball perfectly. Tomorrow I've got nothing to lose, right?"

"Right." He laughed. "You know I'm very, very proud of you."

A lump clogged my throat and I turned away from the guys to face a poster of the Yangtze River that hung on the opposite wall. "Thanks."

"I wondered if you wanted to grab a sandwich or a steak or whatever? Your choice, I'm buying."

I swallowed. "Hmm. Thanks for the offer. Our waitress is on her way with dinner: General Tso's chicken, moo shu pork, and Mandarin shrimp. The scallion pancakes look almost as good as that place in New Jersey last summer."

"You're eating all that by yourself?" His chuckle sounded forced.

"Not just me. Charlie's here. And Greg came with us at the last minute."

"Greg?"

"The security guy—you met him."

Silence. Then: "I don't believe we have met."

"Would you like to come bowling after supper? The family's meeting us in an hour at Northampton Bowl. All of them. I'd really love for you to be there."

"I might stop by. If I don't see you, good luck in the morning."

"Joe," I said, before pressing End and rolling my eyes. I

packed a thin flour pancake with juicy pork and onion stir-fry and drizzled plum sauce over the top. Maybe if I ate enough, fast enough, I could stem the rising confusion of guilt and regret.

"He's invited you to dinner with him every night this week, hasn't he?" Charlie asked.

"Yeah, and so what?" I said around a mouthful of moo shu pork. "It's normal for us to get together after my rounds and talk things over."

Charlie frowned and tapped his chopsticks on his plate. "It's just that if a girl turned me down more than once, I sure wouldn't keep calling her night after night."

I washed the food down with a gulp of beer. "Since when are you the relationship guru?" I muttered. "I haven't seen you with the same girl twice since college."

Charlie glared, stabbed a piece of chicken, and pushed two large chili peppers away from the meat.

"Sorry," I said. "I'm a little touchy tonight."

"Ain't that the truth? Did you see anything suspicious out there on the course today?" he asked Greg.

"Not exactly," he said. "There was a tall blond girl who seemed to be sticking pretty close. Is she a special fan?"

How did he even pick her out in the crowd? "Julie. I've been rooming with her. She got cut yesterday. And she was wondering whether to stay around to watch the weekend. Her caddie found another bag and since they'd driven up together, she felt bad leaving him."

"He couldn't get a ride?" Charlie asked.

"I wondered," I said. "She didn't go to Amber's prayer vigil—I wondered about that, too." I laid my chopsticks down, feeling overfull, bordering on queasy. "I just heard someone say last night that she's gay."

"This is the girl you were trying to set me up with?" Charlie asked. "She's interested in *you*?"

"I don't think so, really." I did a quick mental review of our interactions over the last few days. Julie had been attentive, kind, open, but unless I was dense beyond belief, none of it had felt sexual. I turned back to Greg. "I spoke with Mike last night. He's definitely not sending me those e-mail messages. He just got engaged."

"God bless the poor woman," said Charlie.

I stuck out my tongue. "Have you heard anything more about Amber's death?" I asked Greg.

"Not really." Or not that he was telling civilians.

"Where the hell has Lucien Beccia disappeared to?" I asked.

"It had to be a brutal shock," said Charlie, "losing his top student and future meal ticket. He probably just went home." He handed me and Greg a fortune cookie, broke his open, and read it aloud. " 'You will get a free drop, and then chip in for birdie.' " He held it out to me and smiled. "This must be yours."

"Very funny. What does it really say?"

" 'Your sense of humor reveals itself at just the right times.' " He grinned. "And yours?" he asked Greg.

" 'Love is the glue that holds together everything in the world.' "

"Sweet," I said.

"Say, man," Charlie said, "are you married?"

"Yes."

Was it my imagination or did the word come out almost like a question?

"Either you are or you aren't," Charlie said.

Greg pulled a worn photo out of his wallet: a pretty

brunette, slightly pudgy, two dark-haired kids with round faces, and a pug dog. All adorable—and I bet they felt safe, too.

"My wife insisted on the pug."

"You would have chosen a German shepherd," said Charlie.

"Right." Greg laughed. "At the moment, my wife and I are separated."

"Sorry to hear that," said Charlie.

"What about you?" Greg asked, looking at me.

"Not married, not even close."

A smile played across his lips.

Damn, damn, damn. He wasn't asking about my marital status. He was curious about my fortune cookie. The dreaded blush began to spread up my neck. I shattered the cookie and extracted the fortune.

" 'Face facts with dignity.' " I threw the paper down. "That stinks. Who thinks these dumb things up? It's just the way my week is going."

Northampton Bowl proved to be a Saturday night hot spot, complete with strobes and disco balls. I'd tried to bail out on the bowling party one more time, but Charlie convinced me that a brief appearance would both make our families happy and eat up worrying time.

The lights flickered over the solar system designs on the walls, where Day-Glo bowling balls replaced the planets. A wave of noise hit us; first the rumbling of balls headed down the wooden alleys. And then, horror of horrors, the amplified, amateur wailing of John Denver's "Rocky Mountain

High." I glanced up at the banner strung from the ceiling. Double horrors: Saturday was family karaoke night.

I followed Charlie across the black carpet sprinkled with blue, pink, and yellow confetti. Each step released the aroma of bathroom cleanser, something cheaper than Pine-Sol, if I had to guess. At least we didn't have to put up with the haze of cigarette smoke that still choked bars in the South.

"Oh my God," Charlie yelped, "it's Maureen."

With a glass of wine in one hand, and a microphone in the other, our stepmother closed her eyes and crooned a finale that would have made John Denver weep. Her sons—our brothers—were not among the small group of intoxicated hecklers and enthusiastic fans. As she swooped to a final, wobbling high note, my father grabbed her elbow and pulled her to the lane at the far end of the row.

"She's not a blood relative," I told Greg.

As my eyes adjusted to the intermittent flashes of light, our crowd took shape—Mom, Dave, Mike, Michelle, Lloyd, Dad, and of course, Maureen.

"Where are the boys?" I asked when we reached their lane.

"Video arcade." My father pointed across the room. "Let's get started here."

"I'm not playing," I said. "I can't risk a blister."

"Time for a beer run," said Charlie. "Budweiser?"

I nodded.

"Let's get this show on the road." Mike double-knotted his bowling shoes and stood by the scoring table. "What are the teams?"

"Isn't he the cutest thing?" gushed Maureen. "I want a picture of him while he's still single."

"Me, too," said my mother, lurching to her feet. If she was having her picture taken with Maureen and Mike, she was definitely feeling no pain.

"I'll take one of the three of you," said Lloyd. He gestured for them to squeeze in on either side of Mike.

Keepsake wouldn't do it justice.

The camera flashed. "Now, you get in there, Michelle," said Lloyd.

Grinning, Greg whispered: "Are you next?"

"Let's go check on the boys," I said.

The arcade was crammed with kids and games—skittle ball, monster bash, PGA Tour championship, and a jewelry box with a giant claw. Zack and David were shooting at scantily clad young women and anonymous threatening men with what looked like a rifle or machine gun. Whatever. *Silent Scope—you're a professional sniper,* proclaimed the video game. Sicko special.

I punched the boys' arms. "Nice game you're playing, knuckleheads."

David grinned sheepishly. Zack shrugged one shoulder, the *rat-tat-tat-tat* of the gun not losing a beat. "Got one!"

"These are my brothers. And this is Mr. Merrill. He's with tournament security."

That got Zack to look up from his game. "I bet you use one of these for real."

Greg smiled. "It's a little big to carry under a suit jacket."

David's glance slid down to the slight bulge at Greg's beltline. My stock appeared to have risen by proxy.

"Time to bowl," I said. "Your mother's finished her performance."

On the way back to the bowling lanes, Greg grabbed my wrist. "What did you say was that girl's name?"

My gaze followed his pointing finger. Julie.

"Julie. She's with her caddie and a couple of the other golfers."

"Go say hello," Greg said. "Don't introduce me. I want to get a sense of things from a distance."

He let go of my arm and I was suddenly aware of his scent again—Irish Spring and sweat. Which smelled a lot nicer than it sounds. He dropped back into the shadows.

"Hey, Cassie! Good luck tomorrow," called Jason as I emerged from the crowd. Eyes narrowed, Julie approached their lane with an orange ball. The sign above her read:

> *For your safety.*
>
> **Do not cross the foul line*
>
> **Lanes are conditioned beyond the line*
>
> **Zero score will result if crossed*
>
> **Foul lights are always on*
>
> **Bowling shoes are required*

Every game has its rules.

Julie's ball rolled smoothly down the wooden surface and crashed into the pins. She threw her arms up and whooped.

"Maybe if they had a TV screen out on the course to show the putting line, I would have scored well enough to make the cut," she said, coming over to offer me a hug. "Are you nervous about tomorrow?"

"Absolutely terrified. You decided to stick around?"

"I'd be thinking about it anyway and wondering how all

my buddies are doing. Might as well just stay and watch. Maybe I'll learn something." She grinned.

"Or maybe not," said Jason. Julie socked his arm.

"You'll be awesome next time," I said.

"Did you go to the press conference this afternoon?" Julie asked.

"There wasn't anything new," I said. "Amber's drink was poisoned, just like you said. They're insisting she brought it in from the outside—I doubt it's that clear-cut. See you guys later then. My folks are waiting for me." I pointed to the far lane.

"Could you tell anything from that?" I asked Greg. Julie seemed perfectly normal to me. Except I had so many suspicions swamping my brain that no one—no one—was safe.

"Hard to say. I'll keep a good eye on her."

After watching one game, Charlie and I walked back across the parking lot to our motel room. Greg followed us out, disappeared into a large SUV, and pulled onto the road toward South Hadley.

"You shower first," I told Charlie. I propped up a couple of pillows, relaxed onto the bed, and flipped on the TV. The local ten o'clock news was airing.

"Rockin' Jennifer Rosales has taken the third round lead!" shouted their sports guy, an annoying man with a grating voice and a plaid jacket with matching tam-o'-shanter. "She's got some wild and woolly dress code of her own imagination, but her putter was on fire for the second day. Tour veterans Annika Sorenstam, Kelly Robbins, and Meg Mallon are hanging close on her heels. Don't count any of them out, Barbara," he said to the anchor. "All those ladies know how to win."

"Thanks, Tom." The petite woman with helmet hair and very red lips turned her eyes back to the camera and down-graded the wattage of her smile. "On a more serious note, the FBI has been called in to investigate the recent death of golf amateur sensation, Amber Clancy." Footage of Amber signing hats for a crowd of kids around the putting green flashed onto the screen. "Local officials state that foul play has not been ruled out. One source says the NAACP will be filing a suit regarding the mishandling of her case by the end of next week."

I glanced down at the faint red numbers on my wrist, pressed the TV's Mute button, and dialed Lucien Beccia's cell phone number. Reaching him now was a long shot, but maybe he'd call me back after the tournament tomorrow. I wanted his read on Amber Clancy's life and worries. So far, nothing had been cleared up to my satisfaction. If the FBI was still on the case, obviously the authorities weren't satisfied either.

"The number you dialed has been disconnected or is no longer in service," said a recorded voice. "Please hang up and try your number again."

I tried again but got the same recording—had I copied the number wrong? I certainly wasn't going to skulk around Sarah Washington's office again during the final round of the Open to find out.

Dead damn end.

Chapter 26

⏻ I bolted awake at five A.M.—a good hour ahead of schedule and too early to start the day. Every synapse was on full alert—not a chance in hell of drifting back to sleep. A thousand questions darted through my mind. How would I manage the pressure of the final round? Was the person watching me still at the tournament? If so, who and where? Would I ever see Greg again after today? Why the hell did I care? Why couldn't I just settle into a relationship with a nice golf psychologist like some normal person?

Not that a relationship with a shrink was normal, either. I distracted myself by wondering whether Lucien Beccia had gotten more involved with his star pupil than the teacher's code of ethics said he ought to. I wished I'd gotten through to him last night.

Charlie dragged himself out of bed at six, and we drove to the golf course. I craved carbohydrates and sugar—at the moment my jittery nerves were fueled by adrenalin and not much else. Even at this early hour, crowds jostled for position around the practice area, as big as I'd ever seen at a women's tournament. It was hot and humid and the vestiges of a headache throbbed at the base of my neck. My entire family was camped out on the bleachers behind my station at the driving range, looking strung out and hungover. Mom and Maureen had gone back to maintaining a three-man spread between them. Greg touched his black cap in salute and took up a position halfway between the family and me. I could use a guy like him full-time just to handle my relatives.

"Quite a show your wife put on last night," I said to my father.

He slapped the driver into my palm just harder than he needed to.

Lloyd trotted down the line of players carrying a large Dunkin' Donuts coffee in one hand and a copy of *The Rules of Golf* in the other. He held it up, his forehead creased into worried folds. "Did you review the rules last night? We don't want a replay of the trouble you had yesterday."

"I'll be fine," I said, my heart thumping a little faster. Not only was it too damn late for tips of any kind, the subject of his suggestion made me ill. "It's within my rights to ask for a consultation any time I have a question." I suddenly remembered that I hadn't heard a peep about our man from Titleist. "By the way, did you talk with Aaron about the sponsorship?" I hated to ask, but it seemed worse not to know.

He frowned. "He understands that yesterday wasn't the best you're capable of. He's around today. He'll be watching. They've got a quota of new players they can take on—you're close to making the cut."

There went my "nothing to lose" mantra. Besides the question of personal humiliation, there was plenty to lose. Like multiple thousands in sponsorship dollars and a cute little Titleist logo on my cap and sleeves.

"Let's head on up," said my father. Greg moved quickly to lead the way, clearing a path through the fans clustered around the first tee.

My playing competitor for the day was a large square woman with legs that looked too slender to support her bulk. She chattered about spending the last three years on the Futures Tour and how they were lucky if they got a dozen fans following them. The gallery was obviously getting to her, too.

"Ladies and gentlemen," called the starter. "This is the eight A.M. starting time for the final round of the 59th US Women's Open. On the tee, from Wichita, Kansas, please welcome Lena Smith." Lena saluted the crowd and surged into her swing, very nearly missing the ball completely.

There's a lesson, Cassie, I told myself. *You may have waited your whole life for this minute, but you are going to play like it was any other day.* I waggled the club, sighted down the hill, and took my stance. *Crack:* The ball went sailing out straight and long. The crowd cheered.

Most times, after finishing a round, I can take an interested party through every shot—not that there's all that much call for that level of detail with the average audience. After this morning, though, I felt droopy and thickheaded—the adrenalin had played out, leaving a mental haze behind. The birdies I'd made on six and ten shone crystal clear, and

I could certainly describe the triple I'd taken on sixteen, but the rest was a fog.

I signed my scorecard and left the trailer. No one was waiting to interview me. Even the kid reporter who'd pressed me about the Buick Championship yesterday averted his eyes and drifted by. I hadn't played horribly, considering how it could have gone. But none of the players behind me were going to fret about me sitting on the lead in the clubhouse—I was miles away from that. And I could probably cross off the list concerns about whether Titleist fashions would suit my body type. As for good news, I definitely wouldn't come in last. My friend Lena Smith was a shoo-in for those honors. My first US Open was over: I'd made the cut and managed not to melt down on the weekend. Still, disappointment lingered.

You'll use that for motivation next year, I could imagine Joe saying.

"Do you mind if I go watch some of the golf with the kids and Charlie?" my father asked. "We'll all celebrate later."

"Go right ahead. You've been a trooper this week. And a dream caddie. Thank you." I kissed his cheek and gave him a little push. "Don't forget to take off your caddie bib. A girl having a bad day might try to snatch you out of the gallery."

I hoped I sounded more chipper than I felt. I saw Greg approaching through the crowd, and there was a woman close behind him—Laura.

She bolted toward me and folded me into a bear hug. "You were terrific."

"I survived anyway. I can't believe you're here! How's your dad?"

"He's doing just fine. Much better, really." She glanced at Greg, her eyebrows lifted.

"Have you met Greg Merrill? He's my security guy. This is my best friend, Laura."

He smiled and shook her hand. "Are you going to stay in the clubhouse a while? Sarah Washington asked if I could help out with crowd control for a couple of holes. Annika and Karrie Webb are drawing a bigger crowd than they'd figured on."

I waved him off, a little disappointed, to be honest. I'd allowed myself to imagine an intimate lunch for two.

"Go ahead, we'll get a bite to eat and catch you later."

"I'm starving," said Laura.

It would be two: me and her. Which in the end was probably for the best. Why would I want to get mixed up with a guy who still carried his wife's picture around in his wallet? Besides, I needed to settle things between me and Joe before I took another romantic step.

"I'll keep a close eye on this chick," said Laura, squeezing me again.

I turned my phone on and checked for voice mail messages on the way into the locker room. I felt a jolt of fear hearing a message from Jim Polonski, the California golfer I'd interviewed about Lucien Beccia. He must have captured my number in his phone log.

"Miss Leiner? I hope I have the right number. I thought of something that might be helpful to your story. I've been writing a blog for a year or so. I posted a list of all the players who've left Beccia's academy, some of them you might want to talk with—www.golflosers.com." He snorted a half-laugh. "That's what he thought of us anyway."

I never have understood the concept of blogs—keeping an online diary so anyone in the world—and I do mean anyone—has access to your private ramblings. Rambling in psychotherapy, with only one listener, is bad enough.

The second message was from Audry Longo, the golfer who'd been so excited about scoring a consultation with Lucien Beccia just before the tournament began. She had called to wish me luck in the final round. Bingo! She would definitely have Beccia's phone number. I pressed Redial to return the call.

"Audry, it's Cassie Burdette. Just called to thank you for your good wishes. Sorry you didn't make it to the weekend." I gave her a couple of minutes to describe which putts hadn't dropped and then summarized my own round. "How did it go with Lucien Beccia the other day?"

"You know what, that guy never showed. I'm not saying one lesson makes the difference between playing on the weekend or not, but it's damn unprofessional, don't you think?"

I murmured my consolation. "Do you happen to have his cell phone number? I have a friend who wants to contact him."

She rattled it off. "I hope she has better luck than I did."

"Hang on one more minute," I said to Laura, and dialed Beccia's number, nervous but determined.

"Beccia." His voice was faint and slightly surly. Like who the hell had the nerve to bother the master on a Sunday.

"Umm, it's Cassie Burdette. I'm a golfer, playing at the Open this weekend?"

"I'm not taking any clients on at this point. I will offer one free piece of advice: For God's sake, don't change anything now."

Did he think I'd be dumb enough to hire a new coach the day of the final round? "I was calling about Amber Clancy."

If possible, his voice turned colder. "I have no comment

on Miss Clancy. What did you say your name was?"

"Burdette. Cassie Burdette. Will you please give me three minutes?" I paused. He didn't say no, so I figured the clock was ticking.

"Amber approached me in the locker room earlier this week, asking questions about some detective stuff I'd been involved with. Maybe you saw the piece in the paper?"

"No."

"Fine, but the thing is, she seemed worried, but I never got her to say what about. And then she got called out to the range and left in kind of a huff. That's the last time I saw her alive."

"And why is this my concern? Or yours?"

"Because it looks like someone's stalking me and I don't know who or why and I wondered if there might be a connection. It's a long shot, but you look at what happened to her and maybe you can see why I'd be worried." It was all I could do to press back a sob. I'd been just fine as long as Greg was with me.

"I don't know who Amber's enemies were," said Beccia, "but if you're going to be a star, you can expect to make them. Some people will always be envious to the point that it poisons their minds." He paused. "Losers want winners to fail."

"Just curious," I said. "Do you know anything about the drink in Amber's bag? Aqua Surge, I think it's called. I'd never heard of it."

Silence on the line. "We developed it at the academy. There's been one double-blind study on it already with very positive results," said Beccia. "And we have plans for more. It helps with mental focus and boosts your energy."

"What's in the stuff?"

"Vitamins B, C, E, antioxidants, taurine, and green tea extracts. You can read more about it and obtain a sample from my Web site."

"Do you know where she got that particular bottle?"

"I certainly didn't poison her, if that's what you're suggesting," he snapped.

"Just one last question. Were you in favor of Amber's golf calendar? I wondered what effect that might have had on her status as an amateur."

"Of course I wasn't in favor of it!" he almost shouted. "It was unprofessional and completely distracting from our plans for her future. It brought out all the creeps from the woodwork—I told her this would happen."

"So things weren't going so smoothly between you."

"Bullshit. They were going fine. But ever since she decided to play in the PGA event, I had to get stricter with Amber. And I pushed her father to hire more security. And she objected to all that. But it was for her own good—we heard a lot from crazy fans leading up to the tournament. Naturally it died down some when they saw how she played. She played like a dream."

For the first time, he sounded sad.

"Had she been getting warnings or threats? Did she receive e-mail from someone who called himself Ruleswhiz?"

I heard the whistling of his breath through his teeth. "I wasn't aware of that." The words came out harsh. He had to know more than he was saying.

"If you think of anything else, would you call me? Like I told you, I've been threatened lately, too."

"Then I suggest you take this to the police."

Click.

* * *

Over a roast beef and Swiss cheese sandwich with hot mustard, a mound of chips and pickles on the side, I filled Laura in on the conversation with Beccia and the rest of the crazy week. "He knows something that he wouldn't tell me. We need to look at this golflosers Web site."

"I've been thinking about the snow globe," Laura said, wiping a spot of mayonnaise off her chin with a white napkin. "What's the deal on the photo with the palm tree?"

I shrugged. "I'm guessing it was taken in Hawaii—we played a couple of courses on Maui and they all had palm trees."

"But who would have had access to those photos, Cassie?"

My heart started to beat faster. "Damn. I didn't even think of that. Maybe it was on my LPGA Web page?" Weak. Nothing was on those pages that didn't come through official LPGA channels.

"If we Google 'Cassie Burdette pix,' we can get an idea of what's out there on the Internet."

"Sarah Washington has a computer—she's in charge of tournament security."

I led Laura downstairs to the office. The door was locked. "I guess she got tired of me dropping in."

"We can do this later," Laura said. "Let's go catch the end of the tournament."

"No way. I want this settled. Come with me. I know where there's a whole bank of computers and probably no one using them. Not on a Sunday. Not when they could be watching the best women golfers in the world."

Chapter 27

🏌️ **A** volunteer dropped us off in front of the Mount Holyoke library and we circled the building to the main door on the courtyard, Laura puffing to keep pace.

"I need some caffeine," she said. "A week of nursing took the starch out of me."

"You're in luck. They make a mean latte right here." I pointed to the small coffee shop just inside the wooden doors. "Will you grab one for me, too? Two sugars, please. I'll be up those stairs—the computers are to the left of the reference desk."

I chose a monitor facing the entrance and clicked on the Internet Explorer icon. I hadn't seen anyone following us—we were alone in the shuttle van—but you couldn't be too careful. I tapped "www.golflosers.com" into the Google search bar and glanced around the room, waiting for the page to load. What kind of students would be working on a summer Sunday afternoon? None, actually. Even the reference desk was unmanned.

Then Joe bobbed up the stairs, looking left, then right, then left again. What the hell was he doing here? I shrank lower behind my computer screen. He waved across the room at the librarian, whom I now spotted filing magazines against the far wall. She met him at the reference desk.

"I'm wondering about how you handle your public computers," he said. "I'm a psychologist and I need to send a couple of quick e-mails to patients. Unfortunately my laptop crashed. I'm concerned about confidentiality."

"Not a problem," she said. "We use a self-cleaning program every night that restores the computers to neutral status. It eliminates all loads, software changes, and stored files and images in the cache. Including your e-mail server's address. But you'll have to hurry, we're just about to close up for the weekend."

Fear and adrenalin clenched my stomach into one ugly, pulsing knot. All the suspicions I'd worked so hard to suppress crashed into one hideous possibility: Joe had been sending the anonymous e-mails. He was here to send another one right now. Why the hell else would he be asking the librarian about confidentiality? He doesn't have a caseload of patients.

I dropped down under the table, and crab-walked along a waist-high row of bookshelves, blood pounding in my ears. I paused and peered through the books. Joe was still chatting with the librarian. She looked harried, her brown hair pulled back carelessly with a clip, tortoiseshell glasses askew, and arms piled with books. But she smiled at him.

He has that effect on women—you can't help finding him earnest and likeable. Which was precisely why I was having so much trouble understanding this new theory—how could I be hiding from Joe? Why in the name of God would he send me threatening e-mail?

"I'll be quick. But first, can you direct me to the men's room?" I heard Joe ask.

The librarian tipped her head in the direction of the corridor that led toward the staff offices. Joe ambled off. Then she set the books on the reference counter and went over to lock the main doors. The campus clock tower chimed two times. Where the hell was Laura?

The librarian disappeared behind her desk and I darted across the open area and up the dark wood staircase in front of me. I had to find another way out. Upon reaching the top, I realized that the stairs were an architectural bauble, a dead end. I was on a narrow platform, looking out the window over the indoor courtyard containing the coffee shop. In the other direction, across the open room, cars rushed by on Main Street. Joe returned, wiping his hands on his pants. I quickly crouched down, flattened myself to the floor, and peered through the railing.

The librarian stood and pointed to her wristwatch. Her voice drifted up through the cavernous space. "Closing in fifteen minutes."

Joe nodded, flashed a smile, and settled behind one of the computers. He resembled a professor, not a stalker. I felt like I was going crazy. *Crazy.* But Greg had warned me not to ignore my intuition—and something here felt very wrong.

I considered making a clean break for it—dashing down the stairs, out the door, and into the courtyard. But I'd have to wrestle with the locks, then the heavy doors would bang shut, drawing his attention to my escape. Once outside, where could I hide? Most of the college buildings were locked on the weekend and accessible only with a key card. I'd returned mine to Julie on Friday. I doubted I could out-run Joe.

Where the hell was Laura?

Joe tapped at his keyboard. Looking frustrated, he moved to another computer, this time with his back to me. I tiptoed down the stairs, sprinted past the librarian's desk, and ran the length of the hallway. An elevator door slid open. Julie's tour earlier in the week had included a ride to the lower level where I remembered an emergency exit. I didn't care if the alarm went off when I opened that door—I could cross the main road and reach the safety of the small town. The book-store and cafe would provide friendly staff and a safe haven. Then I heard footsteps and his familiar voice.

"Cassie?"

If I took the elevator now, the clanking and groaning along its path would tell him exactly where I'd gone. But I could hear him approaching from the hallway where I'd seen the stairwell. Directly in front of me was a boxy carved mahogany bench with lions' heads for armrests and an em-broidered tapestry cushion. I pulled on the cushion and the lid creaked open: under the seat was a large wooden chest.

I stepped in, curled down, and shut the lid behind me, leaving a crack for air. I pulled in a deep, musty breath and tried not to panic. Or move. Not so easy with my knees pressed up against one wall of the chest, and my back against the other. The urge to kick and scream and burst out into open air was almost overpowering.

"Cassie? It's Joe. Are you here? Are you okay? I'm here to help."

His footsteps circled my hiding place and stopped near the elevator. "I swear I saw her," he muttered. My sliver of light and air disappeared as his weight dropped onto the bench. I stilled my breath, but my heart picked up the pace, heading toward panic, toward me screaming out loud and banging on the old wood, bursting out of this coffin, the hell with what came after.

A shuffling, scraping sound: Joe had gotten up off the chest. His footsteps receded—in the direction he'd come from, it sounded like. I pushed on the wood, allowing in fresh air and a bright bar of light. When I could hear only my own ragged breathing, I threw open the lid and lunged out. Then I darted into the elevator and jabbed the first-floor button. The door closed and the box creaked downward, finally opening on the basement level. A red glow from the exit light overhead revealed a set of musty stacks. This did not look familiar. The elevator door glided closed behind me and the car began its noisy ascent. Soon all I could hear was the hum of an air conditioner somewhere nearby.

Stay calm, Cassie. You'll find a door, you'll break through the emergency exit, you'll get help.

Probably Laura had already gone for assistance. Joe would never hurt Laura. He loved Laura. He loved me.

I stumbled over the uneven linoleum floor and groped along the wall for a lightswitch. I felt a large knob and twisted it clockwise. *Tick, tick, tick . . .* The lights flickered on. Plain metal shelves on adjustable tracks were crammed with old, oversize books—*Land Tenure,* orange and musty; a set of German encyclopedias with flaking leather bindings;

Great Experiments in Psychology. The spine of one volume had crumbled off and fallen to the floor. With a turn of the crank at the end of a stack, the entire row could be shifted to allow access to more old books. I moved down the aisle toward what I hoped was the front of the library.

The lights went out. Instead of the comforting ticking of the timer, I heard a clacking noise as the stacks on either side of me rolled closer together. I felt my way to the end of the aisle, and squeezed out as they banged together. The sound echoed and died, and then there was a hollow click. A lock? Or . . . Jesus, was it a gun?

Someone—Joe?—was in here with me. Joe didn't carry a gun—did he? I crept past four more stacks of books, able to see only the shadows of the pipes lining the ceiling in the red glimmer of the exit light. I stopped to listen and heard the same whistling breath I remembered from that sleepless night in Hawaii. Joe tended to allergies, in addition to thin eyelids.

Whatever was in his mind, I knew I had no chance of talking him down. Not a snowball's chance in hell. He was a psychologist, for Christ's sake, the king of fast talkers. My only hope was to surprise him. I slid a heavy volume off the shelf in front of me and waited.

I squinted my eyes and tried to make out whether any of the shadows were changing shape in the dim light. Hearing a creak behind me, I raised the book, slammed it down, and ran. Joe slumped to the ground. Then a gunshot rang out and I grabbed my thigh and fell, moaning with pain. Then silence.

"Cassie?" said a man's voice. "Are you all right?"

Chapter 28

I dragged myself to the end of the row and twisted the timer. The light came on. Greg was splayed out on the floor ten yards away. What the hell happened to Joe?

"I think you got him." Jason grinned and pointed at the book next to Greg's head. *Jason?* Then I noticed the gun. The back of my neck prickled and my stomach churned.

"What are you doing here?" I stammered.

"Let's get him tied up and I'll tell you," he said. "Roll him over, will you?"

"You shot me," I said stupidly, pressing my hand to my thigh. It hurt like crazy and a red stain was mushrooming across my favorite khaki shorts. I was beginning to feel queasy and faint.

"Roll him over," Jason said again, raising the gun to my

chest and holding out a length of rope, "and tie his hands behind him."

Greg moaned and his eyelids flickered as I rolled him onto his stomach. I tied the rope into a loose granny knot and tried to puzzle out what was happening and how the hell I'd get out of the mess I'd made this time.

Squatting beside Greg, I glanced back at Jason: "Ruleswhiz?"

Jason nodded. "I tried to warn you off."

"Warn me off what? Why?"

"The Buick gig—it should have been mine."

"But they wanted a girl, Jason. And a tour player."

"I was a player, goddammit, until Lucien Beccia took me down."

Lucien Beccia took him down? What was he talking about? I remembered sitting in the Lenox coffee shop at Kripalu with Jason acting all concerned about that first nasty rules e-mail.

"Did you send me that message right in the coffee shop?" I tried not to sound too indignant—outrage wouldn't help.

"Nah. That was on a timer. But I was curious about how you'd react."

I shook my head quickly. "But, Jason, why?"

He shrugged. "I always thought you and I would be good together, didn't you think it, too, Cassie? Remember how much fun we had at Florida?"

"We had some good times. But you got married, Jason. And you have a sweet little girl."

He sneered. "And I'll never see her again if that bitch has her way. I had a lot of good things going. Then that fucking Lucien Beccia ruined me, and I had to let him know I could hurt him back just as bad. He thought no one could get close to him if he hired big dickheads with guns. But then if you're a caddie, it's not so hard to slip something into a player's bag. Like a little poison in his special golfer's special drink." He lifted his lips into a creepy smile. "How did you like my snow globe, Cassie?"

My whirling mind tried to sort through his bizarre rambling: "You killed Amber because you were mad at Beccia? Are you crazy?" *Smooth, Cassie.*

He started toward me waving the gun. I reached in my pocket and closed my fingers closed over a pointed metal object, the divot repair tool left from this morning's round. Not much of a weapon, but dammit, I'd go down fighting. Just as he grabbed my shoulders, I jabbed the metal prongs into his left eye.

"Arghhh!" he screamed. Curling into a ball, he clapped both hands to his face and dropped the gun. I kicked it across the room.

The door to the stairwell banged open. Joe and two policemen burst into the basement.

"That's him!" Joe shouted. "Jason Palmer!"

The cops rushed over, wrestled Jason down, and cuffed his hands. Joe hurried to me and squatted. "You're hurt?" He reached to touch my thigh.

"Maybe a little. Sure glad you're here."

Joe glanced at Greg—hogtied and groggy with a purple welt on his forehead.

"The cavalry stumbled, eh? Hang tight, I'll run upstairs and make sure the paramedics know where we are."

Chapter 29

Over my protests, I'd been tucked into a hospital bed after three hours in the emergency room.

"Why can't I go home if it's only a flesh wound?"

"Shock," said the nurse, straightening my top sheet and then lining up the cup, the water pitcher, and the old-fashioned land line phone on my bedside table. "Doctor wants to keep an eye on you for a while. Everyone else agrees." She made a clucking noise and placed my Call button in easy reach. "Buzz if you need us."

I looked over at my families. No telling who "everyone" was—the room was packed full of Burdettes and Leiners, plus Laura, and Joe. Other than the bowling outing, I'd certainly never seen them all in such close quarters. No one was arguing, but it felt a little hard to breathe.

The nurse glanced around the room. "You have way too many visitors. I want everyone gone in fifteen minutes." She bustled out the door, passing Lloyd on his way in.

He had a huge grin on his face and a hat in hand, which he came over and offered to me. Navy blue with *Titleist* embroidered in white. "We did it!" he crowed.

My family broke into a flurry of excited questions and congratulations.

And then the nurse returned. "Too many people, Miss Burdette."

"I can't stay anyway," said Lloyd, "just wanted to bring you the news."

"Thanks for everything," I said. "We'll talk soon."

"I'll take Mom and Dave down for a coffee," Charlie offered. "We can take turns in here. How about you guys?" He pointed two fingers at Zack and David. "Want an ice cream?"

"Tell us what happened in the library," said Maureen after the five of them trooped out. She appeared to be torn between pouting over missing another crime scene and wanting to get the dirt. Getting the dirt won.

"Cassie and I went to the library to look up this golfloser guy's blog," said Laura. "But first, I stopped to get coffee. They have the world's worst new employee in their shop. He couldn't figure out the espresso machine and then he started bawling. I finally had to go behind the counter to give him a hand. By the time I came out with the lattes, the librarian had locked the door."

She leaned over to pat my head.

"While I was waiting, I thought about the palm tree in the snow globe photo," Laura added, "and the small world song. I assumed the message had something to do with

Hawaii or the LPGA. But what if it didn't? What other small worlds had Cassie been a part of? The University of Florida golf teams came to mind. That meant Mike, of course. But then I remembered you mentioning Jason. He was a Gator, too—"

"He doesn't deserve the name," I said, spitting into my foam cup.

"Go on," said Maureen to Laura. "What happened in the library?"

"So I banged on the door until the librarian opened up, and I told her I thought my friend was in trouble. We found the computer you'd started working on and the list of Lucien Beccia's former students."

"These were the people who washed out of his academy?" asked my father.

Laura nodded. "The 'losers' log' said Jason signed on with him right after college, but it didn't take long for Beccia to tell him that he was never going to make it on the tour. Beccia told him, and I quote, 'You have neither the talent nor the drive to succeed.' That's when Jason moved to caddying."

Someone tapped on the door and then Greg stepped into the room, his forehead swarned in a bandage. I felt a sheepish smile break out across my face.

"I'm really sorry. I had no idea I was clocking *you*."

He grinned back. "Honestly? It is somewhat embarrassing to be taken down by the lady you're supposed to be watching. Appreciate it if you guys keep this quiet."

I giggled.

Over by the window, Laura made a face and tipped her head at Joe, who had developed the long expression of a hound dog left behind.

"So you saw the list on the computer," Maureen nudged Laura.

I was having trouble going back to the story. My stomach was opening into a yawning pit with both Joe and Greg there. Joe looked seasick, too.

"So then Joe found me in the reference room and I showed him the Web site," said Laura.

I blushed, remembering how I'd run and then hidden from him in the chest, quite certain he meant to harm me.

Laura continued: "So we called the cops. We didn't realise that Jason had already followed Gassie and me to the library."

"Why was he after you?" asked my father.

"Greg told us stalkers most often have relationships of some kind with their victims." I felt my face redden again. "He was right. Jason and I had spent a little time together in Gainesville. Drinking buddies. One night we closed down Richenbacher's and then moved on to breakfast at the Knife and Fork while everyone else went on home. I didn't think much of it. I hardly remembered any of it, to tell you the plain truth. But I guess it set the stage."

"The stage for what?" Maureen asked.

"Stalking starts with a narcissistic linking fantasy," Joe broke in from his seat by the window. "Not that anyone asked my opinion."

"No one asked me, either," my father said, patting Joe's shoulder. "I didn't know a thing about all this and I'm her father. And her caddie."

"I didn't see the point in worrying everyone," I said, pressing one corner of the sheet into tiny folds.

"What the heck is a narcissistic linking fantasy?" Maureen asked.

"Basically, the stalker believes there is more of a connection between himself and the object of his attention than there really is. When she rejects him," Joe continued, "which apparently he felt you did back in college, it brings forth feelings of shame and humiliation. Which he then defends against with his rage."

I wasn't following all this exactly. It suddenly hit me hard that I'd rejected Joe, too. And then I imagined he'd been hurt enough to turn on me. How had we gotten to the point where I actually believed he would harm me? I wanted to think it was just fear. I'd have to explain to Joe later how I'd overheard him questioning the librarian about the computers—how I'd freaked out. How I would have freaked out no matter who asked the question.

"The rage fuels the behavioral pursuit," Joe was continuing. "The stalker is compelled to control and possibly hurt or destroy the object of his narcissistic longing."

"I don't think this would have happened if I hadn't been invited to play in the men's tournament," I said. "The way Jason saw it, they passed him right over and zeroed in on me."

"Maybe not," Joe agreed. "Most stalkers suffer losses—real or imaginary—that finally trigger their bizarre behavior."

Where did he get all this stuff? What an egghead. I felt a rush of affection. "His wife left him recently, and they're fighting over their child."

"This is pretty much what he confessed to the cops," said Greg. "It pissed him off big time when you got the nod for the tournament, just for being a girl." He held his hands up and laughed. "His words, not mine. And his wife filed for divorce around the same time you got the invite to the

Buick Championship. Just like your good doctor said, he was already angry about his life, but now he focused that anger on you. Besides, he thought you'd figured out what he did to Amber."

"Did Jason poison her?" Maureen asked.

"One of the other caddies saw him put a sports drink in Amber's bag a couple of days ago," said Greg. "The cops didn't learn this until recently because the caddie had been in rehab."

"Aahh," I moaned. "Tony the lush. He warned me not to let a caddie fool with my stuff, but I just thought he was mad I hadn't chosen him. I wonder if he saw Jason put the snow globe in my golf bag?" I wrinkled my nose. "But why kill Amber?"

"Lucien Beccia called the police earlier today," Greg said. "He told them that he also had been receiving messages from a guy called Ruleswhiz. They threatened to expose the training tactics Beccia uses in his academy."

"Blackmail?" my father asked.

Greg nodded. "With the poisoned drink, he was showing Beccia that he could get close enough to hurt him where it most mattered: his star pupil. Beccia wasn't just providing antioxidants in his sports drink, he was feeding Amber beta-blockers."

"Beta-blockers?" I said.

"They reduce the effects of adrenalin and slow the heart," said Joe. "They're not illegal in competitive golf yet, but it's definitely bad judgment to force them on a teenager. If that was exposed, it could destroy Lucien's empire."

Greg looked over at me. "Jason thought you'd figured this out, so he had to take you down, too."

I thumped my forehead. "What an idiot. I kept talking to him about all my theories. God, I feel terrible about Amber—if only I'd told someone sooner."

"Told them what?" Greg asked. "She didn't give you anything to go on."

"She was afraid," I said sadly. "I should have seen that when she started to ask me for help in the locker room. Maybe she didn't want to take the drug. I should have convinced her to tell her father everything."

"Good advice for you, too, young lady," said Dad.

"What about the weirdo rules e-mails?" Laura asked.

"You were on the right track," I said. "Jason was warning me about what would happen if I got the idea I was too much of a big shot. He was having fun playing with me. Jesus, he was sitting right across the table when I got the first one."

Laura made a face. "I wish I'd been here this week. Maybe I would have picked up on the Florida connection earlier or noticed that he was behaving oddly."

"He wasn't really, that's the thing," I said. "And Greg and Charlie and I had generated so many possibilities, that I suspected everyone."

I threw a sideways look at Joe, but he was studying his shoes. Or the linoleum. Or something, anything, to avoid looking at me.

"How long are you in town for?" Maureen simpered at Greg.

"On my way home now." He trained his brown eyes on my face. "Just wanted to wish you Godspeed, and tell you I'm sorry I was a little rough on you this week."

"I guess I asked for it," I said. "I thought you were being bossy and nosy. People tell me I have control issues." I shot a quick smile at Joe, but he didn't respond. "I'm working on it."

Greg laughed. "Gotta go, my little girl is in a recital to-night and my wife will kill me if I miss another one." He looked at his watch. "If everything runs like butter, I may make the last half hour."

"Thanks for taking care of *my* little girl," said my father.

Greg shook hands with each of my visitors. "You'll call if you need me? You have my number?"

I nodded, afraid my voice would break if I spoke. We all watched him leave the room.

"We need to get going, too," said Maureen. "We got an earlier plane once we found out you weren't in contention."

"You're a champion in our hearts," said my father, com-ing over for a gentle hug.

"I'll walk them down to the cafeteria," said Laura, mov-ing quickly to the door.

I didn't want to be left alone with Joe just yet, but too late. They were gone.

I cleared my throat. "I'm sorry, Joe. I really am. I was so scared. In my heart of hearts, I never thought it was you. But I panicked. I'm sorry." I laughed, a tinny, false-sounding whinny. "When you asked the librarian about erasing e-mail evidence, I just flipped. You said you were sending stuff to patients—you don't have patients."

"I can sort of understand that, Cassie." Joe shook his head and frowned. "Sort of. But I've had a lot of bad nights lately. Take last night. Did you even notice that I didn't show at the bowling alley? I'm guessing not. You want me around when it's convenient—when I can diffuse the ten-sion with your family, for example. But you don't seem to want me for me."

His eyes met mine, steady and cool. And I realized that maybe even if he understood intellectually how he'd moved in my mind from friend to enemy, I'd cut him bone deep.

"You're absolutely right," I babbled. "I've been a terrible ass. This whole Buick tournament and then the Open. I haven't handled it well. I know that."

"You never said one word to me about the threats, Cassie. I finally made Charlie tell me what was going on. That's why I was in the library. I was trying to help. I could have helped."

"I know you could have helped. You're always helping. I blew it this time. But we'll get through this, right? We always do. I'm so lucky to have you."

"I don't know." He rapped on his chest with his fist. "I'm having some trouble here. It seems like a game for you, Cassie. I don't know what's going on with you and Mr. Testosterone"—he jerked his head in the direction that Greg had gone—"but I'm not hanging around to watch it happen. I love you. I've been afraid to say it. Afraid to put too much pressure on you and scare you away."

I was having trouble processing the whirlwind of feelings—I didn't want to lose him but I couldn't promise anything. I had to buy some time.

"Can we get together next week at the Jamie Farr Classic?"

He stood up and moved to the door. "I don't think so."

Closing my eyes to avoid the sight of him leaving, I felt for the remote control and pressed the Call button. Though it was hard to imagine a pain pill would touch what I was feeling.

My nurse materialized in the doorway. "What is it, dear?"

"I need my cell phone."

She waggled her finger. "No cell phones allowed in patients' rooms. They disrupt the signals in our monitors and IV pumps. Get some rest, dear."

As soon as she left the room, I eased my legs off the side of the bed and slid open the drawer of the bedside table. My phone was there along with my watch and wallet. I speed-dialed Joe's number.

"First of all, there's nothing going on with me and Mr. Testosterone," I said when he answered. "Nothing."

Joe didn't say anything.

"I was scared to death and he made me feel safer."

Still quiet on Joe's end.

"Can I tell you a story?"

"Fine."

"Why in the hell did Amber ever agree to pose for that calendar—that's what I've been wondering. I think she was trying to grow up—and having a hard time figuring out how, with her coach and her father crowding her space. Those guys told her how to make every move—her golf swing, her personal life, everything. She was imprisoned by their ambition. So she blew things up. She didn't see another way to convince them she could make her own choices."

"But—"

"Just listen first, okay? You said it earlier—you're always helping me. If we're ever going to have a real relationship, it has to start on a more level ground. I think Dr. Baxter's been telling me this for months: I don't have to blow things up. I can just say, look, Joe, I love you, too. But I don't know how this is all going to come out and I need some time. I can't ask you to wait while I'm working on this, but I sure would miss your friendship."

More silence.

"He's a smart guy, your shrink. He said all that?"

"Some of it I made up myself."

Joe laughed.

I chuckled back. "If it's possible, I'd like to try taking this relationship one shot at a time."

"They say that's not as easy as those mental golf goons try to make it sound." Joe laughed again. "I'll call you soon."

Glossary

Approach shot: a golf shot used to reach the green, generally demanding accuracy, rather than distance

Back nine: second half of the eighteen-hole golf course; usually holes ten through eighteen

Birdie: a score of one stroke fewer than par for the hole

Bogey: a score of one stroke over par for the hole; double bogey is two over par; triple bogey is three over

Bump-and-run: chip shot for which the aim is to get the ball running quickly along the ground toward the green

Bunker: a depression containing sand; colloquially called a sand trap or trap

Caddie: person designated or hired to carry the golfer's bag and advise him/her on golf course strategy, also called a looper

Card: status that allows the golfer to compete on the PGA or LPGA Tour

Chip: a short, lofted golf shot used to reach the green from a relatively close position

Chunk: to strike the ground inadvertently before hitting the ball; similar to chili-dipping, dubbing, and hitting it fat

Collar: the fringe of grass surrounding the perimeter of the green

Cup: the plastic cylinder lining the inside of the hole; the hole itself

Cut: the point halfway through a tournament at which the number of competitors is reduced based on their cumulative scores

Dewsweeper: an early morning golfer

Divot: a gouge in the turf resulting from a golf shot; also, the chunk of turf that was gouged out

Draw: a golf shot that starts out straight and turns slightly left as it lands (for a right-hander); a draw generally provides more distance than a straight shot or a slice

Drive: the shot used to begin the hole from the tee box, often using the longest club, the driver

Eagle: a score of two strokes under par for the hole

Exempt status: allows a golfer to play in official LPGA tournaments without qualifying in Monday rounds. Exemptions are based on past performance in Q-school, previous tournaments, or position on the money list

Fade: shot that turns slightly from left to right at the end of its trajectory (right-handers)

Fairway: the expanse of short grass between each hole's tee and putting green, excluding the rough and hazards

Fat: a shot struck behind the ball that results in a short, high trajectory

Flag: the pennant attached to a pole used to mark the location of the cup on the green; also known as the pin

Front nine: the first nine holes of a golf course

Futures Tour: a less prestigious and lucrative tour that grooms golfers for the LPGA Tour

Gallery: a group of fans gathered to watch golfers play

Green: the part of the golf course where the grass is cut shortest; most often a putter is used here to advance the ball to the hole

Green in regulation: reaching the green using the number of strokes considered par for the hole; one is regulation for a par three, two for a par four, three for a par five

Greenie: prize for hitting the ball closest to the pin in one shot on a par-three hole

Hacker: an amateur player, generally one who lacks proficiency; also called a duffer

Handicap: a measure of playing ability used in tournaments to allow golfers of varying skill levels to compete with each other; lower handicap, better golfer

Hazard: an obstacle that can hinder the progress of the ball toward the green; includes bodies of water, bunkers, marshy areas, etc.

Hook: a shot that starts out straight, then curves strongly to the left (right-handers)

Irons: golf clubs used to hit shorter than woods; golfers generally carry long and short irons, one (longest) through nine (shortest)

Lag putt: a long putt hit with the intention of leaving the ball a short (tap-in) distance from the hole

Leaderboard: display board on which top players in a tournament are listed

Lie: the position of the ball on the course; killer lie— extremely challenging position; fried egg lie—all but the top of the ball buried in a sand trap; plugged lie— ball sunk into the surface it lands on

Looper: caddie

Money list: cumulative record of which golfers have earned money in the official tournaments and how much

Out of bounds: a ball hit outside of the legal boundary of the golf course, which results in a stroke and distance penalty for the golfer; also called OB

Pairings sheet: sheet listing which golfers will be paired together for the round

Par: the number of strokes set as the standard for a hole, or for an entire course

Pin: the flagstick

Pin high: ball has come to rest on the green level with the flagstick

Pitch: a short, lofted shot most often taken with a wedge

Pre-shot routine: a set of thoughts and actions put into practice before each shot

Proxy: closest to the pin on a par-five hole in regulation (3 shots)

Pull hook: a shot that turns abruptly left (for right-handers)

Putt: a stroke on the green intended to advance the ball toward the hole

Qualifying school (Q-school): a series of rounds of golf played in the fall that produces a small number of top players who will be eligible to play on the LPGA Tour that year

Rainmaker: an unusually high shot

Range: a practice area

Rough: the area of the golf course along the sides of the fairway that is not closely mown; also, the grass in the rough.

Round: eighteen holes of golf

Sandy: a par made after at least one of the shots has been hit out of a bunker

Scramble: team format in which each player hits her

shot from the team's best ball after every stroke until the ball is holed out

Shank: a faulty golf shot hit off the shank or hosel of the club that generally travels sharply right

Short game: golf shots used when the golfer is within 100 yards or so of the green, including pitches, chips, bump-and-run shots, and putts

Skull: a short swing that hits the top half of the ball and results in a line-drive trajectory

Slice: a golf shot that starts out straight and curves to the right (for right-handers)

Solheim Cup: competition pitting the best twelve U.S. golfers against an international team; occurs every two years. Equivalent to the Ryder Cup for men

Swing thought: a simple thought used before hitting a shot intended to distract the golfer from mental chatter

Tee: the area of the golf hole designated as the starting point, delineated by tee markers, behind which the golfer must set up

Tour card: *see* Card

Top: to hit only the top portion of the golf ball, generally resulting in a ground ball

Trap: colloquial term for bunker; *see* Bunker

Two-putt: taking two shots to get the ball in the cup after hitting the green; a hole's par assumes two putts as the norm

Wedge: a short iron used to approach the green

Wingding: an informal tournament with players assigned to teams according to skill

Woods: golf clubs with long shafts and rounded heads used for longer distance than irons. The longest-shafted club with the largest head used on the tee is called the driver

Yips: a condition involving nervous hand movements that result in missed putts

Yardage book: a booklet put together by golfers, caddies, or golf course management describing topography and distances on the course

The Golf Lover's mystery series
featuring Cassie Burdette
by
ROBERTA ISLEIB

SIX STROKES UNDER
0-425-18522-2

A BURIED LIE
0-425-18996-1

PUTT TO DEATH
0-425-19530-9

FAIRWAY TO HEAVEN
0-425-20155-4

"A hole in one."
—Midwest Book Review

"Murder, suspense...and golf.
What more do you need?"
—Award-winning author Steve Hamilton

"Cassie Burdette is delightfully real!"
—Abigail Padgett

Available wherever books are sold or at
penguin.com

PC771